"Show me a dame who's never lied, and I'll find you a man who's never cried," he said. I hoped Rita Delancey wasn't lying about more than her name. I wasn't sure. You never can be.

I went home, poured a drink, got into bed, and dreamed about a full-breasted blonde who kept holding out her hand to me. But every time I reached out to touch it, she'd fend me off with a baseball bat.

Freudian crap...

DEAD IN CENTER FIELD

DEAD IN CENTER FIELD

PAUL ENGLEMAN

Library of Congress Catalog Card Number: 82-90940

ISBN 0-615-52787-6

Manufactured in the United States of America

First Ballantine Books Edition: July 1983

This is for Peg and Joe.

Acknowledgments

Thanks to my brother Mark, Thomas Rayfiel, and Steve Street for their editing; Mike Murphy and Morrie Goldfischer for their help; Lynn Strom and Hank Nuwer for their encouragement and Sue Davey for her typing.

1

It was summer of 1961. I was smoking a pack and a half of cigarettes a day, drinking two and a half cases of beer a week, getting laid three and a half times a month, and following every game the Gents played.

A guy named Marvin Wallace had the town of New York holding its breath, as he slugged home run after home run into the short right-field seats at Yankee Stadium, where the New York Gents played their home games when the Yankees were on the road. They called it the house that Babe Ruth built, but Wallace was the new architect in charge of renovation. He had designs on demolishing the Babe's all-time record of 60 home runs in one season, and at the rate he was going, it looked like he might finish the job by the end of August.

Every day the newspapers ran stories comparing Wallace with Ruth, much to the displeasure of the Babe's most loyal fans. The Sultan of Swat, as Ruth was known, was generally regarded as the greatest baseball player who ever lived. And his home-run records were thought to be unbreakable.

Until Marvin Wallace came along.

Even though he had knocked out 45 home runs the year before, the Gents wiry, black-haired left fielder was considered an upstart by many fans and even some of the baseball writers. They seemed to think it was sacrilegious for a non-Yankee to challenge a legendary figure like the Babe. And if someone other than a Yankee was going to break Ruth's record, it should be Wallace's teammate Jaco Sworpe, who had hit 53 home runs in 1958 and was one of the first black players to break the color line. But here it was, August 20, and Wallace had already cracked an astonishing 47 home runs, with 41 games still left in the season. Some of Wallace's critics were beginning to say he was lucky, but I knew better. I used to play minor-league baseball.

I was killing off another sweltering Sunday with my friend Nate Moore, swilling cold beer and watching the ballgame on my black-and-white TV. Nate had a color set at his place, but I had an air conditioner, and at this point in the season the grass at Yankee Stadium was turning brown anyway. On evenings when it was cool, I usually watched the games at Nate's apartment, but the stifling New York heat hadn't broken for weeks. It was getting so bad that I didn't automatically laugh anymore at rumors that the Russians were conducting atomic testing to turn New York into a giant toaster. Not that I believed such shit, of course.

I know that sitting around watching baseball and waiting to get hemorrhoids may not sound like an exciting existence to some people, but it was a tremendous relief to me. Mainly because it kept my mind off the fact that the telephone hadn't rung in weeks, except for the occasional call from the same confused Oriental who was trying to get Long Wang's Chop Suey Paradise. From my walks past his place, I could see that Wang's eggrolling business was no livelier than my private investigation work. But at least someone called him once in a while.

The Gents were batting in the fourth inning against Dick Donovan and the Cleveland Indians when I heard the knocking at my apartment door.

"Don't answer it," Nate said. He was sprawled full length on my double couch, all 6 feet, 6 inches, and 250 pounds of him, and he dwarfed a 16-ounce beer can in his massive hand.

2

"It's probably a Jehovah's witness. Who else would be crazy enough to go knocking on doors on a Sunday afternoon in New York City when it's a hundred degrees?"

I ignored his suggestion and slowly peeled myself off my sticky pink lounge chair. Nate could afford to be flippant about potential customers because they weren't his customers. He did a lot of work for me when I had a lot of work, but he hadn't been working much lately. Lucky for him, I wasn't his primary source of revenue. Most of what he earned came from painting, a not entirely unprofitable occupation to which he devoted considerable thought but little actual effort. I personally thought he was a better detective than painter, being unable to share his enthusiasm for photorealistic impressionism. I never did finish college, but I was smart enough to know that somewhere in that concept was a basic contradiction in terms. And just on principle I thought it was pretty ridiculous for a forty-year-old man his size to spend the better part of his life painting flowers.

"You'll be sorry," I heard Nate call to me as I began to unlock the door.

But I wasn't. She wasn't a Jehovah's witness, she was a godsend. And the first attractive woman I'd seen in a month who hadn't been coiffed in the spitting image of Jackie Kennedy. I made a mental note to stop by a church at Christmas to offer my thanks.

She was blond, tall, slim, and stacked, the perfect combination for a tit-man like me. She had soft blue eyes, large but unobtrusive, and a peaches 'n' cream complexion reserved for cover girls and the wives of famous men. A solitary lovely freckle loomed just above and to the left of her upper lip, and I was certain there had to be another in a location known only to her intimates.

"Mr. Renzler?" She spoke in a soft, uncertain voice that belied a New Jersey origin.

"The one and only that I know of," I answered.

"Oh, I'm sorry. I guess I was expecting someone older."

"I'm thirty. Is that old enough for you?"

"Oh yes, it's fine. I was just surprised. I wasn't sure if you were open on Sunday."

"I'm not, but I sometimes make exceptions," I answered,

3

hoping my smile didn't look too much like a leer. "You're an exception. Why don't you come in."

As we entered the living room, Nate bounded off the couch faster than I'd seen him move in years. He scattered four beer cans that were lying on the floor and turned down the volume on the TV set. His Gents T-shirt was so wet, it looked like one enormous sweat stain. We must have been making a great first impression.

"This is my associate, Nate Moore," I said.

She nodded anxiously and reluctantly put out her hand as Nate extended his. "Rita Delancey," she said.

"Why don't we go into my office," I suggested.

Not surprisingly, Rita Delancey agreed. I'm sure she figured no place could be as sloppy as the living room. But she hadn't seen my office.

She smiled, nervously, and I smiled back, suavely of course, and asked her to sit down. She sank through the dust in my client's chair and pretended not to notice that we couldn't see each other for a few seconds. I could tell she wasn't exactly comfortable in the surroundings and tried to console her with an offer of the Old Grand-Dad that I kept on hand for special occasions. It was to no avail. She refused with a graceful wave of a long slender hand that I knew I'd like to hold, even if just for a minute, sometime. Soon.

"Do you mind if I do?"

She didn't, and I walked to the small refrigerator in the corner and finessed a few ice cubes out of a rusty metal tray. "What seems to be the problem, Miss Delancey?"

"Mrs.," she corrected, and I felt my heart melt like a Hershey's bar at a summertime matinee.

"I'm sorry."

"That's quite all right. If I weren't married, I probably wouldn't be here right now," she said.

"Someone's trying to blackmail you?"

She nodded, and the nervous smile began to evaporate. In a few seconds it turned into a frown and a few seconds later into a series of sobs that created a steady drizzle of tears from eyes that got prettier as they got wetter.

I offered a tissue. She accepted it and apologized.

"There, there, it's okay," I said in the most soothing, noble

4

voice I could manage. "Anyway, the floors haven't been washed in ages."

That made her chuckle, which was its intention. I personally was tired of the line, having used it many times before. Detectives don't get laid much, but they do get to watch a lot of crying.

"Perhaps if you tell me about it," I said.

She nodded. "I got a call yesterday from a man who said he had pictures. I have to give him five thousand dollars or he'll send them to my husband."

"What kind of pictures are they?"

She blushed. "Not the kind you're thinking of." Her voice was angry. "Maybe I shouldn't have come here, taking up your time, if you think—"

"Hold on a second." I interrupted by raising my hand. "First of all, my time is not so valuable. Second, I have to know what kind of pictures he has if I'm to get them back, as I presume you want me to do."

"I'm sorry, Mr. Renzler. It's just that I don't want you to think I'm that kind..."

Her voice trailed off, and I decided to help her along. "That kind of woman."

"Yes."

"And it's Mark."

"Mark."

"Mrs. Delancey, if you don't mind my saying so, I don't really care what kind of woman you are. I meet all types, and in my business it's bad business to make moral judgments about people."

"I had an affair, Mr. Renzler." She blurted it out, and for a moment I thought she was going to start crying again. She probably got propositioned three times a day, and here she was talking about an affair as if it were an axe murder. Innocence is the soul of temptation. I cleansed my soul with a mouthful of Grand-Dad.

"This man knows about it," she said. "He says he has pictures. I don't know what exactly, but my husband is an important man. He just can't find out."

I nodded reassuringly. "I'll try to make sure he doesn't. But

5

I want you to know that this man might have more than one thing to sell. If you buy this time, he'll try to sell again."

"I suppose that's a chance I'll have to take."

I got up to fix myself another drink, and this time she accepted my offer. She took the glass from me and gulped down the bourbon like it was bad-tasting medicine. "I love my husband, Mr. Renzler, but he's a very jealous man. He's only twenty five but he's been married once before. Now that he's got me, he wants to keep me forever."

I could understand. Rita Delancey was the kind of woman husbands don't allow out of the house alone. I figured he'd probably had plenty of opportunity to feel jealous.

"Does your husband suspect anything?" I asked.

"No, no, he trusts me completely."

"What about the affair? Are you still seeing this, what's-his-name?"

She blushed again. I had a feeling she was a quick-tempered woman. "No. And I don't think you need to know his name."

"That's true. I don't. Unless he has something to do with the man who called you about the pictures."

"No." Her voice was sharp and loud. "Arthur would never—"

She stopped dead in mid-sentence. There would have been an awkward silence if Nate hadn't yelled from the living room. Within seconds he burst into the doorway, beer splashing out of the can like it was an automatic lawn sprinkler.

"Forty-eight," he said. "Wallace just hit number forty-fuck-ing-eight."

I excused myself and dashed into the living room behind Nate. We got there in time to see Wallace round third base and trot across home plate, where he received a congratulatory handshake from Jaco Sworpe, who was waiting to bat next. Then I hurried back to the office.

"I'm sorry." I must have looked as sheepish as a kid who just got caught playing with himself. "We're hopelessly involved in baseball, and this guy Marvin Wallace—"

She nodded her head, smiling, and I didn't bother to finish my explanation. Even Rita Delancey knew about Wallace's quest to break the home-run record. "It's okay," she said. She

6

began fumbling through her purse. "If you'll just recover the pictures, I'll pay you two hundred dollars."

She pulled a stack of bills from her purse and laid it on my desk. I could see Ben Franklin's face peering through a large paper clip.

"There's five thousand, two hundred there," she said. "You can count it if you want."

"I'll take your word for it. Besides, math was never my strong suit."

She smiled, a forced smile, and took a deep breath. "Well, I guess that's all."

"Just one minor matter," I answered. "Where and when am I supposed to meet this guy?"

"Tomorrow night, at ten o'clock, in Passaic. Two thirty-five Chestnut Street."

I groaned. I had once made a vow never to take a job in New Jersey unless I was desperate. I was breaking my vow. I was desperate.

2

Nate convulsed with laughter when I told him about my appointment. "I don't believe it. The last time you worked a case in Jersey, you said you'd rather go to Saudi Arabia."

"I still would. But no one's asked me. You want to come along?"

"When?"

"Tomorrow night."

"Are you kidding? The Gents are playing a doubleheader against the Orioles. Braverman's pitching, and Wallace has a chance to get his fiftieth homer. Can't you change it to Tuesday night?"

That was just like Nate. I hadn't worked for a month, and he was suggesting I take the day off.

"You are really desperate," he said.

I was indeed. And not in the mood to take any abuse about it. I gave Nate the address, so he'd know where to look for my body if I didn't show up in a few days. A little over twenty-four hours later, I was cruising through the Lincoln Tunnel in my blue Corvair. I was an employed man again.

I left about eight o'clock to allow time to stop at a suburban eatery. It was rare that I got an excuse to return to my homeland. When I did, I always tried to soak up as much culture as possible. For me this meant stopping at Howard Johnson's. There was one along Route 3 just past the Passaic River, which, to my refined sense of geography, is an inexplicable distance from the city of Passaic. I took it slow driving through the swamps—the Meadowlands, Governor Meyner liked to call them—to see if I could spot any floaters. Every month or so some stiff in a wash 'n' wear suit would be pulled out of the river. So it was a good bet that three or four thugs a week were getting free swimming lessons. But I couldn't see anything except the usual collection of bald tires, rusted transmissions, and Milky Way wrappers.

Just beyond the swamps, I slowed down to get a look at *The Parent Trap* with Hayley Mills, which was playing at the Route 3 Drive-In. But the screen was obscured by fog as dense as her co-star, Dean Jones.

Ah, New Jersey.

Stuffed to the gills with fried clams and roughly 14 percent of the available flavors, I took off for Passaic. Finding a street in New Jersey is easy, as long as you know you're in the right town. As it was I only had to deal with two other Chestnut Streets before I found Mr. Blackmailer's current address.

It was 9:45 when I pulled up past the house, a brick-and-white ranch affair with no sign of life. I cut the headlights and parked two houses down. I turned up the volume on the radio and watched my rearview mirror.

The Gents had won the first game of the doubleheader on a shutout by Ed Braverman. You had to be doing some great pitching to shut out Jim Gentile, Jackie Brandt, and the Orioles. Braverman was the best in the game. Wallace had knocked in the winning run with a solo home run. It was his 49th of the season. Jaco Sworpe had collected three hits, knocked in two runs, and stolen a base.

The Orioles were leading in the second game, 1–0 in the fourth inning, but Barry Preston was due to lead off for the Gents and Wallace and Sworpe were right behind him. I didn't

9

get a chance to hear if they scored. A white Buick, '61 I thought, pulled up in front of 235 Chestnut. A bulky man in a raincoat stepped out. He was carrying an umbrella. This guy didn't listen to the same weather forecasts I did. It hadn't rained in weeks.

I watched as he crept along the near side of the house and entered through a screen door. I could have followed right after him, but I decided to wait in the car to hear what Wallace would do when he came to bat. Besides, it wouldn't do the bastard any harm to wait a few minutes for his five thou.

It seemed like sound reasoning, but the sounds that came from the house gave me reason to reconsider. Someone was doing a lot of screaming, and it wasn't the kind of screaming you hear at birthday parties. I hopped out of the car and sprinted across the lawn. I carried my gun in my hand.

By the time I reached the front corner of the house, the screams had subsided. I peered through the window into what was probably the living room. There wasn't a stick of furniture inside. That's not to say the room was empty. The man in the raincoat was charging through.

I crouched near the bush as he came out the side door. I suppose I could have shot him, but that's not always the smart thing to do. Especially when you're out of state. You never know when you might end up pumping lead into the mayor's son.

As he ran past, I could see that it was not an umbrella he was carrying. It was a baseball bat. It was stained red and dripping blood. I stayed put until he got into the car. It was too dark to see the plates, but I could make out an orange bumper sticker—*Hughes for NJ Governor*—as he pulled away.

Then I went inside.

Dead bodies are not an easy thing on my stomach. Especially when the body has a crushed, bloodied head and my stomach is full of HoJo clams. His pockets were turned inside out. His left arm was twisted beneath him, the hand broken at the wrist, fingers battered and bloody. I'm no coroner, but I could tell he'd been hit at least ten times. The guy that did it had a pretty hefty slugging percentage.

Except for a Robert Hall suit and desert boots from Thom McAn, there was nothing of value on him. The house was

10

empty and gathering dust. The sports pages of that morning's *Daily News* were on the bathroom floor alongside the commode. Jake L. Franks's column was facing up, and part of it was torn out. Someone had been reading it while taking a shit. I hoped he had used it to wipe. I had read the column earlier in the day. Franks had said that Wallace was already cracking under the pressure and would not be able to break the home-run record.

Bullshit. That's what I thought. Most of the pressure Wallace had on him was due to sportswriters like Jake L. Franks. It was no secret that Franks had it out for Wallace. He'd been on his case all year. I picked up the paper and strolled to my car. Should have followed the batboy.

On my way back to New York I stopped by a phone booth in front of a huge pharmaceutical plant on Route 3 called Hoffman-LaRoche. Naturally the police wanted to know how I knew there had been a murder and naturally I didn't tell them. Instead I hung up. And heard, upon getting back into the car, that Wallace had hit another home run, his 2nd of the night and 50th of the year. He was the first player ever to hit 50 home runs before the end of August.

I stopped by Nate's in time to watch film clips of Wallace's home runs on the news. The Gents had won both games of the doubleheader. But the Detroit Tigers had also won a doubleheader, so the Gents were still only two games ahead of them. No one really doubted that the Gents would win the pennant, but the Tigers were hanging close. The only doubt was whether Wallace would break the record. And he was making more believers every day, Jake L. Franks notwithstanding.

"You think Batman and Thom McAn were working together, and one double-crossed the other?" Nate asked after I'd told him the story.

"I don't know. You'd think he'd wait until after the payoff."

"You can't always assume that a blackmailer will be smart."

"That's true. If it is a double-cross, she'll be hearing from him again soon. Which means I'll have to go meet him, which means I wouldn't mind having some company."

"Sure," Nate said. "You think the guy has pictures to sell?"

"I'm not sure. Something's just not right about this thing. She's nice, very nice. But she's not being straight with me."

I had checked and found that there was no phone registered to Rita Delancey. But I didn't expect her to give me her real name. People who are being blackmailed seldom do.

"You think she was setting you up?"

I said I didn't. I hoped she wasn't. And if she had, what was I being set up for?

"Well, at least we've got intrigue even if we don't have any answers," Nate said. His eyes twinkled as he opened another beer.

In my ten years of playing detective, I'd never met a person as aloof from crime or violence as Nate Moore. And that includes all the cops I've met, and I spent two long years on the New York police force. Nate was in it for the intrigue — and the money, of course. But he thought of detective work as a game, nothing more. He knew it was dangerous, but it didn't bother him. I knew it was dangerous, too. That's why I took him along with me. I could handle myself just fine. But it doesn't hurt to have a little life insurance. Nate was my policy.

"Show me a dame who's never lied and I'll find you a man who's never cried," he said. I hoped Rita Delancey wasn't lying about more than her name. I wasn't sure. You never can be.

I went home, poured a drink, got into bed and dreamed about a full-breasted blonde who kept holding out her hand to me. But every time I reached out to touch it, she'd fend me off with a baseball bat.

Freudian shit.

3

Tuesday morning I was awakened early, too early, by the ringing of my office phone. I rolled over and picked it up, lighting my last Camel in the process. A secretarial voice— the kind that lurks behind blood-red-drenched lips—came through loudly, too loudly, for me for that time of day. It was 8:30 by the Utica Club beer clock on my night table.

"Mr. Mark Renzler, please."

"Speaking, thank you."

"Mr. Arthur Fielding, New York Gents calling."

I had been having some weird dreams lately, but this was a bit too precise for one of those photorealistic dreams Nate had been telling me about. And the male voice that came on the line after probably a full minute pause was too formal and businesslike for even the most boring dream.

"Renzler?" This was no secretary. "Arthur Fielding, owner of the Gents. I want to consult with you on a matter of the utmost importance. I've got a rather busy schedule today, so I'd like you to be down here at, why don't we say, nine-fifteen."

Yes, why don't we. I was about to explain that I rarely made appointments before noon, that I always required prospective clients to provide at least a sketchy outline of their need for my services before I went down to meet them, that it would take me until 9:30 just to get my body out of bed, and that I would likely need a gallon of coffee in me before I could hope to function like the intelligent person I occasionally show flashes of being. But before I could, Lipstick got back on, gave me the address, and hung up.

It was just as well. For a brief moment, I considered calling back and spelling out my ground rules, but I didn't. Turning down Fielding's invitation for policy reasons would be like refusing a tryout with the Gents because they wouldn't let you bring your Jap-made glove to practice. I did a lot of rash things at obscene hours of the morning, but this would not be one of them. Instead, I pulled out my powder blue suit, which I wore year round, and settled on my navy blue tie. It was one of two that I owned. The other, a black-and-white checked affair that I'd picked up at Barney's years before, had fallen behind either the refrigerator or the stove. One of these days I was going to look for it.

I stepped out of my building on West 72nd Street at exactly 9 A.M., according to the Chemical Bank clock. I was carrying a styrofoam cup full of instant coffee, a vile creation to my way of thinking, but the only caffeine I had time for short of tea, which I've always thought of as a sissy drink. I picked up the *Daily News* and *Times* at the corner of Amsterdam and caught a cab to the Gents offices in Rockefeller Plaza.

The back-page banner headline on the *News* was GENTS WIN 2; MARV HITS 2. The story inside had a chart comparing Wallace's home-run pace with Ruth's record pace of 60 home runs in 1927. Ruth hadn't hit his 50th homer until the 138th game of the season, September 11. Wallace had hit his in the 124th game of the season, August 22. He was 14 games ahead of Ruth's record-setting pace. Sworpe, who had 40 home runs, was even with Ruth, but it was unlikely he'd be able to match the Babe's torrid finish. In the month of September in 1927, Ruth had hit 18 home runs. That was a lot of slugging.

The Gents still had 38 games left in the season, and it looked as if Wallace would have no trouble hitting the 11 more homers he'd need to break the record in that time. But the 1961 season had 162 games, 8 games more than the 1927 season. When it began to look as if Wallace had a chance to break the record, acting baseball commissioner Ebel Chapman announced that to surpass Ruth officially, Wallace would have to hit 61 home runs in 154 games, the same number of games that Ruth had played in 1927. This meant that Wallace only had until September 21, not the end of the season, to break the record.

Chapman's announcement was the subject of widespread debate and occasional fist fighting in bars all over the country. The discussions were particularly lethal in New York. What made the decision even more controversial was that Chapman was only acting as commissioner in place of Ford Frick, who was on a leave of absence. There was some belief that Chapman was merely carrying out orders, since Frick was on record as supporting Chapman's ruling. Personally, I thought both of them had taken leave of their senses. It was unfair for any commissioner, no less a temporary one, to make a special ruling about one record for one player. If Wallace could hit 61 homers in one season, the record was his, as far as I was concerned. But I wasn't the commissioner of baseball.

The item about the murder I had phoned in wasn't played up to usual *Daily News* excess, but I wasn't surprised. It was a late-breaking story and a New Jersey one at that. There was only a short blurb from UPI on page 14 about an unidentified body found in a deserted house in Passaic. The story didn't say who the owner of the house was or what time the body was found. Passaic police had found wood fragments near the body and believed that the person had been beaten with a heavy club, possibly a baseball bat.

I tore the clipping out of the paper and paid the cabbie as we pulled up to the building. It was a typically modest New York skyscraper with about five hundred floors. I boarded an elevator and traveled express to the thirty-fourth floor. I got off in front of a block-long sign that read: NEW YORK GENTS, ARTHUR FIELDING III, OWNER AND CHAIRMAN OF THE BOARD.

I had been in plusher offices than Fielding's, but I couldn't remember when. Just that I could recall the feeling of sinking even deeper into another rug at another time. I saw three women sitting at marble-topped desks as I entered the door to the office.

15

I approached the one at the largest desk, a graying mare with bullets for eyes and a faucet for a nose whom I took to be Lipstick—a few unsightly red smears *were* in evidence. She sized me up with an authoritative air that I hadn't encountered since a drunken night years back when I had gotten stuck on the idea of going down to see my local Marine recruiter. He had told me I wasn't Marine material. I felt a similar estimation in the way her eyes regarded me now.

"Mr. Renzler, I assume. Mr. Fielding will see you in a few moments. Why don't you take a seat." She gestured toward a white fluffy chair that looked like a giant marshmallow. I could've slept in it with the Gents chunky outfielder Husky Magill, and neither of us would have noticed that the other was there. "Randy will get you coffee if you like."

"I'd like that a lot," I said, falling at least two feet into the chair.

Randy, as it turned out, seemed to be more my kind of girl. Young, slim, and she smiled. On closer inspection I saw that her left hand sported a diamond the size of a hardball. And her left cheek was the home for a wad of Juicy Fruit that made her look like Nellie Fox, a second baseman for the White Sox whose bubble-gum-card mug had a chaw of tobacco as big as a shot put running down the length of his face. But he could play the field. Randy, I wasn't sure about.

I slurped my coffee approvingly—it wasn't instant—and lit a Camel, which elicited a by-no-means-pleasant grimace from secretary number three, an aging leather-tit terror with a face that had more wrinkles than a jumbo box of raisins. Perhaps I should mention that secretaries as a group are not my favorite people, falling about seventh on my list of most despised occupations behind lawyers, doctors, accountants, bankers, and other professional types.

A buzz came over Lipstick's intercom that I took to be a signal that Fielding was ready for me. I was correct.

The inner sanctum was about the same as the outer office, except that the carpet was thicker and the chairs were bigger. An altogether commodious atmosphere and exactly what you'd expect from the owner of the best baseball team in the world.

Fielding was one of those gray-haired guys who'd be white-

16

haired if it weren't for regular coaching from a big-league stylist. I figured he was in his early sixties. He spoke with a heavy Boston accent and exuded Ivy League confidence. Unlike maverick baseball owners such as Bill Veeck, Fielding rarely was in the public spotlight. But I knew quite a bit about him from having played in the Gents organization.

Arthur Fielding had graduated from Harvard and gone on to become an insurance magnate in Hartford, amassing a small fortune in a short period of time. His father had been a major league ballplayer around the turn of the century. He played for the old Baltimore Orioles, arguably the best team ever assembled. Baseball was Arthur Fielding's first love, and he started the Gents after retiring from the insurance business in 1948. He chose the name Gents, he said, because baseball was a gentleman's sport. He gave me the sort of firm, sincere handshake that only business executives with positive mental attitude can pull off smoothly, and introduced me to the other man in the room. It was the Gents manager, Ed White.

White didn't break my hand with his clasp, and I gave him a cordial hello and congratulations on the season before taking a seat on the marshmallow next to him.

"So you're a baseball fan, right?" Fielding said.

"Correction, Gents fan," I answered.

They both had a chuckle, and Fielding, who seemed to be the get-down-to-business type, got right down to business.

"Renzler, first off I have to tell you that I'm making you privy to a matter of vital importance. Absolutely vital. I can't stress that enough." I thought he was doing a pretty good job of it, but I didn't say anything. "I can't have you talking to anyone else about this. What is said in this room between you and Ed and me goes no further. Is that understood?"

"Naturally." There was something in Fielding's tone that I didn't particularly like. Maybe it was the manner of a guy who's been giving orders all his life.

"You're aware of course that Marvin Wallace is closing in on the single-season home-run record."

I nodded, and Fielding paused and looked toward White. Then he took a deep breath. "We—Ed and I—believe that someone is trying to stop him from doing it."

17

I paused for a second myself, in disbelief. Then I laughed. "They're going to have a tough time, don't you think? He only needs eleven more homers to do it."

Fielding and White were not laughing.

"What makes you think that?" I asked. "Has he received threats?"

"We get threats all the time," Fielding said. "Some people think it's sacrilegious for an unknown to break a record set by an immortal like Babe Ruth."

"That's understandable. But I'd hardly call Wallace an unknown. He did lead the league in home runs last year."

"That's true," Fielding said. I didn't think he sounded convinced. "But we're straying from the point. The point is that someone, a very desperate person, wants to stop him."

"If you get so many threats, what is it that makes this one so special?"

"Show him the note, Ed," Fielding said.

White pulled a sheet of paper out of a folder on his lap and handed it to me.

"This came addressed to Ed," Fielding said. "Someone left it at Big Johnnie's, a bar in New Jersey that's owned by one of our broadcasters."

I read the note. I could see why they were disturbed. It didn't have the tone you'd expect from a crank. It was a professional job, as these things go, neatly typed and single spaced.

TO ED WHITE: 8/21

You're having a great year for a first-year manager. But if you don't stop playing Marvin Wallace, someone may get hurt. Who knows Ed. It might be you. Make sure Wallace isn't in the lineup when you play Chicago Friday or else there's going to be an announcement made that embarrasses your whole organization. This is not a joke. If you can't take care of this on your own, ask Fielding to do the dirty work for you. It's in every one's best interest. Believe me. Do not contact the police. I'll be back in touch.

YOUR #1 FAN

"What do you make of it, Renzler?" White asked when he saw I had finished reading.

I shrugged. "Not much. Except that it looks too intelligent to be from a crank. And I doubt it's some fanatic who's loyal to the memory of Babe Ruth. Unless, of course, you know of someone."

Fielding snapped his fingers. "As a matter of fact, I can think of someone. Two months ago I got a letter from a man who wanted to buy the Babe Ruth monument in center field. I told him it wasn't mine to sell, but he wrote back a crazy note that said everything is available for a price. He had a strange name." Fielding began looking through a file folder on his desk. "Yes, here it is," he said. "The man's name is Tidwell, William Bosworth Tidwell. He offered six million dollars."

"It's a different typewriter," I said, looking over the letters. "I'll check it out. But there's a chance the person who wrote this other note has a more concrete motive. Can you think of one?"

They both struck out. Fielding looked at his wrist watch, a gold-and-diamond job that probably cost him a year of my income.

"This note could have been written by millions of people," I said. "Have you talked to Wallace about it?"

"No, I can't do that. I won't have one of my players upset and worried."

"That's understandable," I said. "And Wallace is playing under enough pressure already. But he's the one this note seems to be about, and he may be the one with the answers. If you don't have anything to go on, except that the note's typed, someone dated it August 21, and left it at Big Johnnie's, there's not a whole lot you can do."

Fielding frowned and picked up a paperweight that was shaped like a baseball. White played with a ring on his finger.

"Besides, I'm not sure I'm the person you want." I was beginning to wonder how he'd chosen me to begin with. "I'm not trying to talk myself out of a job, but don't you have some kind of team security to look into this, or the police?"

"We do have a security force," Fielding said. "But I can't have them in on this. The word will leak back to the players.

I won't allow that. The players are not to know. If we went to the police, it would hit the papers. We've got to go about this from a different angle."

I was hard-pressed to think of one. "There isn't a whole lot I can suggest. I can talk to the bartender at Big Johnnie's to see if he remembers who left the note. I can talk to this fellow Tidwell. There's a possibility that someone might get hurt, though I have a feeling the tactic is to frighten you. There's a threat in here to Ed, too."

"I don't think we have to worry about that," Fielding said.

"I wonder what Ed thinks about it."

"I'm not worried," the manager said. "Unless it gets more serious."

"It could," I said. "Especially if someone in your organization is involved."

"That's ridiculous."

"It's not ridiculous, Mr. Fielding. Whoever's trying to get at Wallace has a motive. I don't know what it is, and you don't seem to either. But someone could be trying to get him for personal reasons. We can't overlook the possibility that it's one of your players."

"I'm sorry. You'll have to do the best you can without involving the players. You can certainly understand that we have a pennant to win and—"

"Yes, I understand. But this problem is a big one, or you wouldn't have bothered to contact me."

Fielding was silent, and White played with his ring some more.

"Which brings up another question, if you don't mind. How did you come to contact me?"

Fielding leaned back in his chair. He was smiling. "I guess basically I just have a good memory for names, but my son deserves some of the credit, too."

John Fielding was the Gents general manager.

"He came across your picture in the newspaper a couple of years ago. The story said you were one of the best investigators in the city. He remembered you from when you were with our Richmond team. And he happened to mention it to me. Before then, I hadn't known about your accident."

Fielding looked as awkward as I felt. "I'm sorry about it," he said. "I was told by more than one person that you were a good prospect."

He was right. I had been a good prospect. I played second base on the Gents AA team for two years. At one time there was even some talk about bringing me up to the major leagues. I was a better fielder than hitter. Great glove, poor schtick, they used to say.

One of my weaknesses at the plate was picking up the flight of the ball. Some people don't understand how a batter can freeze when a ball is hurled ninety miles an hour at his head. Take it from me. It's easy. You never see the goddamn thing.

I suppose that's not exactly true. I do recall a brief, and I mean very brief, white blur. I must have seen something, because I turned my head just enough to take it full force on the left eye. The doctors said it probably saved my life, turning that little bit. It did absolutely nothing for my eyesight—or my batting average. Didn't help my fielding either. After a year of sulking and dreaming about what could have been, I got to the point where I was glad that I had lived. But it hurt like hell to have to give up baseball.

Other guys had come back from being beaned. Jimmy Piersall. Don Zimmer. But they hadn't been blinded. They also were better baseball players than I was.

As it turned out, the guy who hit me did get to spend some time in the majors. He was a crazy Mexican. First name was Manuel, I could never pronounce the second. He played in the Pittsburgh Pirates minor-league system when he plugged me. Eventually, he got up to the Pirates, but they traded him to Kansas City. I think he finished up with the Cleveland Indians in 1954. They said he had control problems. No shit.

I didn't think about the accident anymore. The only time I did was when someone else brought it up.

"How long has it been?" White asked.

"Twelve years now."

"That's a tough break. I hate to see someone's career ended by an injury," Fielding said.

"It kept me out of the army."

White chuckled a bit at that, but Fielding seemed a bit uneasy. Maybe he was a military man. I hoped not.

I picked up the note. "We're pretty much handcuffed until he tries something else. This basically amounts to blackmail. But a blackmailer usually reveals what he has to sell before making his demands. I suggest we wait him out, let him make another move. But it's risky. He's telling you there's going to be trouble if you *don't* do something. He's not telling you what the payoff is, so he may just spring what he has if you keep playing Wallace."

"Are you saying we can't resolve this?" Fielding was back to his haughty manner.

"Not exactly. This thing could turn to shit right in our hands. But more likely, what he's got to sell is not going to get Wallace out of the lineup. If it worked that way, he probably wouldn't be going through this whole pen-pal routine with you. He'd just blurt out what he knows."

"I see." Fielding nodded emphatically. He seemed to be impressed with my logic. I hoped he was. One thing I had learned about important people who hired detectives: Too often they wanted to run the investigation themselves. That isn't the way I work.

Fielding buzzed Lipstick, whom he called Mrs. Grayson, and told her to pay me and give me four box seats for the rest of the season. That gave me a good feeling about him in a small way. The man was not cheap.

I wanted to talk over some more details with White, so we made an appointment to eat dinner at six P.M. in the Yankee Stadium dining room.

It may have been my imagination, but I think the old biddy smiled a little on my way out. Or maybe it was my mood. I had broken out of a month-long slump with two cases to work on. One with the prettiest thing I'd seen in a year, and the other with the owner of the best baseball team of all time. I usually didn't double up like that, but I couldn't turn either of these two down. I treated myself to steak and eggs at Schrafft's and then walked uptown through Central Park and back to 72nd Street. It was turning out to be a good day.

4

When I got back to 72nd Street, Pressie, our combination security, door, and elevator man, winked at me with his good eye. Between the two of us, we managed to have perfect vision for one person. And we managed to agree on what we saw: This old world was indeed fucked up.

Black, arthritic, and courting death with every attempt to breathe, Pressie must have been eighty years old. He had no idea. He spent most of his days sitting still in the inner lobby, listening to Miles Davis on a portable reel-to-reel tape recorder. As a result he was generally oblivious to what went on around him. But he still had an eye, as it were, for attractive ladies.

"She was here again, Mr. Renzler," he said. "Same clump of pretty whiskers came to visit you yesterday."

"What time?" I asked, knowing the inevitable reply.

"I wasn't watching no time, Mr. Renzler. You know I never pay no attention to no time."

It was true. I always wondered how Pressie knew when it was time to go home. "Leave a message?"

I had to wait through the end of "Green Haze" by Miles Davis for a reply. "You know," he said. "Just for you to call her."

I thanked him and picked up the mail. He guffawed as I stepped onto the elevator. "If a man answers, Mr. Renzler, you remember to hang up."

Pressie had unknowingly touched a sensitive button. Mrs. Delancey—Rita, if I may—had said that she would contact *me*, because her husband was often home during the day. If I did have to call her, she said I should hang up if he answered the phone.

I got a Rheingold out of the refrigerator and dialed her number. I expected that she wouldn't be home, because if Pressie had remembered her being there, it had to have been fairly recent. But she was just good-looking enough to make him exceed his ordinary limits of recall. So, what the hell, I called her.

Wrong move. He sounded like one of the guys on the after shave commercials. Maybe that's why he was important. An actor. I couldn't place the face, though.

I called Nate to tell him to find a date and join me at Yankee Stadium to watch the Gents beat the Orioles. He was suitably excited—overwhelmed by his usual standards—when I told him about the morning's events. He declared his intention to write a personal note of thanks to Fielding as soon as *Seven Keys*, his favorite TV quiz show, was over.

I had to get myself a date, and I knew exactly who to ask. Melissa Kramer had a soft spot for me, which meant that I, by comparison, had a cotton plantation for her. She also covered New Jersey politics for the *New York Times*. It was crime, not politics, that interested me, but in New Jersey they're basically the same profession. She'd be able to check the wire-service machines for me to find out if there was any more information about the murder. But the best thing of all about her—she liked baseball. A woman with that kind of taste is hard to find.

"Are you working a case?" Her surprise was mildly insulting, and I now remembered that she could be brutally forthright at times. She put me on hold for a few minutes before returning with a report. "His name was Rudy Appell. Had a record seven

miles long and two miles wide. Assault, robbery, armed robbery, racketeering, gambling. You want his AKA? It's a good
one."

"Sure."

"Butch Bender. Last known address was Newark."

"Very good. You're getting to sound just like a cop."

"You like it?" She laughed. "I've got something else here
a cop wouldn't know."

"Such as?"

"If it's the same Appell from Newark I'm thinking of, he's
the son or nephew of Ray Appell."

"Doesn't ring a bell."

"I'm not surprised." Another insult, but it was in jest. "He
used to be an aide to the next mayor of Newark, Hugh Addonizio."

"I thought Addonizio was a congressman."

"He is."

"But it's not an election year."

"Right. But it's being set up now. He won't announce until
October or November. Believe me, Renzler, he's going to be
the next mayor."

"Okay, I believe you. But what about Appell? What does
he do now?"

"Oh, he's dead. Two months ago. Found him in the parking
lot of some diner up near the Tappan Zee Bridge. He was shot,
I think."

"I'm surprised it hasn't been in the papers."

"It has, dummy. Your problem is that you only read the
sports pages." She wasn't exactly right, but she was too close
to argue about it.

"No, not the murder," I said. "I remember hearing about
that. I mean the son or nephew. I'm surprised no one has
connected last night's murder to the other one."

"Doesn't surprise me a bit. You'd be amazed by what the
police miss."

"You forget, honey, that I was once a cop. I'm never amazed
by what they miss. I'm talking about the reporters."

"You forget, sonny, that I *am* a reporter. You'd be amazed
by what they miss. But you did notice that I didn't miss it."

25

She was a snob, a complete snob. But her heart was pure gold, and she had a pair of legs that could cure the blind.

"Did you know they found a baseball bat?" she asked.

I didn't.

"They found a baseball bat in some bushes across the street. Covered with blood."

"They usually are when they've been used to beat someone's brains in."

"Well it doesn't sound like this guy Appell had many brains. What are you working on anyway, Renzler?"

"I'm not sure exactly. Two things it looks like. But it's kind of involved. I'll tell you about it sometime. But that's not why I called."

"Oh, I suppose this is a social call."

"As a matter of fact it is. As luck would have it, I am now in the employ of the New York Gents. And I have box seats to tonight's game."

"You're working for the Gents?" This time her surprise was not affected. "What's it all about?"

"Some other time, soon. Do you want to see the Orioles play or not?"

"Will Nate be there?"

"Of course. He wouldn't pass up a free baseball game. But Neta's coming along, so he'll be a little restrained." Neta Simpson was the only nice woman Nate ever went out with. And she was the only woman who could tolerate his excesses.

"Last time we went to a ballgame, he ran out on the field," Melissa said.

"He'll behave this time, I promise."

"I'm a fool to believe you, but you always sound so honest. I'll go."

I called back the Delancey residence twice. The aftershave man answered twice. Three strikes and you're out. I decided to wait until she called me.

She did, just as I was leaving to meet Ed White. "I saw the paper," she said. "It was on the front page." She had been reading a New Jersey paper. "It's terrible." She sounded as if she were ready to cry.

"It's not that bad, actually," I answered. "The guy was just a punk. Does the name Appell mean anything to you?"

26

She said it didn't.

"What about Butch Bender?"

"No. Why? Who are they?"

"Appell's the name of the guy who got killed. Bender's what he called himself before he got killed."

"I'm glad you're all right. When I first saw the paper I thought . . ."

"You thought it was me."

"Yes."

"Well it wasn't. But it could have been. Did you tell me everything he told you?" I tried to make my voice sound firm, not angry.

"Oh yes, I did. Mr. Renzler, I'm sorry. I didn't know anyone would get hurt. You have to believe me."

I did. And I told her so. That might have been a mistake. I'd find out soon enough if it was.

"So who killed him? You didn't, did you?"

"Me? Hell no. Listen, Mrs. Delancey, I've gotten into a couple of tight spots here and there where I've had to use my gun. But I don't make a practice of killing people. And not with a goddamn baseball bat."

"Oh, I'm sorry." I think she thought she had offended me. Actually I was amused. "What do we do now?" she asked.

"We wait. It looks as if two people were putting the heat on you. One got greedy, decided to take all the money himself. He didn't wait around for me last night. But you'll probably be hearing from him soon. When you do, call me, okay?"

"Sure. But one more thing, Mr. Renzler. I don't think you should call me here. My husband was very upset. When I got home he said someone had called five times and just hung up when he answered."

"I'm sorry," I said. "When I heard you'd been to my office, I thought it might be important. I won't call again."

"Thank you, Mr. Renzler, for all your help."

"It's Mark. You're welcome."

"Mark. I'll be seeing you again soon."

"I hope," I added after she had hung up. She was the sweetest thing. *The* sweetest. I wondered how many other people she had told to hang up if her husband answered. It was no wonder the guy was jealous.

5

I got off the D train with about six million other people on their way to the game. At least I assumed they were going to the game. I didn't know anyone who went to the Bronx just for the hell of it.

I was about fifteen minutes late when I got to the ballpark, and it took me another fifteen minutes to find my way to the Empire Room. It was a pretty classy joint, complete with barmaids and waitresses dressed in cute Gents outfits that afforded fairly generous views of home plate. And I'm not talking about baseball. I saw White at a booth in the back engaging one of the barmaids in a bit of infield chatter. I thought he looked a bit disappointed when I arrived, and I figured he was just getting around to inviting her to his house for a little batting practice. I ordered a gimlet with Bombay gin, and we watched as she did a sprint to the bar that took the wind out of both of us. It was the best table in the house, and it looked like the most private, too. We could see the Orioles working out down on the field.

I ordered the prime rib at White's suggestion, and we chatted about baseball over our drinks. I could see that White was nervous, and I couldn't blame him.

"I'd like to cooperate with you any way I can, Renzler. But Mr. Fielding doesn't want the players involved in any way."

"I understand his concern," I told White, "but you have to give me some background if you want to get anything done."

"I know," he said. "But Fielding called me up and told me not to say anything that would get you poking around in team business."

I liked White, but I could see that things were going nowhere fast. "I'm not going to go into the locker room sniffing everybody's jockstrap," I said, smiling so my sarcasm wouldn't seem snotty. "But it would help a lot if you could tell me anything unusual that you've noticed. Like Wallace, for instance. Does he get along with everyone? Is there anyone on the team who doesn't like him? Anyone on the team who doesn't like him enough to threaten him?"

White sighed and took a long sip of his drink. He looked down below as Brooks Robinson, the Orioles young third baseman, slammed a pitch into the upper-deck seats in left field. "He's going to be a helluva ball player," White said.

I nodded, then interrupted his musings. "Listen, Ed, you work for Mr. Fielding, and I'm working for Mr. Fielding. I'm also working for you and for Marvin Wallace and for the whole team. I have the feeling you'd like to be helpful, and I can promise you that anything you tell me is confidential. I'm not going to go around confronting players with accusations, and I'm not going to tell Fielding every single item of gossip I get from you."

"Okay," he said reluctantly. "I figure you're going to find out what you want anyhow."

I nodded my approval, and he continued.

"Marvin Wallace has been playing baseball under tremendous pressure. The only guy I've ever seen play under more, I'd say, was DiMaggio when he had the fifty-six-game hit streak. Our team has been playing good ball, but we're still only a couple games in front of Detroit. I guess you've seen the stories in the papers that Wallace is just shooting for the record, that he's not playing for the team."

"They write stories like that about Sworpe, too," I said.

"That's right." His voice was getting louder. "Personally, I think it's a pile of horseshit. Complete horseshit." He spoke just as the waitress brought more drinks.

"Something wrong with the meat?" She was cuter than a button and appeared to be missing a few threads.

"No, no." White looked sheepish. He waited for her to retreat to a safe distance before talking again. "But I'm not sure everyone on the team would agree with me," he said.

"Have there been any incidents that make you think that?"

"You got to see this thing the right way, Renzler. These guys are pro athletes. They've got their pride."

"I know. I almost was one."

"That's right, you do know." He smiled. My familiarity with baseball was putting White more at ease.

"Every time Wallace or Sworpe hits a home run, they've got writers crawling all over them. So guys like Coffman Maxwell, who's only got the highest batting average in the majors, or Ed Braverman, who's already won eighteen games—it's only normal for these guys to resent it."

I knew what he was talking about, but I didn't think it was normal. In little league, kids envy each other's skills. In high school it gets worse. The petty jealousies among jocks only get more intense as the level of competition gets better. You'd think it would be the other way around, but it's not. White's team might turn out to be the best of all time. That meant the infighting and squabbling might be the worst, too.

"Anything in particular you're thinking of?" Gradually, I was working White to where I wanted him.

The Gents manager smothered a chunk of prime rib in horseradish and began looking down toward the field. For a moment I thought he was going to start talking about Brooks Robinson again. He didn't.

"There is one player, a young kid," he said. "He's going to be a helluva pitcher someday. We called him up from Columbus a couple weeks ago. His control's off a bit, but he's got a live fastball. You know, one that really jumps. Anyway, he and Wallace got into it real good the other day. It was no big deal, I guess. But I don't know the kid well enough to say what he'd do."

"What was the argument about?"

"I didn't really get the details. Otto Croaker, our batting coach, saw it happen and cooled them off. But I guess Marvin slugged him a couple good shots. I doubt Otto could tell you what happened. Just between you and me, Croak has a helluva baseball mind, but off the field he ain't too sharp."

That I could believe. Otto Croaker had been a baseball coach for as long as I could remember. He'd been with at least six other teams before coming over to the Gents. Prior to that he had been a journeyman player, but that was before my time. He had to be a hundred and fifty years old.

"I just let it pass," White said. "I didn't want anybody gettin' excited, and I especially didn't want it in the goddamn papers. Wallace gets real sulky sometimes, but I think there might be something wrong with the kid's attitude. Some of the players seem to think he's a real flake."

"What's his name?" I asked, knowing the reply before he answered. The Gents had only brought up one pitcher recently.

"Bidwell," he said. "Curt Bidwell."

"What's wrong with his attitude?"

"I'm not sure exactly. I can only go by what I hear, because he's been okay with me. But I hear some of the players been saying he's real flaky. They say he asks a lot of questions. Not about baseball. Personal questions. The kind a rookie isn't supposed to ask."

White looked a bit embarrassed. "When we go out on the road, and I'm not saying everyone, but you know, some of the players have a drink here or there, maybe meet someone here or there. You know, a waitress or something."

I knew precisely. Only it wasn't merely a drink or two, and it wasn't just someone here or there.

"It's kind of an unwritten rule that you don't bug another player about what he's doing on the side, if you know what I mean."

I did. "What about Wallace? Was Bidwell bugging him about something he was doing on the side?"

White chuckled. "No, not exactly. You see, we got this other thing some of the guys like to do on the road. It's called beaver shooting. You heard of it?"

"Yes." I had even done a little of it myself. It gets lonely

31

on the road, believe me. A few guys would go up onto the roof of the hotel they were staying in. It helped to have a telescope. If you found a good spot, you could see into any room that didn't have the curtains closed. If you got lucky, you could see a naked lady. If you got very lucky, you could see a nice-looking naked lady. And if you got really lucky, you could see a nice-looking lady engaged in some sort of sexual act.

White chuckled some more. "I guess Bidwell said something to Marvin about how he'd like to beaver-shoot his wife."

"And Wallace slugged him."

"Right."

"You said you think Bidwell may have a bad attitude."

"Well, I don't know. He'd probably get away with it if he wasn't a rookie."

"Have you thought about sending him back to the minors?"

"Yeah, I have, I sure have." White was going over something in his mind. "But to do that, I'd have to tell Mr. Fielding. He never interferes with the way I run the team, but this kind of thing would upset him a lot. He really hates dissension among the players. I'd have to tell him why. Bidwell could be a helluva pitcher real soon. But Mr. Fielding is kind of a military guy. He believes in discipline. If I sent Bidwell down and Fielding doesn't like him, he may never make it back to the majors again."

White sounded as if he'd seen it happen before. He looked at his watch. "Seven o'clock. I've got to go downstairs and make my lineup."

White signed the bill, and I walked with him to the clubhouse. As we got to the entrance to the box seats along the first-base line where I would be sitting, White saw some people he knew. I recognized them, too. Nobody who knew anything about baseball wouldn't know Mickey Mantle and Roger Maris, two damn good home-run hitters in their own right. They were with a much older fellow, Frank Crosetti, the Yankee third-base coach. They were heading out to Kansas City the next day for a series with the A's, and they were spending their night off at the Gents game.

We chatted for a few moments before they went to their

32

seats. As soon as they left, Ed White's expression became serious.

"I'd appreciate it if you wouldn't tell Mr. Fielding all of what I told you," he said. "He and I get along pretty well, but I don't want him thinking I'm working against him."

"You've been real cooperative, Ed. Fielding doesn't need to know what we talked about. He wants this thing solved, and that's what I intend to do. Without involving the players, if that's possible."

White looked relieved. We shook hands, and I wished him luck. I watched him walk slowly down the long concrete hallway to the Gents clubhouse. He had a lot on his mind.

6

Down behind the Gents dugout, Nate didn't appear to have anything on his mind except finding the beer man. I could see Melissa and Neta looking over their programs while he stood on his seat whistling at an elderly vendor.

"Hey Pops, three more hops," he yelled as I walked down the aisle.

I recognized the vendor from years back when I used to come to games as a kid, and I decided to save him the extra steps. He looked like he could use help back then. I scrounged in my pocket for two bills, asked for four beers, and told him to keep the change.

"You with that loon in the front row?" he asked.

I admitted my guilt, and he shook his head sympathetically. "Guy's got some thirst," he said. "He'll be spending the whole night in the pisshouse."

I got a kiss from Melissa when I got to the seats, along with hugs from Nate and Neta. She was the most even-tempered woman I'd ever met. Nate was euphoric over the accommodations and told me so repeatedly between bites of what he claimed was his fifth hot dog. "Three-fifty seats," he said. "This guy Fielding doesn't hold back."

It was fun to be at the ballgame, and I almost forgot I was working until Wallace came to bat in the bottom of the first inning against Chuck Estrada. He was greeted with a deafening chorus of catcalls and cheers that must have lasted a full two minutes. More than sixty thousand people had turned out for the game, and every one of them had an opinion to register. From our seats I could see Wallace close up, and his face looked even more tired and nervous than the pictures in the newspaper would lead you to believe.

Grounding out into a double play probably didn't make him feel any better. He struck out when he came to bat in the third inning and grounded into another double play in the fifth. That was the story of the ballgame. Every time the Gents got men on base, the Orioles seemed to come up with a double play.

Baltimore got off to a 3–0 lead when Jim Gentile homered off Bob Shermis with Jackie Brandt and the third baseman, Robinson, on base in the fourth inning. The score stayed that way until our tenth beer, the seventh inning.

We had to restrain Nate physically from prostrating himself across the top of the Gents dugout when Ned "Mule" Muhlsinger tied the score with a three-run homer. Muhlsinger was Nate's favorite player, and Nate asked if I'd use my new connections to introduce them sometime. My favorite, second baseman Barry Preston, didn't fare as well. The Orioles had scored another run in the top of the ninth, and Preston came to bat in the bottom half of the inning with a chance to win a game. But Hoyt Wilhelm, Baltimore's knuckleball relief pitcher, got him to hit into a double play to end the game.

Wallace had gone 0 for 4 on the night, and Sworpe had managed only a lousy single. The Tigers had won up in Boston against the Red Sox, and though I and most of New York loved to see Boston lose, it meant the Tigers were only one game behind the Gents. The crowd wasn't exactly ecstatic on the way out. The fans had come to see Wallace hit home runs, and they expected the Gents to win. We pushed and shoved our way through the aisles, with Neta tugging Nate behind her and Melissa clutching my hand so we wouldn't get separated.

35

As we got to the top of the stairs leading from the box seats to the exit, I thought I saw a familiar face. She was standing about twenty rows away, waiting for the line to the exit to start moving. As it did, she turned slightly in my direction, and there was no doubt about it. Rita Delancey was my type of woman, a baseball fan.

We walked through the scenic Bronx to the subway station, and I fished out forty cents for our tokens. Nate and Neta got off at 79th Street, and I invited Melissa back to my place for coffee, which wasn't all I had in mind. She accepted, and we drank Old Grand-Dad instead and crawled into bed.

It wasn't the first time for us, but it didn't happen on an everyday basis, either. She had some things to work out with her ex-husband and I helped her along once in a while. She'd been divorced for six months. I thought back on mine and I realized that it would be three years next week. I lay on my back and stared up into her crystal-green eyes and thought of Amy. Amy had the same eyes, the same mouth, but she was an entirely different person. She didn't have Melissa's long brown hair. She wasn't as pretty, and her sense of humor wasn't as sharp. I wondered what she was doing. Probably asleep, or maybe getting up to feed the baby. Amy had wanted babies, but I didn't. She had wanted a house in Connecticut with a garage and two cars, but I didn't. She had wanted a man who worked steady hours, came home every night for dinner at six o'clock, and mowed the lawn on weekends. She had everything she wanted now.

I hadn't blamed her four years before when she got fed up with the bullshit. I was never home, and she never knew when I'd be coming home. She never knew *if* I'd be coming home. She'd wait up for me till two in the morning. We'd scream and fight till three. I'd go for a walk till four, and she'd have to be at work by eight. When she got home, I'd be out again. Our marriage didn't have a rat's chance in the Ritz. It hadn't worked from day one.

We met when I was a cop, three years out of City College. I'd quit that shit after two years, and wanted to save the world. The army wouldn't take me, thanks to my glass eye, but the New York police couldn't afford to be particular in 1952 when every able-bodied guy was off in Korea shooting gooks. I'd never really liked cops, and I wanted to find out why. I found out fast.

Most cops are jocks who never made it. Getting on the force is like making the high-school football team. You think it will be exciting, but pretty soon you find out you've got to be a full-time asshole to get along with anyone you work with. It's what growing up in the U.S. is all about. It starts with Boy Scouts, gets stronger with high-school sports, climaxes in the army. The real jocks—the ones with talent—go pro. The rejects become cops. The others, the ones that don't make it at all, become little-league baseball managers.

I felt important for a couple of years, especially after Amy came along. I was a hero to her, and that's all that mattered. But I got sick of the backroom bullshit, got tired of playing cards, eating candy bars for dinner, cleaning my uniform, and busting the wrong people's heads. Then I met Larry Sturgin.

Larry was a private detective, the best in the business around the end of the war. Those were the glory days for privates. GIs were coming home and paying anything to check up on what their sweethearts had been doing while they were off fighting for the red, white, and blue. Larry hated cops, and mostly for the same reasons I did. He'd been one, too. I signed on as his assistant. I learned a lot from him and had a good time for a while. Amy didn't like it, but I didn't care. She thought I should quit when Larry was killed. I thought about it but didn't. I got the guy who killed Larry, the only guy I've ever killed. And nobody asked any questions.

Except Amy. We patched things up, and it worked for a few years, but it was never the same again. Four years ago she moved out. Three years ago I became a single man. And two years ago she married an accountant for some corporation. He had job security.

"What are you thinking about, Renzler?" Melissa was lying on top of me, investigating the more interesting details of my otherwise uninteresting face with a very attractive finger.

I took a bite of it, and she squealed in mock pain.

"I'm thinking about how much I'd like to do it again."

We did.

7

There's nothing like a little good sex to make a two-bit private eye feel like a million-dollar dick. And it's a good thing I felt that way, too, because the phone was already ringing and it was only 8:30. I hoped these calls weren't going to become a daily routine.

I braced myself for the worst and expected Mrs. Grayson. So I was pleased to hear Rita Delancey's voice as I lit my first Camel of the day and stumbled with the phone to the stove to boil water for coffee.

She sounded upset, but her voice hadn't lost any of its sexiness. "Mr. Renzler? How are you?"

"It's Mark," I told her for the fourth or fifth time. "I'm fine. I'm just reading the paper. The Gents lost last night." She didn't say anything. "Do you like baseball?" I asked.

"Uh, no. I really don't know anything about it."

I couldn't figure out why she was feeding me a line, but for some reason I had expected her to dodge the question. I was getting the uneasy feeling that Rita Delancey was hiding more than her name.

"Of course you didn't call to talk about baseball," I said.

"No." Her voice trembled a bit, which sounded nice, because it had a throaty quality about it, and I happen to like throaty voices. I wondered if it was my question about baseball that was making her nervous.

"He called again," she said.

"The same guy?"

"I think so. He called last evening, right after I talked to you. I called you back, but you were gone."

"What's the message this time?"

"He said to go to another house. I have the address. He said last time things got botched up. He said he didn't want any mistakes this time." She paused.

"Anything else?"

"He said if I didn't cooperate, he'd . . ." She began to blubber. If she was putting on an act, it was a first-rate performance. "He said he'd make me company for the other man. The one at the house."

"He's just trying to scare you. Don't you worry. He's not even going to get close." I didn't know this for a fact, of course, but she seemed to be reassured, and that's what I wanted. "Did he say anything else?"

"Just to bring the money if I wanted the photographs. You still have the money, don't you?"

I told her I did, but I didn't tell her that I was beginning to think there weren't any photographs. I didn't know how far I could trust her, if I could trust her at all. And even if I could, it wouldn't do any good to confuse her with a list of possibilities.

I would have laid odds that the place was in New Jersey. It was. In a town called Totowa, which was getting very close to my old stomping ground, Wayne, and uncomfortably close to Paterson, one of the poorest excuses for a city I've ever seen.

She gave me the address, 2340 Totowa Road, and the time,

39

nine P.M. I told her I'd be there and that she should call me the next day to find out how it went.

She still sounded upset, so I thought to humor her with a bit of small talk.

"Are you from Jersey originally?" I asked.

"Yes."

"Let me guess. Union City."

"No. North Bergen."

I chuckled. "That's just this side of Paradise. What about your husband?"

"He's from Hackensack."

"Now that *is* Paradise." Since she didn't laugh, I said, "I won't keep you any longer but be sure to call me tomorrow."

"Mark," she blurted as I was about to hang up. "Be careful."

"I will," I promised. "I will."

8

Famous last words. If I had listened to the lady's advice, I might not have wound up sprawled across the front seat of my Corvair in the parking lot of the Golden Star Diner with a hunk of stick shift in my mouth and a lump on my head the size of a bowling ball.

I'd decided to make a day of it in New Jersey and had gone out to Big Johnnie's early in the afternoon to talk with Ray Gurella, the bartender who'd found the note to White two days before. It had started out as a nice day. Melissa had left right after Rita Delancey called, but not before promising another round of unlimited sex within forty-eight hours.

Ray Gurella was a talkative guy, and he was generous with the vodka in his Bloody Marys. Gurella said he hadn't taken note of the man who'd left the envelope for Ed White, but he might recognize him if he showed up again.

About four o'clock a tall, oily fellow walked up to the bar and took a seat a few stools down from me. He was wearing an open-neck T-shirt that we used to call an Italian dinner jacket when I was in high school. We also would have called him pizza face, because his mug was covered with acne scars that looked like first-degree burns. He ordered a beer and sang "Travelin' Man" along with Rick Nelson on the jukebox. His voice sounded as bad as he looked. What caught my attention, though, was the envelope he held in his lap.

"This isn't the guy," Gurella said, as he leaned over to refill my glass. "But he was in here Monday. I remember. I wouldn't forget a face like that. There was someone with him, a big guy. He wasn't too handsome, either. I think he left the note."

Pizza Face strolled to the jukebox and punched up "Quarter to Three" by Gary U.S. Bonds. Instead of returning to the bar, he headed straight for the main door.

I ran to the jukebox and picked up the envelope. It was addressed to Ed White. I started after him just as he went out the door. He walked to a white Chevy Impala and pulled leisurely out onto Route 3. Apparently, he didn't know I was following him.

We drove a few miles west to the junction of Route 46, and I kept my distance as he turned into the Golden Star Diner parking lot. When he got out of the car, he walked around to the back of the diner. I parked the Corvair and did the same.

If it had been during the evening, and if I hadn't had five Bloody Marys, and if he hadn't looked like such a scrawny kid, I might have been more alert. But I'm not used to being slugged during daylight hours. There must have been two of them after all, because as I walked up behind Pizza Face, something with a Brooklyn accent called me a motherfucker and put a dent through the back of my day-old haircut.

Coming to in the car was a lot like waking up earlier in the day. The only difference was that this time I heard five telephones instead of one, but nobody was trying to call me. The note for Ed White I had picked up was not in my pocket. My wallet was. My money wasn't. I checked under the seat. Rita Delancey's cash was still there.

The Golden Star was not my idea of haute cuisine. But when your head feels like a handball court, a cup of coffee usually helps. It took four cups and a cold cloth to bring me back. The meat loaf and mashed potatoes almost sent me away

42

again, but I balanced it out with two slabs of coconut cream pie that must have been baked by the day chef three days ago.

I called Nate and asked him to meet me at the Golden Star. The appointment I had with the blackmailer was only a couple of miles and hours away. He promised to bring a six-pack. I drank more coffee while I waited.

The *Passaic Herald News* had the story I was looking for on page 3.

POLICE HAVE LEADS IN
BASEBALL BAT KILLING

Passaic police say they have uncovered important clues in the investigation of Monday's brutal baseball bat murder in a deserted home on the city's affluent west side.

Police said the bat used to kill reputed mobster Rudy Appell was a special model used only by major-league ball clubs. Appell was the nephew of Ray Appell, a former aide to Congressman Hugh Addonizio (D., Newark).

Lieutenant Warren Chester of the Passaic police said the bat was a 38-ounce major-league model and probably is only available through the commissioner of baseball's office. The bat was found across the street from the house in the bushes, Chester said.

Last May, the body of Appell's uncle was found in the parking lot of Billy Hogan's diner in Orangeburg, New York. Appell had worked for Addonizio since May 1959 but resigned in March. Sources reported at that time that Appell was running a bookie parlor, but Addonizio's press secretary denied the charges. The FBI was called in to investigate the death, but no indictments or arrests have been made.

Lieutenant Chester said Passaic police are looking into connections between the two killings. He said the FBI may join the investigation of Monday night's murder.

The younger Appell was 37, police said, and his last known address was in Newark. He was unemployed and had a lengthy arrest record. Appell had been serving a six-month sentence for racketeering in the Essex County

43

Corrections Center, but was released on parole last month, police said.

I made a note to myself to ask Melissa to check whether Appell had ever been arrested for blackmail. Something strange was going on, and it had to do with Rita Delancey and blackmail and baseball, but I couldn't figure out what it was. For some reason, she didn't want me to know she had been at the baseball game the night before. In an hour, I would be meeting a man she said was blackmailing her. I was glad Nate was coming along.

I showed him the clipping when he arrived. He was wearing sunglasses and a trench coat that had seen more rain than the weatherman. It was his detective outfit, he said.

Nate paid my check, and we left my car in the parking lot and drove in his. We went past the Gladiators' Arena in Totowa, and Nate made me promise to accompany him to the next week's special feature, professional wrestling with Antonina Rocca, the Fabulous Kangaroos, and Brute Bernard and Skull Murphy. I said I would, knowing full well that he'd have forgotten all about it by the next day. Nate had a great memory for details but a terrible mind for plans.

Totowa Road is one of those long suburban routes that pass through one town and then winds out past a parade of model homes into the next, where the name of the road changes to something original, like Main Street. In this case, it changed to Riverview Drive, which was something of a mind-boggler, because the only body of water for miles was a dried-up creek that crossed the Passaic County golf course, just to our left.

Nate recognized the area from years back when his parents had dragged him out to see the Dey Mansion, one of a thousand old homes where George Washington was said to have stayed with his troops during the Revolutionary War. I'd been through the Dey Mansion a few times myself during Boy Scout days, since it was a favorite historical landmark for local Scout leaders.

Nate was slowing down to make sure his beer can would land close to the old homestead when we noticed that the car coming toward us was speeding. If ever there was something wrong about a car, this was it. I would have recognized that

Buick in my sleep. As I told Nate to turn around, I saw the *Hughes for NJ Governor* sticker on the back bumper. The car didn't have any plates.

With remarkable reflexes Nate made a magnificent 180-degree turn in his Oldsmobile that took in a considerable part of the Dey Mansion's perfectly manicured front lawn. But the driver of the Buick had a lead, and he got the luck of the light a mile down the road. We could have followed farther, but we had an appointment with a blackmailer that I didn't want to miss. I had a feeling we were late already.

It was five minutes to nine when we arrived at 2340 Totowa Road. Nate pulled over into a dirt road leading to the golf course, and we got out. A brand new Ford with Jersey plates was parked in the driveway. Nate checked the hood. It was warm. We edged along the side of the house to the back door.

The house had a familiar look, dark and deserted, but we could see a light coming from deep inside. I could make out a refrigerator and a stove as I went in the back door with Nate right behind me. We froze as a shadow moved slowly along the hallway in our direction. We pressed ourselves against the wall and tried to stay out of sight. His footsteps were loud as he entered the kitchen. Apparently, he wasn't expecting anyone.

Nate cut in front of him just before he reached the back door and landed a couple of body blows that would have dented a truck tire. As he doubled over, I rammed his back with my head, driving him into the stove. He crumpled and slumped to the floor, letting out a low groan. When he hit it I aimed my flash in his face.

"Jesus Christ," Nate said.

But it wasn't Jesus Christ. It was Marvin Wallace.

Nate switched on the light. I helped Wallace to his feet and showed him my ID. He was groggy, his face was bruised, and by the next morning his ribs would feel like someone had pried them apart with a crowbar. Other than that, he was in fine shape.

Wallace said a man had called him earlier in the day and told him to come to the house. The man told him he had photographs to sell that could ruin Wallace's marriage. When he arrived Wallace heard a scuffle inside. A man in a raincoat came running out of the house. Wallace went inside to see what had happened. A man was dead, he said, in the next room.

Indeed he was.

Pizza Face had looked ugly enough when he was singing "Travelin' Man" at Hot Rod Alleys. He looked even worse with half his face crushed like red pepper. Someone had treated him to the works. He wouldn't be doing any more singing or traveling, and I wouldn't be eating pizza for a long while. His

T-shirt was soaked red with blood that had dripped from his mouth and nose. His head was turned at an angle that no normal neck could achieve. His neck wasn't normal. It was broken.

A baseball bat was on the floor beside the body. The blond wood was caked with clumps of hair and blood.

"Did you touch this?" I asked.

Wallace was frightened, confused. First he said yes, then no, then he said he didn't know.

"Did you touch anything else?"

"I don't know. I can't remember."

"You've been set up," I said. "Someone wants someone to think you spent your night off taking batting practice on this guy's skull. You know why anyone would want to do that?"

He didn't. But I figured he might come up with a few ideas in another place at another time.

I gave him my card. "Tomorrow, early, call me. Go right home, and don't tell anyone where you've been or what's happened."

Wallace didn't put up any argument. He nodded and walked toward the kitchen door. He would have listened to a Girl Scout right about then. And a Girl Scout might have been more help than Renzler. There were cops at the door with New Jersey accents. Wallace wasn't going anywhere.

Suburban cops are small-timers. They're rarely called upon to do anything more strenuous than write traffic tickets and drag drunks downtown. Most of them can't get a gun out of a holster without shooting off a toe.

As luck would have it, the cop in charge managed to draw his gun without incident. Our good fortune ended there. He was pointing it shakily at us. His name was Wally Winkler, and he was an officious sort. He wanted us to call him Sergeant and stand at attention and kiss his shoes, which looked like his wife had just shined them with Johnson's Scuff-Kote.

After staring at the body for two or three minutes he called for backup help from the nearby Wayne police. Totowa, it turned out, had only one squad car. Thanks to us, it was already in use.

Winkler held the gun on us while his assistant, Sherman, searched us. He couldn't have been more than fifteen, and his complexion suggested he went to the same dermatologist as

Pizza Face. He handed Winkler our wallets. The sergeant gasped as if he were having an asthma attack when he saw Wallace's identification.

Winkler was a punk, and he became suddenly polite when he realized he was standing face to face with the man who was about to break Babe Ruth's home-run record.

"You have to understand, Mr. Wallace. We're just doing our job," he said. "If you like we can go to the police station to talk after the other policemen arrive."

"Does that go for us, too, Wink?" Nate asked.

"Shut up. I'm running this investigation," Winkler snapped.

"Doing a pretty good job of it," I observed. "Telling people to shut up is a great way of getting them to talk."

Winkler grunted. "Okay. Let's hear your story. But no bullshit."

"First, why don't you tell Sherm to keep his mitts off the evidence," Nate said.

The younger cop's face turned as red as a slice of pepperoni when Winkler spun around and saw him holding the bat.

"Goddamn it, Sherm. Put down the fucking bat."

Nate grinned. "Hey, Wink, maybe Sherm's your man. His prints are all over the murder weapon."

Winkler was not amused. Neither was Wallace, whose face was turning sallow as he stared at the mutilated body on the floor.

"Can we move to the next room?" I suggested. "The atmosphere in here leaves a little to be desired."

"Maybe some music would help," Nate said, pointing to Winkler's radio. "Can you get WPAT on that thing? I could really dig hearing a little Ray Conniff Singers right about now."

"Why don't you get on the radio and put out a call for one white sixty-one Buick, one white fellow driving," I said.

"Why should I?"

"Because that's the kind of car the guy was driving who pulled away from here just as we arrived."

"How convenient," Winkler said. His voice was as ironic as it would ever get. "I suppose you got the license number."

"There was no plate on the back."

"How curious." He was being ironic again.

"Jesus Christ, you don't really think we did this," I said.

"Why not? I've got you standing over the body."

"Let's see," I said. "The three of us took turns bashing in the guy's head. Then, after we got sick of it, we decided to call the cops just for the hell of it. Then we decided to wait for you to arrive. That is why you came, right? Somebody gave you a call?"

"Yeah. That's right."

"Doesn't that suggest something to you?" Nate asked.

We didn't find out if it did, because just then the Wayne cops arrived, and it began to look like a police academy reunion. The assistant police chief, a stocky, balding fellow named George Grimaldi, persuaded Winkler to let him take us down to the Wayne police station for questioning.

Grimaldi was hardly what you'd call a prodigy, but he seemed to have more on the ball than Winkler. He was in his fifties, probably, and if he lost thirty pounds, his wife wouldn't have complained. But, unlike Winkler, he wasn't intimidated by Wallace, and he went to work on the home-run slugger right away.

"You know, Mr. Wallace, this is the second guy this week that's been found killed with a baseball bat. Found another one over in Passaic Monday night. They say the bat used to kill that guy was a major-league model. You can't buy it in a store. The only place you can get one of them bats is from the commissioner's office—or from a major-league team. The bat they picked up tonight has your name on it. It's *your* bat."

Grimaldi leaned back in his swivel chair and listened as Wallace told him about the phone call he had received. He slowly unwrapped a stick of Juicy Fruit and offered it to us. Getting no takers, he folded it into a tiny square and placed it carefully on his tongue.

"I hate this shit, myself," he said. "But I had to do something after I quit smoking. That's not a bad story, Mr. Wallace. The only problem is, it does give you a motive for hitting the guy, and it doesn't explain the murder two nights ago. Between you and me, I don't blame you. If a guy was putting the heat on me, I'd be tempted to knock him around a little, too. But you've been doing a pretty messy job of it."

Wallace looked to Nate and me for help. Grimaldi was on stage. He was toying with Wallace the way a good relief pitcher plays with a weak hitter. He was pushing around a baseball star, and he appeared to be enjoying it.

"I think Marvin was playing baseball Monday night," I said.

"Yeah," Nate added, "maybe you think he did that one during a pitching change."

Our sarcasm warmed Wallace up. He was regaining some of the composure he had lost after finding the body. "I don't think I have to answer any of these questions without a lawyer," he said. "Are you going to press charges or what?"

"Come on, Marv," Grimaldi said. "I'm just asking a few routine questions. I been thinking these two friends of yours been having a bad influence on you."

"I don't know these guys. First time I ever met them was tonight." He rubbed his chin and looked at Nate.

"That's right," I said. "Take a good look at him, Grimaldi. You know he didn't kill anybody. He even parked his goddamn car in the driveway."

"Well what about you? You two smartasses have been giving off a lot of lip."

"Christ, we didn't do it," Nate said. "Just ask Marv. We didn't get there till after he did. The guy you want drove off in a white Buick. He's probably in Pennsylvania by now. We told Winkler about it, but he didn't know how to work his radio."

Grimaldi glowered at Nate and peeled another stick of gum. He picked up the phone and ordered the desk sergeant to put out a bulletin on the car.

"Who you working for, Renzler?"

I didn't have to tell him, but it was beginning to look like we might not be released before Labor Day. And I didn't want to involve Rita Delancey, either. "Arthur Fielding," I said. "Owner of the New York Gents."

Wallace looked as if he'd just been called out on a third strike, but Grimaldi was undaunted. "Why did he hire you?"

"To keep an eye on Marvin. The team has been getting some threats, just crank calls it looks like, but Mr. Fielding doesn't want to take any chances."

"You guys been doing a great job of keeping him out of trouble. Ha! Look at him," Grimaldi said, nodding toward Wallace. "He don't even know about it."

"That's the idea," I said. "Marvin's got enough on his mind without worrying about guys tailing him. Fielding just wanted us to watch him from a distance. He didn't want Marvin to know about the threats. Now it looks like someone's trying to frame him for murder."

To make the story convincing I asked to call Fielding. Even if Grimaldi didn't arrest us, there was a chance something would leak to the papers. Fielding would not like that at all.

The night operator at Fielding's office wasn't eager to give out his home number. With a little prodding—"I'm his stock-broker; you want him to lose a hundred thou on account of you?"—I got it from her.

The Gents owner did not sound happy to be awakened at one A.M. "I expected you to call, but I thought you'd at least wait until the morning," he said curtly. "I suppose you got the message from your tape recorder."

"What message?"

"I got a phone call early this evening. A man told me to take you off the case. Under the circumstances I don't think I have any choice but to follow his orders."

"The circumstances have changed, Mr. Fielding. I'm at the Wayne police station with Marvin Wallace. There's been a murder over in Totowa, and Marvin and I were there. I don't think there are going to be any charges made, but there could be some publicity—"

"I'll be right down," he said.

I hit on the magic word. Men like Arthur Fielding III do not like publicity. At least not bad publicity.

We drank coffee while waiting for Fielding, and Wallace called his wife to tell her he'd be late. He was going to have a lot of explaining to do when he got home.

"He sounds different in person than he does on the aftershave commercials," Nate said.

He was right. Wallace did sound different. But his voice sounded the same to me as it had when I had called his wife the previous day. I wondered if her voice still sounded sexy when she responded to his hushed explanation of why he wasn't home. It seemed ironic that I had learned Rita Delancey's identity by going out to meet the blackmailer and running into her husband instead. But it was no accident that he was there.

51

And it was no accident that she had been at the ballgame. Rita and Marvin Wallace may have had their differences in marriage, but now they had something in common—they both were being blackmailed, probably by the same person.

Fielding lived in nearby Upper Montclair, so it took him only a few minutes to arrive. Grimaldi unwittingly did us a favor by retelling our story to Fielding, rather than making Fielding explain his version. The Gents owner was shrewd enough to confirm the tale in detail. He offered to post our bond, but Grimaldi decided not to hold us. The FBI was taking over the investigation of the murder in Passaic, he said, because it was believed to be a mob killing. He expected to be taken off the case.

Fielding announced that the team was leaving for a series in Chicago on Friday, but he promised to contact the FBI beforehand. "We want to cooperate to the fullest," he said, "but we do have a pennant to win." He smiled broadly at Wallace. "And we have records to break."

The Gents owner was a slick PR man, and Grimaldi ate up his schtick as if he were dishing out ice cream sundaes. He promised to keep the story out of the local papers, and he asked for and got Wallace's autograph for his son. Where before he had been gruff and moody, he now became garrulous and friendly. If it hadn't been for a phone call from his wife, he probably would have kept us there all night, chewing the fat like old buddies.

Before Wallace and Fielding drove off, we scheduled a meeting for Thursday morning at nine o'clock. Nate and I discussed Rita Delancey's conjugal affiliation with Marvin Wallace as he drove me to the Golden Star Diner.

"It takes a blackmailer with a crude sense of humor to invite husband and wife to the same meeting," Nate said.

"Yes. The kind of person you'd expect to go around bashing people's skulls with baseball bats."

It didn't make any sense. Someone was trying to frame Wallace for murder and blackmail his wife at the same time. But whoever it was seemed more interested in killing hoods than in collecting money. And if he did have something to sell, he wasn't staying around to reveal what it was. But he had found the time to put a new part in my hair and to tell Fielding to put me on unemployment.

One thing was sure: If his intention was to upset Wallace, he was doing a good job of it. According to the newspapers, the home-run hitter was already so nervous that clumps of his hair were falling out. He was being subjected to incredible pressure—from the booing fans, from the hostile press. Turning up next to a dead body with his baseball bat was not going to help his concentration at the plate. I wondered what would happen if he found out someone was trying to blackmail his wife.

It was three o'clock by the time I crossed the George Washington Bridge and headed down the West Side Highway. New Jersey was shrouded in darkness, but the lights were blazing in Manhattan. The city that never sleeps was wide awake, as usual. Me, I was dead tired.

10

Thursday morning, like all mornings, came too soon. Pressie had actually crossed the lobby to the intercom to call me, and that could only mean one thing.

I told him to send Rita Wallace up and pulled myself to a sitting position within seconds. Once out of bed, I put on my charcoal trousers and indulged my lungs with a breath of fresh Camel smoke. I didn't have to look at a clock to know it was 8:30. I decided against a shave and got the coffee brewing as she arrived at the door to my apartment.

If I had Rita Wallace to wake up with every morning, I'd never need stimulants. I was sure she had been up late, but she looked fresh as a fruit salad, contrasting sharply with me. I felt like a foldaway bed of wilted lettuce.

Not one strand of her lovely blond hair was out of place, and her blue eyes sparkled like the ocean at noon. She wore a light blue cotton dress that clung tightly to her figure, and the

54

neckline plunged just enough to reveal the line of demarcation between her separate but equally luscious breasts. My adrenalin had begun to flow.

"I had to come see you right away," she gushed. "I wanted to find out what happened last night."

"Coffee, Mrs. Wallace? I have a meeting with your husband and Arthur Fielding in half an hour, so I have to hurry."

Her face didn't turn as red as I had expected. She didn't answer the question, but I poured her some anyway. She had come to find out if I had found out who she was. My discovery may have surprised her a bit, but she wasn't shocked.

"I suppose it's useless for me to continue this charade," she said.

"Perfect." I laughed. "That's exactly what you're supposed to say. That line turns up in every detective book. And I hear the TV shows are using it now, too."

She didn't share my amusement.

"Yes, Mrs. Wallace, the charade didn't work. But that's okay. I didn't think your name was Rita Delancey in the first place."

"You can certainly understand why I didn't want you to know," she said penitently.

"Sure, I understand." I was leaning back on my couch, and she had sat down beside me. In a few minutes I'd be meeting with her husband. The temptation was strong to cancel the appointment and demonstrate to her just how understanding I could be. I opted for caffeine instead.

"Mr. Renzler, I don't know how to ask you this." She paused.

"Sure you do, Mrs. Wallace. But you needn't ask. You can worry all you want about what I'm going to tell your husband about you, but it's a waste of your energy."

Her face brightened considerably, though it hadn't seemed dim by any means when she came in. "I appreciate that, Mark," she said. She rubbed a slender finger along the back of my neck, and I could feel the vertebrae along my spine shudder with silent applause. I hated nine o'clock meetings.

It took a lot of effort, but I got up to leave before her

demonstration of appreciation went any further. "Mrs. Wallace, I won't tell your husband anything he doesn't have to know. I don't know what he told you about last night, but I'd like to find out. Someone is trying to blackmail both of you, and someone is trying to stop him from breaking the home-run record. I'll keep your name quiet if you play ball with me. I have to leave now, but I want to talk to you when I get back."

I showed her the TV set and the record player and poured her more coffee. "I'll be back in an hour or so," I said. "Wait for me."

She said she would, and I believed her.

When I walked out of the lobby, Pressie flashed me a grin that would have revealed a full set of teeth if he had any left. His was the only happy face I saw for the next three hours.

Wallace, White, and Fielding were all waiting for me when Mrs. Grayson escorted me in. I took up residence on my regular marshmallow and asked her for coffee.

Fielding managed to force a smile. "Nothing in the New York papers," he said, holding up the *Daily News* and the *Herald Tribune*. "And there was no news in the Jersey papers, either."

The Gents owner seemed to be a person who looked on the bright side of things at all times. If I had his money, I'd probably find that attitude a lot more feasible. But his happiness was obviously affected.

"I called the FBI," he told me. "Inspector Kleindienst. He said someone from the Midwest office is going to interview members of the team about both murders. Not just Marvin, the whole team! Just because the bats used in the killings were major-league models, they seem to think that someone on my team is a murderer."

Fielding's voice was angry, and I tried to calm him down. "I don't think anyone on the team is a suspect," I said. "The FBI is just checking out leads. I'd like to know about the bats myself. Marvin, have you noticed any of yours missing?"

"No," he said, "but I never think to keep track."

White hadn't heard about any bats being stolen, either, but he said it was hardly the sort of thing anyone would take note of.

56

"Who, if anyone, would?" I asked.

"Try Ernie Mandel. He or the batboys may be able to tell you," White said.

"I'm not sure you should talk to anybody," Fielding said. "I still have to decide about you."

"What's there to decide? I suggest that Marvin give his account of what happened so we know where we stand."

Wallace nodded and began to speak, but Fielding interrupted. "Yesterday a man called me and told me to take you off the case, Renzler. He said there would be serious consequences if I didn't. I'm inclined to follow his instructions."

"What's he going to do? Frame Marvin for murder and bash in the back of my head? He's already done that, Mr. Fielding. I think you should come to grips with the fact that the consequences are serious already."

Fielding took a long noisy breath and stared into the coffee mug on his desk. He wasn't used to being talked down, certainly not by an employee in front of other employees. I felt certain I would have the opportunity to test his patience sometime soon.

"Go ahead, Marvin," he said. "Tell him your story."

"I got a call on Sunday the first time," Wallace said. "The guy told me to meet him at some house in Passaic Monday night. I couldn't, though, because we had the doubleheader with Baltimore. Then yesterday some guy kept calling. Every time I picked up the phone, there was nothing. Then he called later and told me I had one more chance. He told me to go to that house where I met you and your buddy. I didn't want the guy calling my wife, so I said I'd go. I'm sorry I did."

I felt sorry about spooking Wallace by hanging up, but it seemed a mild indiscretion compared with his other trouble.

"Then yesterday again I got this note in the mail," Wallace said. He pulled out a scrap of paper the size of an index card. A message was printed crudely in pencil:

RECORDS WERE NOT MADE TO BE BROKE.
HOME RUN HITTERS ARE.

57

"Do you have the envelope this came in?" I asked.

He didn't.

"Did you see where it was mailed from?"

"No. I just put all my mail in one pile and throw out all the envelopes."

Fielding showed Wallace the note White had received at Big Johnnie's bar. Either it was the work of a different person, or the same person had deliberately changed the style to make it look that way.

"Marvin, can you tell me about the guys on the team? Is there anyone who you think would like to frighten you?"

Fielding began waving his arms madly as if he were a third-base coach trying to stop a runner from dashing home.

I pleaded my case. "Mr. Fielding, you said you didn't want me questioning your team. That's fine, except that the FBI is going to be doing that in a day or so, and you can't prevent it. As long as Marvin's here, I'd like to take the opportunity to speak with him."

Fielding was trying to look on the bright side of things again, but his tone belied the success of his effort. "Okay. But I don't want you talking about this to that friend of yours."

"He works for me, Mr. Fielding. When you buy my services, you get his, too."

Fielding picked up the baseball paperweight on his desk and began squeezing it. For a moment I thought he was going to throw it at me. I had taken him to a full count, and he wasn't liking it one bit.

White broke the uncomfortable silence. "Arthur, I think you ought to let Renzler stay on. And I think you should let him come to Chicago and talk with the players."

Wallace nodded in agreement. I had a feeling it was one of the few democratic decisions that had ever been made in Fielding's office.

Wallace's dislikes on the team were numerous. Nate would have been disappointed to learn that he wasn't particularly fond of Ned Muhlsinger, the Gents first baseman. He also didn't care for Coffman Maxwell, the starting catcher, or his backup, Mutton Moran. Harry "Hawk" Harkness, the Gents third baseman, and two of the team's broadcasters, Johnnie Haller and Al Lewis, also made the list. They accused him of loafing in the field while they were on the air, but in person they were sickeningly friendly, he said.

"I guess some of the guys on the team don't like me, either," Wallace said. "But I don't think any of them would wanna get at me. Except..." He looked at White, who nodded. "Except maybe for this new guy," he said. "Curt Bidwell."

"What's the problem with Bidwell?" Fielding had been listening quietly until now.

Wallace shrugged. "We had a couple arguments. Nothing major, I guess."

"Why didn't you tell Ed about him?"

Wallace studied his hands in his lap before he answered Fielding's question. "I did tell Ed," he said.

Fielding buzzed Grayson and told her to make more coffee. While he spoke to her, his gaze remained fixed on White.

The Gents manager sank back into his marshmallow chair. His ass was burning so badly he could have toasted it. "Marvin did tell me," he said at last. "But I thought it would be better if I didn't say anything. Bidwell apologized, and Marvin didn't think it was important."

"Marvin's job isn't to decide what's important. Marvin's job is to hit home runs."

Wallace and White stared into their laps while Fielding talked.

"I can have Bidwell taken care of," the Gents owner said. "He's not so special. Promising pitchers are a dime a dozen."

White looked up abruptly. He knew more about pitchers than Fielding ever would. "If you don't mind my saying so, Arthur, that's just the reason I didn't tell you. I didn't want you sending him down. He might be a flake, but he's a good young pitcher."

"And he might be harassing one of my star players, and he could be a murderer." Fielding had lost his control. His pitches weren't even coming close to the plate.

"Hold on a sec." It was my turn at bat. "Mr. Fielding, you

59

don't know if Bidwell has done anything. But if he has, you're not going to find out by sending him off to play minor-league baseball in Columbus. Let him stay. That way we can keep an eye on him."

Logic seemed like a better line of appeal than mercy to take up with Fielding. He sipped his coffee and took my motion into consideration. His intercom buzzed, and he answered in a brittle voice. "I told you to hold all calls."

His anger didn't faze Mrs. Grayson. "Tell that to Mr. Russo," she shot back.

Fielding's face flushed. "I'll call him back in ten minutes."

The interruption seemed to soften Fielding's contempt for Bidwell. "Okay," he said, "Bidwell stays."

We agreed that we would only tell the FBI about the phone calls Wallace had received and not about the notes to him or to White. Wallace promised to call me right away if he got any more threats.

It was 11:30 by the time we finished. It wasn't the day for another Schrafft's special, and I didn't have time for a walk through the park. When I got to the lobby of my building, Pressie told me what I didn't want to hear.

"You been stood up, Mr. Renzler. She left right after you did."

Rita Wallace was making quite an impression on Pressie. I decided to buy him a bottle of J. W. Dant before I went away. He liked to sip it on winter mornings, and his circulation was so bad, it always felt like winter to him. He wasn't much of a doorman, and security obviously was not one of his strengths, but he did have fine taste in women.

"Did she leave a message?"

"Just to say that she'd call you. If I was you, Mr. Renzler, I'd wait right by that phone. You don't want to miss no calls from that pretty lady."

He was right. I didn't. But I had a few matters to attend to before I headed to Chicago. During our first meeting, Fielding had mentioned that a man named William Bosworth Tidwell had offered to buy the Babe Ruth monument in center field at Yankee Stadium. I had meant to check him out sooner, but I'd

60

been too busy getting bashed over the head, arrested, and lied to.

Tidwell seemed like a long shot, but he also sounded like Babe Ruth's biggest fan. I had to make sure he wasn't Marvin Wallace's biggest enemy.

11

William Bosworth Tidwell's estate was about half the size of Rhode Island. It started at the top of the New Jersey Palisades and sloped all the way down to the Hudson River, about five miles south of the Tappan Zee Bridge. It was what developers call a nice chunk of real estate.

The trail leading to Tidwell's house was about three miles long and steeper than the price of front-row seats at a heavyweight-championship boxing match. At several points along the main drive were other, smaller trails, all indicated with signs in the shape of baseball bats. The street names were right out of the Hall of Fame register—Babe Ruth Road, Lou Gehrig Lane, Bill Dickey Boulevard, Joe DiMaggio Drive. I felt like I was driving into a sports chapter in *Ripley's Believe It or Not*.

At the bottom of the trail just in front of the house was a diamond-shaped drive. It surrounded a grassy area that looked like a baseball infield. I parked the Corvair on the first-base side and got out my camera and tape recorder. When I called earlier I had told Tidwell I was doing a story for the *Chicago Tribune Magazine*. It seemed a good idea not to tell him I was a private investigator. A friend of mine, Rolph Laxman, was a sports editor for the *Tribune*, and I had asked him to cover for me if Tidwell did any checking. As it was, he barely seemed interested in being interviewed.

I walked toward a door marked VISITORS DUGOUT. Mounted on it at eye level was a mahogany bust of Babe Ruth. It was the only thing on the porch that even remotely resembled a doorbell, so I ran my hands along the contours of the Babe's face, hoping to find a switch that would announce me as a guest. As I stood back to get a better angle, I stepped across the welcome mat, a facsimile of home plate that looked to be about regulation size. In doing so, I triggered a recording, which blared out of two tiny speakers housed in Babe's nasal cavity.

"Here's the pitch. The mighty Babe swings, and there it goes. It's going, going, gone!"

At the conclusion of the tape the door opened, and I was standing face to face with a heavyset man of about thirty. He had dark hair and a chubby face, and he was wearing a New York Yankees baseball uniform, complete with pinstripes, socks, a cap, and spiked black shoes. He doffed the cap. If I hadn't known that he died years before, I would have sworn that the man standing before me was George Herman "Babe" Ruth himself.

"Mr. Renzler? I'm Robbie Tidwell. Uncle Billy—I mean, Mr. Tidwell—is expecting you. He's in the computer room. Come this way."

I was expecting Tidwell to be nuttier than a Snickers bar, but I wasn't prepared for the condition to be congenital. I looked uncomprehendingly at Robbie, but he seemed not to notice. No wonder. People probably mistook him for Babe Ruth all the time.

As he turned around I saw that the numeral 3 was sewn into the back of his shirt. It looked like an authentic uniform. If Tidwell could afford to offer six million bucks for the monument to Babe Ruth in Yankee Stadium, he could probably afford real uniforms for his help.

Robbie led me down a long hallway that was covered with

black-and-white photos of Babe Ruth. As we turned the corner at the end, we passed through the kitchen. Another man dressed in a Yankee uniform was sitting at a small table. He was eating a hot dog and drinking a Yoo-Hoo chocolate drink. He wore number 5 on his back and was hunched over the sports section of the *Daily News*. He looked up as I brushed past him. There was no doubt about it. The guy was a fucking ringer for Joe DiMaggio, the Yankee Clipper. I took a look around, but there was no sign of Marilyn Monroe. I wondered if he was another relative or if Tidwell had to buy him from someone.

Lou Gehrig was leaving the computer room as we entered. He was carrying the remnants of a tuna fish sandwich and two empty bottles of Yoo-Hoo on a metal tray that read "New York Yankees, World Champions 1928."

Tidwell was sitting in a leather lounge chair eating a salted nut roll and washing it down with a Rheingold. He was not dressed in Yankee pinstripes. He wore a navy blue silk robe that dragged along the floor as he came forward to greet me. He extended his hand. It felt like cold cream of wheat.

Tidwell had bags under his eyes as big as bases. Gigantic tufts of gray fuzz bracketed his eyes on top. His skin was wrinkled and pale, as if he hadn't been outside for several years. I would have estimated his age at eighty, but he had a full head of hair that hadn't all turned gray.

He held his arm out in front of me. "You like it?" he asked.

It took me a few seconds to realize he was talking about the gold cuff link on his sleeve. "Very nice," I said. Actually it looked like any gold cuff link to me.

"Look at it closer."

I did. And I had to admit it, it was distinctive. Engraved in diamonds on the upper side of the cuff link was Babe Ruth's face. This guy definitely had a thing for Ruth.

"It's gold. Solid gold." His speech was slightly slurred, and he spit as he talked. I politely dodged a miniature tuna missile and stepped back a few paces. "And those are diamonds," he said. "Fine cut diamonds. Not your cheap store stones. You know how much one of these costs?"

I figured about two thousand dollars, but I didn't want to guess incorrectly and run the chance of embarrassing one of us.

"Five thousand dollars. That's apiece." He held up the other to show me. "I had two pairs made. I gave one of them to my nephew. He's a pissant in the Gents organization."

"What's his name?"

"You wouldn't know him. And he's not using my name, so who cares? Right? He's just a pissant. I ought to take the cuff links back from him. He's such a little pissant."

He motioned to a chair. "Sit down. You want a beer?"

I said I did. He strode across the room and stepped on home plate twice. On the back of his robe was an embroidered emblem in the shape of a baseball. Around the ball were stitched the words "Sultan of Swat." That was Babe Ruth's nickname. Moments later, Lou Gehrig appeared at the doorway with two Rheingolds.

"So you're a writer, huh? What kind of way is that to make a living? I would have thought you would come up with something better than that to do, Renzler. After all, you were a pretty fair second baseman for a while."

Tidwell knew his baseball better than I expected. It's one thing to know about Babe Ruth. It's quite another to know of Mark Renzler.

"You know what your problem was, Renzler? Besides the eye, I mean." He spoke with the authority of one who always has the right answer.

"Hitting," I said.

"Hell no. I mean besides that. Everyone knew you couldn't hit the toilet with your turds. I'm talking about fielding. Let me tell you, Renzler. I saw you play a couple of times, and I swear you couldn't go to your right fast enough to get those balls hit up the middle."

He hesitated. I think he thought he was hurting my feelings. "Don't mind me," he said. "I bet you're a good writer. It's funny I've never seen your byline. I'm sure I would have noticed it." His voice trailed off. "But I guess I don't read much sports anymore. Players just aren't as good, you know."

"What about Marvin Wallace?" I asked.

"What about him?"

"It looks as if he's going to break the single-season home-run record."

"No way. No way." Tidwell got up from his chair. His

voice was loud. "You think that curly haired pissant's going to break the record set by Babe Ruth? You've got another think coming there. Why that Wallace couldn't carry Babe Ruth's jockstrap."

"He's been doing a lot better than carrying Ruth's jockstrap this season," I said. I was enjoying Tidwell's performance.

"Bah. Flash Wallace? He's not going to break the home-run record. That's what I call him—Flash. That's short for Flash in the pan."

"What do you mean, Flash in the pan? He hit forty-five home runs last year."

Tidwell was exasperated. He jumped up and down three times and clutched his fists together. The man was charming, absolutely charming. But he had the emotional composure of an eight-year-old child.

"Home runs! You want to talk about home runs? Listen to this, Renzler. You just listen." He began counting on his fingers. "Four times Ruth hit more than fifty home runs in a season. Four times, dang it! Eleven times—that's right, Renzler, eleven times—he hit more than forty home runs in a season. We're not talking about one good season. We're talking about brilliance; total, complete brilliance, for twenty-one years. Tell that to Wallace!"

Tidwell slumped back into his chair, exhausted. He closed his eyes and leaned his head back. His breathing was deep and regular. I wondered if he was going to sleep. Finally, he opened his eyes, slowly, as if to do so required intense muscle concentration.

"You want to see something?" His voice was now as soft and peaceful as it had been loud and violent before. "Come here," he said.

I followed Tidwell across the room to a huge console type-writer. "Look at this." He was smiling so hard, his eyebrows almost covered his eyes.

I looked at the paper he had torn out of the machine. It was a game-by-game comparison of Babe Ruth's home runs in 1927 and Marvin Wallace's home runs in 1961. Along with numbers on the page were computer drawings of the two sluggers. On the left side was the squat, rotund Ruth. Across from him was the tall, wiry Wallace. His black hair was a sickly shade of

66

gray on the printout. The information on the page showed that Wallace was well ahead of Ruth's record pace.

"This is why I rarely read the papers," Tidwell said. He patted the computer fondly. "I have my own sports information network right here. It gives me all the statistics, all the records I need. And it's programmed to pick up sports news off the radio wires."

Tidwell touched a few typewriter keys and chuckled smugly as another printout eased out of the machine. "Yes, yes," he said. "Just as I thought."

Tidwell shoved the paper into my hands. It had the same art work and information as the other printout. But added at the bottom were stats for Wallace for games that he hadn't played yet. The total at the bottom of the sheet for Wallace was 59 home runs. The sheet showed 58 home runs for Wallace in 154 games, the cutoff point that had been set by baseball commissioner Ebel Chapman.

"My computer is so much more sophisticated than that rusty contraption at NBC," Tidwell said. He laughed as he walked across the room and stepped on home plate.

Every morning on *The Today Show*, NBC featured "Casey the Computer," which compared Wallace and Ruth's home-run pace. On Tuesday morning, after Wallace had hit 2 home runs the night before to reach 50 for the season, Casey had predicted that, barring injury, Wallace would break Ruth's record within 154 games. I mentioned Casey's prognostication to Tidwell while he took two more Rheingolds from Gehrig.

He sputtered with laughter and handed me the beer. He took another deep breath and stared through my eyes. I got ready for another philippic.

"That computer of theirs is a pile of junk," he said. "They don't have the technology I do. They're in the Dark Ages over there, dang it. Their machine doesn't factor in stress. Mine does. My computer is the sultan of swat in information technology. That heap of scrap metal at NBC is in the minor leagues. Right where Marvin Wallace belongs."

I must have looked dubious, because Tidwell adopted a persuasive tone. "Believe me, Renzler, Wallace is not going to break the record."

"What makes you so sure?"

"My machine. I trust my machine. Wallace does not have the character of a champion."

As if to show me what character was, Tidwell lifted himself out of the chair and motioned for me to follow him across the room. Built onto a square glass table was a baseball game. It was about a yard long and two feet wide. The lettering along the side of it said "Home Run Derby." Two characters, each about six inches tall, were inside a batting cage. One stood at a tiny pitcher's mound, the other was anchored to the right side of home plate. The batter bore an uncanny, even if not coincidental, resemblance to Babe Ruth.

"Pitch me some, Renzler," Tidwell said. He pointed to a metal lever on the left side of the machine.

I turned the lever and watched as the pitcher hurled a tiny steel ball toward the batter. Tidwell cranked the batter's lever. Ruth's bat made contact with the pitch, and the ball sailed over a foot-high fence and into a crowd of miniature plastic spectators. I flipped the lever again. Once more Tidwell turned his switch, and Ruth cracked one into the seats.

"Come on, Renzler, keep 'em coming," he said. His eyes were fixed on the playing field.

I cranked again, and he hit another home run. Again, and he hit another. Again. Another.

"I owe my life to this game, Renzler." He spoke without breaking his concentration. "Every mechanical baseball game you ever played in your life was designed by me. That's how I made all my money." His voice was matter-of-fact, with no trace of pride or sense of accomplishment.

"Really?" was all I could think to say, as I paused to take a sip of my beer.

"Hurry up," Tidwell said. "You're spoiling my rhythm."

In all he slugged out 17 consecutive home runs before we were interrupted by Robbie and Joe DiMaggio. "Uncle Billy, it's time for *Abbott and Costello*," the nephew said.

Tidwell stopped in mid-swing. He extended his hand. "Thank you, Renzler," he said. "I must be going. It's time for my TV program. Today is the episode with who's on first. I've seen it a hundred times, but I still love it."

I reached out to grab his arm as he turned abruptly away.

"Just one more thing, Mr. Tidwell. I understand that you tried to purchase the Babe Ruth monument in Yankee Stadium."

"That's right. I offered Arthur Fielding six million dollars for that monument, but he wouldn't sell it to me. The bastard. And don't think he couldn't use that dough. Mark my words, Renzler. In a few months I may just have myself that statue. I might make that bastard an offer he can't refuse. I'm going to put it right out front in the middle of the diamond. And another thing, Renzler. That Wallace. He's not going to break the record. And I'll tell you what. If he does break the record, I'll give you my cuff links. That's in a hundred fifty-four games, of course.

Of course. It was a deal. But he didn't bother to consummate it with an offer of his cream-of-wheat hand. He left quickly, off to watch *Abbott and Costello*.

Robbie and Joe DiMaggio walked me back through the hallway and out the exit to the Visitors Dugout. I finished off my roll of pictures with shots of them on either side of the Babe Ruth bust on the door.

The two men in the baseball uniforms watched as I got into the Corvair, circled the bases, and started back up the trail. I looked in my rearview mirror and saw that they were still watching as I crossed DiMaggio Drive. My visit was probably the most entertainment they'd had in weeks.

It takes all kinds, I guess.

12

It took me three phone calls and a couple of favors owed to find out that the Roxanne West Realty Company was handling the vacant house in Passaic where Rudy Appell had been murdered. It took me two more calls to find out that the same company was responsible for the house in Totowa where Nate and I had discovered Wallace and Pizza Face. It took me one call to find out that Roxanne West's phone had been disconnected. And one more to find her address.

It was in Ridgewood, a small town between Paramus and Paterson, for whatever that's worth. All it meant to me was that I had to make another trip to New Jersey. If this kept up, I was going to have to see about getting a summer home there. Perhaps I'd ask Roxanne West about it.

To qualify for a real-estate license in New Jersey, you have to be dumb and greedy. It helps to be unattractive, too, but that is an optional requirement. Of course you have to pass the exam, for which you must know the alphabet and your numbers from one to a hundred. Roxanne West looked to meet all the criteria, and I figured that with sedulous preparation she probably could have passed the test.

Actually, I didn't meet the woman. Not formally, at least.

Her office was a small storefront three blocks from the center of downtown Ridgewood. I use the term downtown loosely, because if you went three blocks farther, you'd be in the center of the next town. Glen Rock, I think it's called.

The sign in the window was freshly painted, and beneath it were capsule descriptions of about a half-dozen homes for sale. I studied the listings, but none were for the houses that interested me. Perhaps they only rented those out for murders.

Inside, the office was sparsely furnished. There were four chairs with desktops, like the kind used by schoolchildren. These were for the customers to sit in. At the moment, they were unoccupied. Yellow pencils that looked to have been assaulted by a band of starved beavers were attached with string to the desktops. Toward the back of the room was a large blue desk that was shedding paint the way middle-aged men lose their hair. Someone had tried to refinish it with coffee stains, to no avail. Behind the desk sat a large woman with bluish hair and flaking skin. She looked like she came with the desk.

The air was redolent with wallpapering cement, indicating recent redecoration efforts. Someone shouldn't have bothered. The wallpaper was a montage of assorted fruit painted in sickly pastels, without regard for natural color. There were blue oranges, purple bananas, gray watermelons, and green cherries. Very impressionistic.

The theme of the place was completed at the back of the room, where a very big woman was making a very big impression on a formica-topped counter. Actually, she was making two big impressions, because she was leaning on the counter with both elbows. Two forearms formed uprights as wide as goalposts to support her head. The head was nestled in a pair of hands that looked like a double set of catcher's mitts. Her face must have been a foot and a half wide, and though I'm not a great judge of weight, I'd say that her head alone probably weighed forty pounds. On a day with low humidity she probably tipped the scales at three hundred pounds. If the other woman came with the desk, this one must have come with the office.

She was drinking coffee from a mug that was festooned

71

with lipstick smears. As I got closer I could see droplets of sweat seeping down the vast expanse of her forehead and into her eyes. It was still relatively early. By noon she'd look like a gigantic red sponge. I could feel my breakfast trying to take cover as I proceeded to the counter with caution. I was going to make this as quick as possible.

"I tried to call earlier, but your phone was disconnected," I said.

"That's right." Her voice was deeper than the ocean and thick with the sound of shifting phlegm.

"I'm interested in talking to Roxanne West about a house," I said.

"Which house are you talking about?"

"It's in Passaic. Two thirty-five Chestnut Street."

"Only Roxanne can show that house," she said. "And she ain't here."

"I don't want to see it." I smiled my charming smile. "I've already seen it. I just want to find out how much Roxanne is asking for it. And I was hoping to learn who owns it."

"I can't give out that information."

"I see. Only Roxanne can give out that information, I'll bet."

She was not taken with my attempts at friendliness. "That's right," she said, staring into the grooves in the formica.

"What about that house in Totowa? Twenty-three forty Totowa Road, I think it is."

For the first time, she moved her elbows off the counter, revealing breasts that looked like twin German submarines underneath her army-green blouse. I was making her restless, and she looked toward her companion for help.

"Lilly," she said, "do you know anything about this house in Totowa he's talking about?"

Lilly answered in a frosty voice. "Only Roxanne can help with that one."

"When will Roxanne be back?" I directed my question to big fatty.

"I don't know."

I looked toward Lilly. "I don't know either," she said.

"Well, I hope she comes back soon. You girls seem pretty helpless without her."

72

Neither one of them answered. You couldn't even insult them. I pulled a business card out of my wallet and got set to leave. As I did, the office door opened and the mailman came in. He carried a thick bundle of envelopes to Lilly's desk.

"Nice day, eh, girls," he said, as he handed the envelopes to Lilly. He nodded politely to me, and I returned the gesture.

We all watched him walk to the door. "Have a good day, Lilly. You too, Roxanne," he said.

I turned back to big fatty and smiled my charming smile again. Her blowsy face was three shades redder than a fire truck.

I handed her my card. "When Roxanne feels like talking to me, she can give me a call. I'd like to talk to the owner of those houses. About baseball. There might be some money in it for her. Maybe she could buy some new wallpaper." I looked at her sweat-soaked shirt. "Or maybe an air conditioner."

I could feel their eyes boring through my back as I left. I caught up with the mailman two doors down. I asked him if Roxanne West's realty company did much business.

"It's not too busy during the day," he said. "But it sure gets busy at night. There's always people in there when I drive by. One thing's for sure. They sure get a lot of mail in that place."

"Thanks," I said.

"Sure enough. Have a good day."

As I headed back to the Corvair, I saw Roxanne West standing outside her office. I waved to her, and she tried to hustle her butt back inside, but it was no easy task. The last I saw of her was her unwieldy rear end wriggling through the door like a huge clump of dust being sucked into a vacuum cleaner.

Melissa was up to her pretty ass in a drought story when I called. The reservoirs in New Jersey had all dried up, and mass hysteria had set in among homeowners who couldn't use their automatic lawn sprinklers. I had spoken to Melissa on better days.

"This is the third fucking drought piece I've done this week," she said. "If this keeps up I'm going to have water on the brain."

"Bitch, bitch, bitch."

"Not now, Renzler. I'm not in the mood."

She could be so sweet at times. This was not one of them.

"What do you want?" she asked. "The second murder?"

I said yes, and she put me on hold for half a Camel while she went to check the story. I had to be at Idlewild Airport in two hours, and there wasn't much time to pack. Fielding had scheduled a short team meeting for before the flight to introduce me and to brief the players about the FBI's investigation. It would be bad form to show up late. The thought of airplane food made lunch seem like a good idea, but my stomach was still reeling from the morning's encounter with Roxanne West.

"His name was Tommy Leon," Melissa said. "He was thirty-one. Another small-timer. Lots of arrests, only one conviction. The arrests were assault and battery, robbery, and gambling. It looks like he served six months for the gambling rap."

Tommy Leon was a hood all right. I had a feeling the world would survive without him.

"It's a little weird," she said. "This is the second murder with a baseball bat in a couple of days, but there's not much in on it. The police found the bat beside the body. But there's nothing here about fingerprints or suspects or leads."

"Good," I said. Grimaldi was doing his job.

"Renzler, how much do you know about this?" She sounded mildly alarmed.

"Plenty," I said, "but not enough."

"Are you in trouble?"

"No. But I appreciate your concern on such a busy day."

"Fuck you."

"That's better," I said. "Now you sound like the friendly sweet girl I know and love. Have you heard of this guy Leon before?"

"Never. But I think this gambling arrest may have been with that guy Appell who was killed the other night. He got out of prison a month ago. It looks like Leon got out at the same time."

"I think you're right. Will you check it out?"

"Of course. But when are you going to let me know what you're working on?"

"Sunday night, when I get back."

"Back from where?"
"Chicago."
"Isn't that a city in Illinois?"
"I think so."

13

Chicago. City of gangsters and crooked cops, steelworkers and crooked union leaders. Crooked politicans and crooked judges, crooked landlords and crooked businessmen. Chicago. Melting pot of unsightly elements. Bad air, bad vibes, bad water. Home of the blues, the White Sox, and the Cubs. Frank Sinatra's kind of town.

And I was on my way there.

Fielding and White had been brief at the meeting. They told the players about the two murders and said the FBI was investigating only because the bats used in the killings were 38-ounce major-league models. They did not mention the threats Wallace had received. Fielding said that he hired me just as a precaution, but he did not explain the details. He asked the players to cooperate by answering my questions.

I learned quickly that the players didn't have much interest in talking to me, regardless of Fielding's request. While we were waiting to board the plane, I approached Coffman Maxwell, the Gents catcher, and Ned Muhlsinger, who were chat-

76

ting away in a corner. Both of them were on Wallace's list of dislikes, and both used 38-ounce bats.

The Gents big black catcher waved me off as soon as I got close.

"I didn't murder no one, and I ain't missing no bats, and I ain't answering no more questions," he said, before I could even ask him one.

To make sure I didn't persuade him to reconsider, Maxwell bolted away, leaving Ned Muhlsinger to pick up the slack in conversation. From interviews I'd seen him do, I knew this wasn't Mule's strong point.

"Don't mind Coffee," he said. "He just gets riled real easy."

"I guess so," I said, reaching into my carrying case for the baseball I had brought along. "I have a friend named Nate Moore, and you're his favorite player, Mule. Would you mind autographing this for him?"

"Not one bit," the first baseman said. He was grinning vacantly.

"I know it might be a sensitive point, but I'd also like to know if you've noticed any of your bats missing lately."

Mule seemed to be devoting full attention to the task of signing the ball, and I had a feeling he hadn't heard the question. I was wrong.

"Tell you what, Renzler," he said, as he handed me the baseball. "I'm not missin' any bats, I didn't kill nobody, and if you ask any more questions, you're pressin' your luck."

I figured that by pressing my luck, I would also be trying the first baseman's patience, so I put the ball away and headed for the boarding ramp before I found out. As I got there I was stopped by Johnnie Haller, the former Detroit second baseman who was now a Gents announcer and owner of Big Johnnie's.

When I was a kid, Haller was one of my two favorite players. The other was Phil Rizzuto, an all-star shortstop who had gone on to become a broadcaster for the Yankees. Haller was the tallest infielder in the league, and Rizzuto was the shortest. I had alternated between copying both their batting styles, which may explain why I never learned to hit.

"I don't know if I can help you, but I'll be glad to try," Haller said.

"That's the nicest offer I've had all day," I told him.

77

"I understand someone delivered a note to Ed White to my bar the other day. Is that why you're investigating?"

Like Maxwell and Muhlsinger, I didn't care much for answering questions, either. "I heard about that, but I doubt there's a connection."

"But you came out to the bar on Wednesday. My bartender told me."

My former idol was beginning to earn my idle disregard. "What else did your bartender tell you?" I asked Haller. I tried to sound friendly but disinterested.

"He said you followed a guy out. A real ugly guy, he said."

"Anything else?"

"Yeah. He said you tip real good."

"He's right. If you hear anything else, let me know, okay?"

I began walking along the boarding ramp, with Haller following me. I was hoping he wouldn't turn out to be a pest, but he was not doing much to reassure me. I was also hoping he didn't know that the ugly kid I followed out of his bowling alley wound up being killed with Marvin Wallace's bat. If he did, I felt sure he'd spread the word around the clubhouse. I was wondering what he had already said.

Fielding had arranged for me to sit with Ernie Mandel, the Gents equipment manager, and Perry Powers, the public relations director. If Mandel was helpful, there was a chance I wouldn't have to speak with many players. After the reaction I'd gotten from Maxwell and Muhlsinger, that was looking like a pleasant possibility.

Mandel and Powers were already seated when Haller and I arrived at their aisle. He continued to his seat in the back, while I climbed over Mandel. He and Powers could have been nice guys and left me the aisle, but they didn't. I made a point to take my time getting settled.

Perry Powers was the kind of person who gives PR a bad name—not that I've ever met anyone who gives PR a good name. He was short and thin, and his blond hair was cut about an eighth of an inch off his scalp. It's beyond me how he managed to develop a full head of dandruff, but I was polite enough not to ask. He wore red-and-green plaid pants that made him look like a giant Scotch-tape dispenser. And he bottomed

78

it off with a pair of white bucks that were cleaner than Pat Boone's reputation.

Mandel wasn't much in the looks department, either, but he could hold his own in a runoff against Powers. We chatted during takeoff, and I waited until our drinks arrived before starting in on him with my questions.

"Have you noticed any bats missing?" I asked.

"No."

"Well, what about the players? Has anyone mentioned anything to you about missing any bats?"

"No."

"Do you ever take a count to keep track of how many you have in stock?"

"Not too often."

Mandel was a man of few words. I like that, but I hate to play Twenty Questions. "When was the last time you took a count?"

"I can't remember."

"Try." I smiled my or-else smile and spoke in my or-else voice.

Mandel avoided my stare and sipped at his drink. "I think it was about a month ago."

"That's good," I said. "Maybe you could recall how many you counted."

"I don't think so. It was almost a month ago."

I searched the equipment manager's face with a long silent stare. I was looking for something that would tell me whether he was being intentionally uncooperative. I couldn't find it. His expression was so absent, he might just as well have worn a no-vacancy sign on his forehead. This was the time for Powers to volunteer his skills at communication, but he was engrossed in *The Carpetbaggers*. I decided my own approach to communications would be more effective.

"Listen, Ernie," I said. "I'm getting the distinct feeling you don't want to answer my questions. That's too fucking bad for you. We're going to be flying for another two hours, so I've got plenty of time to find out all I need to know. And what I don't get from you, I'll get from the batboy."

As my tone changed, Powers stopped reading his book and began listening to me. But I don't think he found me more interesting than Harold Robbins. I flagged down the stewardess and ordered another drink. Powers had barely touched his Coke, but Mandel had drained his glass quickly.

"That's a gin and tonic for me, and a scotch and water for my friend Ernie," I told the stewardess. As she turned to leave I winked at Mandel. "Be a nice guy, huh, Ernie?"

"Wait just a minute," Powers said. His voice was seething with indignation. "You can't talk to him like that."

"Shut up. This is none of your fuckin' business, Perry." No one would ever accuse Mandel of being indirect. Vacuous, perhaps, but not indirect.

For a moment I thought they were going to fight across me. The PR director looked bruised and insulted; Mandel, mean and mad. I didn't think either of them was capable of inflicting serious physical damage, but in close quarters anything is possible. Sitting between them with a drink tray on my lap, I felt like I was caught in a rundown.

"Let's not argue," I suggested. "Let's just talk." It sounded like the sort of thing Harriet Nelson would say to settle a dispute between David and Ricky.

Mandel took a gulp of his drink. "Okay," he said, "what do you want to know?"

"Everything. I want to know how and where you get your bats. I want to know how many each player has. I want to know where they're kept, who has access to them, and who would notice if any of them were missing."

I still had to do some tooth pulling, but in the next half hour Mandel told me everything I needed. He wasn't much help, however. Just about everyone who went into the Gents clubhouse could walk off with a bat. The bats were ordered through the commissioner's office and shipped directly from the factory in Louisville. Once they arrived it was anybody's guess how many of them were broken or stolen or used.

I didn't have much trouble understanding why Mandel was reluctant to talk about his job: He didn't do it. His system of keeping supplies was so sloppy that anyone could take anything without being noticed. If Fielding had any idea how much money he stood to lose from theft or waste, it was a good bet Ernie Mandel would not be working for him.

As I was getting on the charter bus from Midway Airport

to the Palmer House, Otto Croaker waved to me from the second row. Croaker was the ancient third-base coach who had broken up the fight between Wallace and Bidwell.

"Hey, young man," he crackled at me. "If you don't mind sittin' next to old Croaker, you can set yourself right down here."

Even though White had told me Croaker wasn't playing with a full deck, I thought I should chat with him anyway. As I took the seat beside him, he flashed me a toothless smile. "Ribbit, ribbit," he said as he extended his hand.

Croak's frog imitation was legendary. Back in his playing days, he used to drive opposing pitchers crazy with his piercing, guttural grunts. His volume had faded over the years, however, and I was barely able to make out the sound above the roar of his asthmatic breathing.

"Ribbit, ribbit. Ribbit, ribbit." Croaker grinned at me again while he struggled to steady his hands enough to light a cigarette.

I lit it for him and he thanked me with another croak.

"Do you mind if I ask you a few questions?" I said.

"Do you mind if I answer them?" He laughed hard at his remark. "Ribbit, ribbit."

"Not at all." I smiled to let Croaker know I was enjoying his antics, though I don't think it occurred to him that anybody would *not* find him funny. That's probably because no one had ever taken him seriously.

"I understand you broke up a fight between the new kid, Bidwell, and Marvin Wallace." I kept my voice low, hoping Croaker wouldn't answer in a higher volume. Most of the players were sitting toward the back of the bus, but I didn't want to take any chances.

"Oh, yeah," Croaker said deliberately, as if he were recalling an event from his childhood. "Kid was askin' Marvin about his wife's beaver. You shoulda seen Marvin's face. Turned red as a beet. You ever seen Marvin's wife?"

I said I hadn't.

"Got a pair of knockers make your spit turn to resin. Ribbit, ribbit. I guess Marvin don't like nobody sayin' nothin' about her. Can't blame him."

I nodded in agreement and waited for the third-base coach to continue.

"Marvin slugged him a couple good ones. Flattened him out smoother than a pancake. That's when Old Croak had to step in. Marvin's been kind of tense, you know, shootin' for the home-run record and all."

Croaker lit another cigarette, with an assist from me. "Are you Catholic?" he asked.

I said I wasn't, without bothering to mention that I once was.

"Too bad. If you was, you could come to Mass with us. Ernie and me, we go every mornin' when we're on the road. Got one at seven o'clock in Chicago."

"That's kind of early," I said, hoping not to offend. But Croaker was already thinking of something else to say.

"Hey, I'll tell you a secret if you promise not to say nothin' to Marvin," he said.

"My lips are sealed."

"I'm hopin' Marvin won't break that record," he whispered.

"Why?"

"Cause I got me a bet down says he don't. Ten dollars. Ribbit, ribbit."

"That's a lot of cash. Where would I make a bet if I wanted?"

"Same place I did, I guess. You know Big Johnnie? He's got a bar out in Jersey. You go there and talk to the bartender. Name of Ray."

"Does Johnnie know about it?"

"I don't know. You know why I bet against Marvin?"

I said I didn't.

"Babe Ruth was a buddy of mine. We used to go out for hot dogs together, and he'd make me do my frog sound for everybody. Ribbit, ribbit." Croaker began grinning again, and I realized that he was tuning me out and tuning himself back in to the good old days. Within moments he was snoring away, sawing off the rotting logs of the distant past.

As I listened to his noisy breathing, I thought over my next move. When I got back to New York, I'd have to pay a visit to Ray Gurella. In the meantime, I'd have to keep an eye on his boss. But I was also faced with the prospect of interviewing a team of hostile players. Probably all of them had taken bats

82

at one time or another, and this wasn't the time to ask about it.

I decided to take another approach. Only one player on the team seemed to dislike Wallace openly. And I knew one person on the team was related to a Babe Ruth fanatic. William Bosworth Tidwell said his nephew was a pissant. He also said something about changing his name. But I didn't think he changed it much. It was time for me to talk to the rookie pitcher, Curt Bidwell.

14

Traveling with the Gents was a lot more luxurious than traveling with the Richmond Sailors. When I played for the Sailors, we used to stay in fleabag motels with one bathroom on each floor. The soda machines were usually empty, and the radios were always broken. Things were a little different at the Palmer House. It was Chicago's finest hotel.

I called down for some beers as soon as I hit my room. The players and coaches had roommates, but I had a room all to myself. It seemed like the life of Riley, and Nate would have loved it. The only problem was, I had to work. He would not have liked that at all.

I was starting to call him when I heard some whistling outside my door. I figured it was room service and waited to hear the knock. The whistling got louder as I walked slowly toward the door. It was a crude rendition of the theme song to *Peter Gunn*, the corny TV show starring Craig Stevens as a private eye. Someone had a sense of humor. I opened the door to see who.

I hadn't been introduced to Curt Bidwell, but I recognized him immediately. He had flaming red hair and his face was spotted with freckles. You don't forget a mug like that. He had pitched the previous week against the Washington Senators in a game I had seen on TV. Bidwell had turned in a pretty decent performance, except that he gave up a lot of walks. The Gents had won the game, though Bidwell was not credited with the victory. He hadn't gotten in to pitch since.

"Mark Renzler, right?" Bidwell was grinning like a kid who's just been kissed for the first time. It was called a smirk.

I said I was and asked him in.

"I came here to confess," he said.

"To what?"

"You name it, I'll confess to it. But I was thinking about murder, blackmail, and just being a generally intolerable pain in the ass." Bidwell had his hands in his pockets. He was tall and thin, about six-foot-five and no more than one hundred and seventy-five pounds. He had the posture of a kid who had repeatedly ignored his teachers' suggestions to stand up straight.

"Are you sure you don't want to reconsider? Being an intolerable pain in the ass is a pretty serious charge. I hear they can fry you for that in Illinois."

He pulled the right hand out of his pocket and offered it to me. His fingers were long and calloused. They looked like they had spent a good part of their life wrapped around a baseball.

Room service arrived with the beers, and I offered one to Bidwell.

"I don't usually drink before a game, but I doubt they'll use me tonight," he said as he took the bottle from me. "I did nine tough innings of batting practice yesterday afternoon."

"You sound kind of cynical for a rookie pitcher who's getting a chance to play for the best baseball team in the league."

"Yeah, I know. Everywhere I go people tell me I have a bad attitude."

"Maybe they're right." I could identify with Bidwell. I often got accused of having a bad attitude myself.

"Why don't you tell me about this blackmail," I suggested. "I heard about a couple of murders, but I didn't hear anything about blackmail."

"Some private eye you are. It looks like a clear-cut case of blackmail to me, and I'm not even an investigator."

"But that's because you knew about it already," I reminded him. "You did say you wanted to confess."

"Isn't that what happened to those two guys who got murdered? Someone was trying to blackmail them. How else do you lure somebody to a vacant house?"

"You put a for-sale sign on it," I said. "You're right that it happens that way sometimes, but not with this one, I don't think."

"This two," he corrected. "The one last Wednesday happened near where I used to live. You know Ridgewood?"

I did. It was where Roxanne West had her realty company. "Do you still live near there?"

"Hell no. I moved to the city. But a lot of guys on the team are from out that way. They seem to dig the suburban life."

"Who on the team is from New Jersey?"

"Lots of guys. Husky Magill, Marvin Wallace, Hawk Harkness, Ed Braverman. Even our beloved owner, Arthur Fielding the third."

"Anyone else?"

"Those are the only ones I can think of. I've only been up for a couple of weeks. I try to keep my ears open, but I don't hear everything."

"You seem to be doing pretty well," I said. I opened another beer.

"I manage. You've got to talk to the right people to get the dirt."

"The dirt?"

"Sure. You know—who's sleeping with who. Who's hitting the bottle instead of the ball. I just heard a few days ago that the owner of this team was slipping the salami to the star player's wife."

"Indeed. Which star player?"

"I can't tell you everything, Renzler. You're the detective."

"Is Jaco Sworpe married?"

"Nope."

Bidwell's reputation for nosiness was not exaggerated. I could see why a lot of people wouldn't like him. "Who are the right people to talk to?" I asked.

"It varies. My roommate, Mutton Moran, has a mouth like a sewer pipe. He'll pass along any shit he hears about anybody. He's also got the worst breath in the history of baseball." Bidwell squeezed his nostrils. I smiled. He seemed the sort who'd keep talking as long as you made him feel like he was entertaining you.

"Some guys you have to catch at the right time," Bidwell continued. "Like Husky Magill. You talk to him in the morning, and he acts like he gets paid by the word. But if you catch him with a few drinks under his belt...." He laughed smugly at his reference to the chunky outfielder's waistline.

"I hear you haven't always been able to catch Marvin Wallace at the right time."

Bidwell's face was congenitally red, but nature allowed him an extra shade of crimson for moments of embarrassment. I had taken him by surprise, but he didn't seem angry. "Boy are you ever right about that. There's never a right time for that guy. He's a bundle of live wires. I don't want to be around when he shorts out." He paused. "So who told you I was having problems with him anyway?"

"Do you like him?" I didn't feel like I was risking anything by being direct with Bidwell. I may have been wrong.

"Hell no, I don't like him. As a matter of fact, I can't stand the guy." Bidwell's voice was loud at first, and his inflection reminded me of William Bosworth Tidwell. But unlike Tidwell, he had enough control to check himself, and he turned the volume down. I was tempted to ask him about Tidwell, but I decided to save it for later. When I wanted to surprise him, that would work just fine.

"I guess basically I feel sorry for him," Bidwell said. "He's going to be a first-class nut case by the time the season's over. He's a nut case already, if you ask me. He just can't deal with all this fuss everybody's making over him. And now I hear he's getting these threats—"

Now it was my turn to act surprised, and Bidwell didn't miss it.

"Oh, that's right, I'm not supposed to know," he said sarcastically. "I got news for you, Renzler. Just about everyone on the team knows Wallace has been getting threats. And everyone knows it has something to do with those killings."

87

"Who was your source for this dirt?" I asked.

"Husky. The man knows more gossip than Earl Wilson. And he'll spill his guts if—"

"—you catch him with a few drinks under his belt."

"That's right." The smirk had returned to Bidwell's face. "I think he gets his information from Johnnie Haller. He's another nosy sonofabitch. They're buddies. Husky hangs out at Big Johnnie's all the time."

Bidwell looked at his watch and got up to leave. He had to be at the ballpark in an hour. I still had time for dinner.

"You seem to get your nose into a lot of places, too," I said.

"Yeah, I guess I do. My mom always said I was the most curious kid in the family. That's no small accomplishment considering there were ten of us."

"Do they all look like you?"

He grinned. "Nope. Not a one of them. Personally, I suspect the milkman was involved. But even I'm not curious enough to ask my mom about that."

"I admire your restraint," I said.

15

By the time Bidwell left, my stomach was near revolt. I'd been treating it with a liquid diet all day, but I hadn't been able to down the queasy memory of Roxanne West.

I walked down State Street to Adams and headed half a block west to the Berghoff Restaurant. I'd spent three months in Chicago in 1957 and had gotten to know the place pretty well. As far as I'm concerned, there's no better restaurant in the city. But no one's ever accused me of being a gourmet.

My thinking became a little sharper after a mouthful of mashed potatoes and creamed spinach.

So far there had been two murders, three threats against Wallace, and two blackmail threats against his wife. I had a baseball team full of unlikely suspects on my hands and no answers in my head. If what Bidwell said was true, most of the team knew about the threats Wallace had received. That would not make Arthur Fielding III happy. I wondered how many players had heard the talk that Fielding had run the bases with Wallace's wife. That would not make the Gents owner happy, either.

If Bidwell had found out about Wallace and Fielding after being on the team only two weeks, it seemed likely that quite a few players knew. The man who first called Rita Wallace had dug up some inside dirt, and he probably got help shoveling from someone close to the team. Arthur Fielding had said it was unthinkable that any of his players would threaten Wallace. Yet he himself had done the unthinkable by shtupping Wallace's wife. Despite what the Gents owner said, I had a feeling his ballplayers were not just a bunch of nice guys. And that went double for Arthur.

I thought for a moment about Bidwell. Somehow I couldn't see him as a murderer. But he did dislike Wallace, and the home-run hitter had only begun receiving threats after he had punched Bidwell out. For those reasons alone Bidwell could not be eliminated from suspicion.

Bidwell did not have to be bashing people's skulls with baseball bats to be involved. Someone was stealing bats, and someone was threatening Wallace. Both dead hoods had been involved in illegal gambling before, and it was a good bet they had been at it again. Somebody they knew probably stood to lose a good deal of money if Wallace broke the record. I wondered if any of their funds were passing through Big Johnnies.

Was Bidwell a gambler? Was someone paying him just to harass Wallace? And what of his uncle, William Bosworth Tidwell, assuming Tidwell was his uncle? Bidwell had not sung any hosannahs to Babe Ruth. But he shared Tidwell's aversion to Wallace. So, I had a feeling, did a lot of other players.

I went back to the Palmer House and called Nate before leaving for Comiskey Park. It was eight o'clock in New York, but I managed to catch him in the middle of a nap. He accused me of interrupting a dream that was dripping with great meaning. A large-breasted woman in a nylon robe had been whispering secrets about the origin of the universe in his ear. She had given him inspiration for a painting, he said, but the idea had slipped into the cosmos when the phone rang. It was nothing less than a tragedy, and it was all my fault.

I reminded him that if I hadn't called, he would have missed the baseball game on TV. But he countered by telling me his TV was wired to an automatic timer that was set to go off just after the conclusion of the national anthem. His main regret now, it seemed, was that he might have to listen to it.

Nate had also wired my telephone to a tape recorder, and I asked him to stop by my office on Saturday to check for messages. His enthusiasm for the task increased considerably when I told him about the autographed baseball from Ned Muhlsinger that I'd be bringing back for him. I wasn't expecting any messages, but I was hoping Rita Wallace had called. She had blown me off the day before, so there was no reason to expect she would. The lady was involved in this thing right up to her gorgeous ass, and I wanted to have a chat with her. I could have called her on the phone, of course. But I preferred to see her in person when I asked her how well she knew Arthur Fielding.

Nate said he'd watch for me in the box seats on TV and agreed to get together with Melissa and me for dinner Sunday night.

I took a taxicab south on State Street to Comiskey Park, but by the time we reached 35th Street, the traffic was backed up for blocks. The Gents were attracting sell-out crowds wherever they played, and the biggest attraction of all was Wallace. Chicago fans loved to turn out to show their hatred for the Gents. This was the last time the New York team would be coming to Chicago for the season—and the last chance fans would have to see Babe Ruth's successor.

I decided to get out on State Street and walk the remaining four blocks to the stadium. Comiskey Park was the oldest baseball field in the major leagues. With its crumbling concrete walls and peeling white paint, it was a monument to the national pastime.

I could hear the starting lineups being announced as I got up to the entrance gate. Thousands of people who were unable to buy tickets were milling outside. People who had tickets said the park was so crowded they couldn't get to their seats. Across 35th Street, hundreds of people were trying to push and shove their way into a bar to watch the game on TV. The Gents would be batting first, and Wallace would be the third batter up. No one wanted to miss his turn at bat, including me.

"This kind of thing would never happen if Bill Veeck still owned the team," one patron grumbled as he hunkered out of the park. He was wearing an extra-large Sox cap and forcing half a hot dog into his extra-large mouth. Trailing behind him single file were three chubby boys, each one a head smaller than the next. With bad looks identical to their father, they were proof positive that God had a sense of humor.

I fought my way through the crowd and eventually got to the door marked AUTHORIZED PERSONNEL. I had a special pass and that made me authorized personnel. But I had to wait in line for beer just like any unauthorized customer. By the time I made it to my seat, Billy Pratt had grounded out to third and Barry Preston had grounded out to first.

The chorus of boos from the crowd was deafening when Wallace came to bat. He stepped into the batter's box and got ready to hit, but the noise did not stop, so he stepped out until it died down. As soon as he stepped back up to the plate, the boos started again. Juan Pizarro, the White Sox pitcher, looked in at catcher Sherm Lollar for the sign. Pizarro was a left-handed pitcher with a burning fastball and a great slow curve. Wallace stepped away from the plate as the pitch came at his head. He was not ready to swing when the ball broke sharply over the plate. The umpire signaled a strike, and Wallace scowled at him. He moved out of the batter's box, and boos began again. The noise of the crowd was so loud I could barely concentrate on drinking my beer. I couldn't imagine how Wallace was able to keep his concentration at bat.

On the next pitch Pizarro tried to sneak a fastball past Wallace. It was a mistake. Marvin swung his smooth, perfect swing, and the crack of the bat meeting the ball cut through the crowd noise like a knife slicing through raw meat. The ball rose off the bat in a steep arc and carried far out into right field. Floyd Robinson, the Sox right fielder, stood by the wall and watched as the ball carried high and deep into the upper deck. As the towering fly ball neared the stands, it got caught in the winds blowing from the northwest. Wallace stood perfectly still between home plate and first base and watched as the ball landed in the upper deck, foul by a matter of feet.

All fifty thousand spectators gasped, then the noise suddenly resumed. For the five seconds it had taken the ball to travel

92

four hundred feet in the air, the entire crowd had been audibly holding its breath.

Wallace slammed his bat to the ground angrily and kicked at the dirt in the batter's box. Pizarro's next pitch was the slow curve, and Wallace swung like he was trying to swat a fly. He hurled his batting helmet in the air and beat the bat against the turf. As he walked to his position in left field, the ear-shattering boos and catcalls became a well-ordered chant: "WALLACE SUCKS . . . WALLACE SUCKS . . . WALLACE SUCKS."

Nice fans, Chicago has.

And so the game went. Luis Aparicio led off for the White Sox with a single and stole second base. Jim Landis knocked him in with a single to center, and Floyd Robinson followed with a two-run homer. The Sox had scored three runs before the Gents starting pitcher, Frank Steiner, could retire a batter. Aparicio got on base every time up. He stole two more bases and twice robbed the Gents of base hits while playing the field. He was the best shortstop in baseball, no doubt about it.

The Sox scored two more runs in the fifth inning, but they didn't need them. Pizarro pitched masterfully, giving up but one run, a homer to Ned Muhlsinger in the sixth inning. Wallace looked more confused every time he came to bat, striking out four times. Jaco Sworpe didn't do much better, with only a scratch single, and even friendly Coffman Maxwell, the league's leading hitter, went 0 for 4.

The mood of the players when we got back to the Palmer House was less than cheery. In the course of a major-league season, even the best teams lose fifty or sixty games, so it was no crisis not to beat the Sox. But the Gents had lost two games in a row, and this was the time of the season when every game was important. Everyone on the team was undoubtedly feeling the pressure of Wallace's run at the record, but there was even more wrong than that. I couldn't put my finger on it, but I was sure it had something to do with the threats against Wallace. And I felt almost certain that someone on the team was involved.

It didn't seem like an opportune time to interview players, but I did have to do my job. I staked myself out at the bar near the entrance to the lounge and sipped at a Bombay and tonic.

I was hoping Husky Magill would stroll in and I could help him get a few drinks under his belt. He didn't.

Hawk Harkness did. The Gents third baseman stood by the entrance and craned his neck to look for someone at the tables in back. He didn't seem to see the person he was looking for, because he shrugged and ambled up to the bar. He took the seat beside me, but I don't think he noticed I was there. When he did see me, he tried to avert his eyes, but it was to no avail. I had him dead to rights, for one drink at least.

I should say that he had me.

It was generally thought that Harry Harkness was called Hawk because of his sharp batting eye. That was not true. Billy Pratt, the Gents shortstop, had told me the players nicknamed him Hawk because of his noisy habit of clearing phlegm. He warned me not to sit beside Hawk during meals if I wanted to keep my appetite. His performance at the bar made it difficult even to drink.

Harkness began hawking after his first sip of beer. It had to be one of the most disgusting sounds I've ever heard a human being make. He reached over the bar and grabbed a fistful of cocktail napkins that had maps indicating the historic sights in the Loop on them. Slowly he separated the top napkin from the rest of the pile and set it next to his glass. Then he leaned over the napkin and took aim. A yellowish green hairball the size of a nickel slid off the pink ridges of his tongue and dropped squarely onto the center of the napkin. Hawk carefully folded the napkin into a ball and hurled it over the bar and into a wastebasket under the cash register, while the bartender and I watched in stone-faced amazement. If the bartender had been bigger and Harkness smaller, there might have been a confrontation. But the fact was, Hawk was a great shot.

"I hear you want to ask some questions," he said to me.

Between his hawking and shooting, I managed to learn that Harkness, like everyone else on the team, was not missing any bats. If he was, he hadn't noticed.

After we talked for five minutes or so, Mutton Moran, the reserve catcher and Bidwell's roommate, entered the lounge. He came right to the bar.

"Come on, Hawk. Stop gabbing with the snoop and let's get a move on," he said.

94

"Yep, it's about that time." Harkness looked at his watch.

Moran did not speak but stared at me icily. I gazed back at him. The way my left eye wanders, it was hard for him to tell where I was looking.

Harkness picked up his stack of napkins and put them in the pocket of his blue Gents blazer. He extended a colossal hand to me. It was slightly damp. "Nice chatting with you, partner," he said. "We're going to go do us a little beaver shooting."

It was understood that I wasn't invited, and I wasn't the slightest bit insulted. Beaver shooting was not my idea of a peak sexual experience, especially in the company of Hawk Harkness and Mutton Moran.

I finished off my second Bombay and tonic and left the bartender a hefty tip for his tolerance. I was packing it in for the night.

The cute little blond clerk at the front desk chuckled when I asked for my room key. She had a southern accent so sweet, you could almost hear the sound of her words melting as they dribbled off her tongue. She couldn't have been more than sixteen years old.

"My, my," she drawled, "you can't decide whether you're comin' or goin', can you?"

"Beg your pardon."

"Why I just gave out the key to eight-fifteen a half-hour ago, I could have sworn I did. Then you left the key right back here on the desk."

Indeed.

When I got back to the room, everything appeared to be in order. I went carefully through my clothes, checking every pocket. I figured that whoever had come in my room had been looking for something, but there was always the chance someone had left me a present. Something small that ticks, perhaps.

I couldn't find one. But I did find something even better. and I didn't think it had been left there on purpose.

As I looked near the door, something shiny in the carpet caught my eye, the right one, of course. It was small, but it didn't tick. It was gold, and it was decorated with diamonds. They were arranged in a pattern to form a face. It was Babe Ruth's face.

There was a chance Bidwell had dropped it earlier in the day. And there was a chance the person who'd taken my room key had dropped it on his way out. There was a chance that the person was Bidwell.

I wasn't taking any chances. I slept with the cuff link under my pillow. Alongside my gun. I expected someone to come back for the cuff link. When he did, we were going to have a little chat.

16

I dreamed that when I woke up, I looked under the pillow. The cuff link was gone and so was my gun. In their place someone had left two teeth.

That's not the way it happened.

My travel alarm clock showed 8 A.M. when the ringing of the phone blasted me awake. It was Arthur Fielding. Despite my grogginess, I could tell from his voice that he wasn't very happy.

"Renzler, be in my room in twenty minutes. Marvin's been threatened again."

"Was it a phone call or a note?"

"A phone call."

"When did he get it?"

"Just a few minutes ago. Why don't you hurry up here. We can discuss the details then. I'm in nine-fourteen."

I called room service and asked to have a pot of coffee sent to Fielding's room. I assumed he'd have some there, but you can never be too sure about some things. Then I took out a sheet I was given when I checked in. It was a list of the room numbers of all the Gents. Everyone was on the eighth and ninth floors. Wallace was in 812. His roommate was pitcher Bob Shermis.

I called the hotel operator. It was a long shot, but you never know.

"A few minutes ago Mr. Wallace got a call in eight-twelve. Is there any way to find out if that was a local or a long-distance call?"

The operator's voice was businesslike but not unfriendly. "I think that was an inside call, sir."

"Do you mean inside the hotel?"

"That's right, sir."

"How can you tell?"

"The lights on my board light up at the same time, sir. All the eighth-floor rooms are together on my board. But I can't be positive, you know. It's so busy down here."

"I see. Do you remember which room lit up?"

"Well, sir, I can't be positive. But I think it was eight twenty-three. Yes, sir, I think it was eight twenty-three."

I checked the sheet. Mutton Moran and Curt Bidwell were in 823. Ed Braverman and Jaco Sworpe were next to them in 825, and Perry Powers and Ernie Mandel were next door on the other side in 821. Across the hall in 824 were Billy Pratt and Barry Preston. Hawk Harkness and Mule Muhlsinger were in 822.

If the operator was right about the call coming from inside, it probably came from one of those rooms. She said she wasn't sure, but I had a feeling she was right about 823.

Ed White was leaving his room as I came out of mine. We were on our way to the same meeting. It was just like old times.

The coffee, White, and I arrived at Fielding's room simultaneously. The Gents owner was on the phone, and his door was open. As I sat down on the edge of the bed I picked up his *New York Times*. A story on the lower left-hand corner of the front page had been clipped out. Wallace came into the room moments later, and Fielding got off the phone. The home-run hitter was not looking too happy.

"Someone called about seven-thirty," he said. "It was a muffled voice, and I couldn't understand what he was saying.

98

Then I figured it out. He said if I played in any more games, I wouldn't see my wife or my boy again."

Wallace was almost sobbing. He looked like a wrecked man.

"I got this in the mail this morning," he said, handing me a small envelope.

The postmark was from Oradell, New Jersey, a small town near Ridgewood. Inside was a small note printed in the same crude style as the other note he had received:

THE NEXT HOME RUN YOU HIT WILL BE YOURE LAST

I passed the note to Fielding and White. Neither of them said anything.

I did. To Wallace. "Have you told your wife about this?"

He nodded. "I called her right away. To make sure she was all right. She said she was okay."

I tried to be reassuring. "I think it was just an attempt to frighten you," I said.

"It did the job," he replied. There was no trace of irony in his voice.

"I don't think anybody will try anything, but just in case I want Nate Moore to stay at your house until you get back."

"Sure," he said as Fielding and White both nodded their approval.

I spoke to the Gents owner. "You said you didn't want the players involved, but I'm afraid that's already happened. I've learned that quite a few players have heard about Marvin being threatened."

"That's ridiculous," Fielding said. It seemed to be his favorite response to my remarks. "How could they possibly find out?"

"The word travels fast in a small group. Plus I gather that Johnnie Haller found out about the note that was left at his bar."

"That shit. I ought to kick that bastard's ass." Wallace had stopped sulking and come out fighting.

"Now wait just a second, Marvin." White was the most sensible of the three. "Let's hear what Renzler has to say."

I took a deep breath. "That phone call you received this

morning, Marvin, may have come from inside the hotel. It looks as if one of your teammates made the call."

"That's ridiculous." Fielding was cranking again. "How could you find that out anyway?"

"I called the switchboard operator. She wasn't positive which room it came from, but she sounded pretty certain it came from inside."

"How could she tell?" It was White's turn to be skeptical.

"The lights on her switchboard go on at the same time."

Wallace and White looked dumbfounded, but Fielding reacted with straight-faced anger. "Which room did it come from?" he demanded.

I held up my arms for a time out. I was going to tell them what I knew, but I wanted to preface my remarks. "She wasn't certain about the room, but she seemed to have a good idea. But the thing you have to bear in mind is that one of the players may have called you as a joke."

"A joke!" White was exasperated. "I don't think it's very damn funny." Wallace looked like he agreed, but he didn't say anything.

"I don't think it's funny either," I said. "But I don't think beaver shooting is a barrel of laughs, and quite a few of the players seem to get a kick—"

Fielding interrupted. "Which room?"

"She thinks it was eight twenty-three. But it could have been one of the surrounding rooms."

Fielding opened his desk drawer and began reading down his room list. I saved him the trouble.

"That's Curt Bidwell and Mutton Moran's room," I said.

The Gents owner picked up the phone like a fielder stabbing a line drive. White stared at me in silent disbelief, but Wallace couldn't contain his anger. "I should pound that bastard," he said. "Break his goddamn nosy head."

"Let's hold on a minute." I was appealing for mercy and reason. "Would you put down that goddamn phone?" I had raised my voice, and Fielding didn't like it one bit. "We can't be sure that one of them made the call. Why don't you wait until we have something certain to go on."

Fielding shook his head. "This is a question of discipline. I'm going to have a talk with both of them, right now."

100

Fielding picked up the phone again, and this time I didn't try to stop him. It would be a while before I told him about the cuff link I had found in my room. For all his suavity and sophistication, he wasn't being much more thoughtful than his beaver-shooting players.

"I want the two of you," Fielding blurted into the mouthpiece. "In my room, right away."

I called Nate while we were waiting for Bidwell and Moran. Fielding had pissed me off, and talking on the phone was the only thing preventing me from showing it—and probably getting myself fired in the process.

Naturally my call woke him up, but Nate was more than willing to spend the weekend with Rita Wallace. His enthusiasm waned somewhat when I told him she had a six-year-old son, but the revelation didn't change his mind.

"It's okay," he said. "We'll just send the little brat out to play in traffic. Why don't you ask Marvin if Rita gives good head."

Conversing with Nate cheered me up, as it usually did. But when Bidwell and Moran came into the room, the temperature dropped about thirty degrees.

Moran looked sullen and glared straight ahead as he entered. Bidwell trailed behind him. He had a smirk on his face that he tried to conceal by looking at the floor. It didn't work. He walked directly to the coffeepot and poured himself a cup. Then he sat down next to White, on the other side from Wallace. Marvin looked at Bidwell as if he were ready to slug him, but he sat still in his chair and sipped coffee. His left hand was balled into a fist so tight that his blood had to take a circulation detour at his wrist.

I was tempted to ask the questions, but I decided to let Fielding handle it. It was his idea to fuck things up in the first place. He could figure out *how* to fuck things up by himself.

"One of you two called Marvin this morning and threatened his wife. Which one of you was it?" This was the subtle school of interrogation.

I've seen a lot of people squirm under questioning in my time, and I can usually tell when someone is lying. Both Bidwell and Moran looked genuinely shocked by Fielding's question, and neither of them answered.

101

"Moran, where were you at seven-thirty?"

Mutton's voice was sulky and belligerent. "I was eating breakfast. With Hawk. You can ask him yourself. I just got back."

Moran's alibi was airtight. No one in his right mind would admit to dining with Hawk Harkness, especially in the early hours of the morning. The very thought of it nauseated me.

"Okay, Bidwell, what about you?"

"I was sleeping," Bidwell said smugly.

"Oh, how convenient. You can do better than that, rookie."

"I *was*." Bidwell raised his voice. He looked to White and Wallace for support but got none. "I didn't wake up until just now when you called me."

Fielding did not look convinced. It was a lame excuse, and Bidwell knew it. He got up and poured himself more coffee. I passed him my cup, and he poured some for me. Our eyes did not meet.

"Okay, Moran, you can go. But I'm going to check with Harkness about that excuse. If I find out you were lying, you're never going to play major-league baseball again. Is that understood?"

Moran nodded, staring at his feet. As he stood up, he continued to look down. Fielding's voice stopped him dead as he headed for the door.

"Moran, I want to see you hustling on that ballfield," the Gents owner said. "If I see you dogging it, you're gone."

For the first time, Moran looked up and faced Fielding. His expression was a cross between hatred and fear. The fear appeared to dominate. The Gents owner glanced away. That was the reserve catcher's signal to leave. Bidwell was next. Fielding would be harder on him.

I tried another appeal to logic. "Mr. Fielding, I think we should bear in mind that the operator wasn't sure the call came from Curt's room. There's even a possibility she was wrong altogether."

The quality of Fielding's mercy was strained at best. He considered my point for all of three seconds, if he considered it at all.

"Bidwell, you're the worst troublemaker I've ever seen in baseball. Everyone tells me you've got a rotten attitude. I think

102

they're right. You heard what I told Moran. That goes double for you. The only difference is, he's a washed-up catcher. You've got a whole future ahead of you. If you so much as breathe in a way I don't like, you won't even find a team in the *minor* leagues that's willing to take you."

Bidwell returned Fielding's glare. Unlike Moran, he didn't seem frightened of the Gents owner. There was even a trace of a smirk returning on his face. I had a feeling he wasn't going to last in the major leagues. He turned deliberately and stalked out of the room, taking his cup of coffee with him.

I picked up a *New York Times* at the newsstand and went back to my room for breakfast. I wanted to be around in case anyone came to reclaim a lost cuff link.

I usually read the sports section first. This time I went right to the front page. The story Fielding had clipped out was short. But it wasn't without interest:

IRS NEARS INDICTMENTS
IN TAX EVASION PROBE

Internal Revenue Service officials revealed yesterday that they have completed an investigation of several prominent New York businessmen and said they expect to issue indictments by the end of next month.

"When the charges come out, some famous heads are going to roll," one IRS source said.

IRS officials were reluctant to talk about the investigation but acknowledged that it centers on returns from 1959 and 1960 in which certain assets were improperly deferred to reduce liability.

A similar investigation last year led to the convictions of Warner Barnett and Thomas Broder, owners of an East Orange, N.J. construction company. The pair, who are major contributors to the New Jersey Republican Party, are appealing the convictions.

They allege that the chief IRS witness, accountant Aaron Russo, implicated them as part of a political witch hunt initiated by the state Democratic Party. Mr. Russo has been active in Democratic politics, including the campaign of Congressman Hugh Addonizio.

103

Mr. Russo has denied the charges, calling them "wishful thinking by two desperate tax evaders."

The story didn't mean much to me, but it might have meant something to Fielding. My idea of an asset was a savings account, and I had deferred starting one for years. Fielding's finances, I was sure, were a bit more complex than mine. William Bosworth Tidwell had said the Gents owner could use some money, but I didn't know whether that was his opinion or if he was privy to Fielding's affairs. Tidwell's preoccupation with computers and statistics lent some credibility to his remarks, but his devotion to *Abbott and Costello* gave me second thoughts.

My first thought, of course, was that Fielding might be under investigation. But it was possible that he had clipped the story because he knew someone mentioned in the article. I'd heard Aaron Russo's name mentioned before, and sometime soon I would have to confer with Arthur Fielding III about it. When I did he was going to be very surprised—and I don't think pleasantly.

Around noontime I ambled down to the lounge and took my regular seat near the front of the bar. The night bartender was not in yet, so I didn't have to suffer any guilt by association with Hawk Harkness when I asked for a beer. From my seat I could see all the way out the main entrance to the hotel, and I watched the players gather in the lobby before leaving for the game.

I waited five minutes after I saw Bidwell and Moran leave before I went to the front desk. It would have been safer to wait until the game started, but I didn't want to miss any of it. Besides, I thought I should be around in case anything happened at the ballpark.

Jailbait had been replaced at the desk by an officious middle-aged woman. She demanded to know my name when I asked for the key to 823.

"Bidwell," I said, "Curt Bidwell." You wouldn't catch this guy impersonating Mutton Moran.

17

I didn't expect Moran to be a tidy housekeeper. Bidwell wasn't much better. And I'm not what you call fastidious, by any stretch of the imagination.

Empty and half-empty Coke bottles were strewn about the room. A deck of cards had spilled onto the floor, as if someone had started a game of 52 Pickup and lost interest. Candy-bar wrappers littered the tables and desk, some still containing remnants of licorice and chocolate. On the night stand near one of the beds, a discarded banana split was doing double duty as an ashtray. All this since the maid had come by at 11:00.

I wasn't sure which drawers were Moran's or which were Bidwell's, so I checked all of them. I found a Gents tie clasp in one and a cheap baseball wristwatch in another, but I couldn't find any cuff links. I checked underneath the desk and went through both their suitcases. I went through their shaving kits and searched the bathroom cabinet. I turned the whole goddamn place upside down without success.

While snooping around the night table I managed to get the telephone cord caught in the drawer. The receiver crashed to the floor, and the room shook for about a half a minute. Sometimes I'm just not cut out for the job.

I had to tug on the cord to put the phone back on the table. It was stuck under the corner of the door adjoining the next room. That would be Ernie Mandel and Perry Powers's place of residence. The door on my side was unlocked. I opened it to free the wire. Just for fun I pushed against the second door leading to Mandel's room. It was also open. A nice cozy arrangement. If I roomed next to Powers or Moran, you can be sure my door would stay locked.

I thought to browse through their room, too, but I suddenly sensed trouble. I'm not a nervous guy, so when my instincts tell me something is wrong, I trust them. They're usually right. This time was no exception.

Mutton Moran was about two rooms down when I came out the door to his room. He did not look happy to see me.

Moran was about six feet, so I had two inches on him in height. But he must have been pushing 240, and I weigh a svelte 175. I'm also a man of dashing good looks, whereas Moran would frighten young children just by smiling. He wasn't smiling as he came toward me.

From the little I had learned about anthropology before dropping out of college, I could tell Moran was one of a few extant specimens that fly in the face of evolution. The facial development of his ancestors had been arrested around the Cro-Magnon stage.

"What the fuck were you doing in my room, Snoop?" He was leaning in close against me. I could see the remnants of his breakfast in the cracks between his yellowing teeth. He was probably heading back to the room to finish his banana split.

"I stopped by to pick up something Bidwell was supposed to leave at the desk for me," I said.

"And just what was it?" The fumes from his last few meals stung like a punch in the nose, causing me some difficulty in breathing. Bidwell was right. This man's sense of personal hygiene left something to be desired.

"That's between Bidwell and me." My voice was firm, but

106

I hoped not hostile. There was a chance I'd be able to talk my way out.

But not much of one.

Moran pushed my chest with his left hand and swung with his right. I anticipated it coming and moved my head to my right. His fist glanced off the left side of my head, wasting most of its impact on the wall behind me. It hurt like a bitch just the same.

Bracing myself against the wall, I ducked with my head and charged his stomach. It was soft and mushy. I felt like I had collided with a truckload of whipped cream. It seemed like it took me forever to push him across the hall and slam him into the other wall. If that didn't knock the wind out of him, nothing would.

Moran lost his grip on me when he smashed backward into the wall. I pulled away two steps and took aim, smacking his ugly face with three pretty fair shots. He didn't seem to notice. I was beginning to sense real trouble.

He blocked my fourth shot with his forearm, and I felt like I had punched a cinder block. He was breathing too heavily to get hold of me, but I wasn't doing a very effective job of hurting him. I danced away from him and jabbed, hoping to tire him out. It would probably take me about an hour and a half.

If I wasn't managing to inflict any damage, I was doing a very good job of pissing him off. As I circled him, landing soft, swift jabs, he began to swing wildly. I got underneath a roundhouse left and caught him on the temple with an overhand right. He let out a howl. That one hurt.

Mutton staggered back against the wall, rocking on his heels. He regained his balance and charged at me with his head down and his arms outstretched. I sidestepped and put out my leg in a move that would have made acrobatic wrestler Antonina Rocca turn cartwheels with envy. Mutton fell to the floor in a heap, but the bastard managed to grab my arm and pull me down with him. Luckily I landed on top, but the odds were turning in his favor. This was not the guy for me to wrestle.

It was fortunate that Jaco Sworpe came along.

I was still on top when the superstar outfielder strolled down the hall, but Moran was yanking on my arm as if he were pulling an electrical plug out of a wall socket. Jaco was notorious for oversleeping and showing up late for games. I was glad he was true to form. When you're the best player in baseball, you can afford to do that. He was also a strong sonofabitch, and once he had his black stovepipe arms wrapped around Moran, Mutton knew it was time to quit.

That's not to say he accepted his defeat with dignity. Mutton Moran did not do anything with dignity.

"First chance I have, you're dead, motherfucker," he said. "And you can bet Mr. Fielding's going to hear about this."

"Come off it, Moran," I said. "Fielding told you to cooperate with me. Starting fights is not the way to do it. And you're at the top of his shit list. You go whining to him, and you'll be playing in the Southern League next week."

"Come on, Mutton," Sworpe said. "Get yourself cleaned up, and let's go down to the game."

I thanked Sworpe for intervening as we watched Moran skulk to his room.

"Think nothing of it," he said. "Mutton just gets this way sometimes. Everyone's a little nervous with you here and all this talk of threats and investigations."

"Well, try not to let it bother you," I said.

"Not me. It doesn't faze me in the least. I just keep knocking in runs and hitting my three hundred." He took a right-handed cut at an imaginary pitch and grinned. "By the way," he said, "I'm not missing any bats that I know of."

I nodded. "Thanks again," I said. Then I headed back to my room before Moran came out and took my presence as an invitation for continuing the combat. I couldn't possibly look as bad as he did, but I had some cleaning up to do myself.

18

I was expecting beers from room service, so when I answered the door I was surprised to see a man in a three-piece suit. He was holding a badge instead of a check. He hadn't brought any beer.

He was Jack Slater of the FBI, and he was doing his best to look and talk like Eliot Ness, as portrayed on *The Untouchables* by Robert Stack. I figured the show was a big hit in Chicago.

"You're Mark Renzler?"

I admitted my guilt before he could work me over with his brass knuckles.

"I'd like to ask you a few questions."

"Do you mind if I dry off first?" I was wrapped in a towel. Slater had caught me on the rinse cycle of my shower. That's how my day was going: nothing but interruptions.

I told Slater the story we had agreed on, and he seemed to believe it. I also asked if he had learned anything about Tommy Leon.

He hadn't, and he didn't seem to like my asking.

"I'm kind of curious as to what sort of guy would want to blackmail a baseball star," I said.

"Just a punk, a two-bit punk." Slater was a bit young to be calling anyone a punk. I figured he was about twenty-six. "He must have been reading something in the gossip columns, and he thought he'd be a big shot. Only he didn't turn out to be such a big shot."

"The FBI is spending a lot of effort trying to figure out who killed a punk," I said.

"Just routine. And it's not my idea. I'm just checking out the connection between this killing and the other one."

"Appell."

"That's right, Appell."

"Do you think the mob's involved?"

"You ask an awful lot of questions, Renzler."

I nodded. "You can't get information unless you ask."

Room service arrived with the beers. I opened one for myself and offered one to Slater.

"I can't. Not on duty."

"Yeah, I know how it is." I took a long swallow. Beer was just what I needed.

"You don't have much to do around here, do you, Renzler? You're just hanging around, watching ballgames, jawing with the team."

"I know," I said. "It's almost boring." The less Slater knew about what I did, the better. If he wanted to think I was a lazy bodyguard, it was fine by me.

"You know what I think?"

I said I did.

"I think this whole thing's a joke. I think someone wants some hood rubbed out and says, 'Hey, why don't we frame Marvin Wallace for it. Wouldn't that be a laugh.'"

"I take it Wallace isn't a suspect then."

"No. And if you don't tell anyone who you heard it from, neither are you or your friend Moore. It looks funny at first, with Wallace being there and this guy being killed with a bat. But we figured out anyone can get a baseball bat if he knows someone."

"That's what I hear."

110

"You hear a lot. If you hear anything we should know about, make sure you tell me. I think you're okay, but my opinion of a person can change awful fast."

I got dressed quicker than Slater's opinion could change and hauled my ass down to Comiskey Park. I was feeling a little bruised from my encounter with Moran, but it was nothing that sunshine, baseball, and beer couldn't fix. Some of the discomfort was offset by the satisfaction of having kicked his fat ass.

As it turned out, I only had a few scratches on the right side of my face and a bruise on the left where he had slugged me. His injuries would be a lot more visible. I wondered what White had said to him when he arrived late for the game. For that matter, I wondered what his teammates had said. I was sure Sworpe would tell them what had happened. And I had a feeling some of them would be glad Moran had taken his lumps. The guy couldn't win a popularity contest if his parents were the judges.

It was a hot day in Chicago, and the traffic was worse than the night before. I walked the last few blocks to the park again, and by the time I got to my seat behind the Gents dugout I felt like I had pitched eight innings. I arrived in time to witness further evidence that the national anthem should not be sung. Chicago is basically a cow town at heart, and one of them had wandered out of the barn to milk the song for all it was worth— not much. I hoped she would manage to intersect the path of a stray foul ball at the nearest opportunity.

I drowned my dislike for Francis Scott Key in a beer and chased it down with a hot dog. Preston and Pratt both grounded out before Wallace came to bat against Billy Pierce, another hard-throwing lefty. The fans didn't wait until Wallace struck out to start their chant, and it was at least three minutes before they quieted down enough for Marvin to step into the batter's box. By quiet, I mean you might have been able to hear a gunshot if you were listening for it. That's what was worrying me. If someone wanted to shoot Wallace, he was as good as dead. I figured he knew it, too.

Wallace swung feebly at three pitches, missing them all. He was so distracted, I could have struck him out. He slammed down his helmet in disgust and walked slowly out to left field.

111

It was a long walk. He hadn't gotten a base hit since hitting the two home runs against Baltimore on Monday night. In his last ten at-bats, he had struck out six times. If he wanted to break any records, he had to get his mind off the threats and back on baseball. That was obvious. It was also easier said than done.

The White Sox got right to work on the Gents pitcher, Charlie Ross, in the first inning. Once again it was Aparicio who started things, with a bunt single and a stolen base. He came home on a single by Landis. The score stayed 1–0 until the sixth. Pierce had only allowed two walks and a single, and he was looking as sharp as Juan Pizarro the night before. The Gents bats were dead, and Wallace's had been the deadest of all.

Preston led off the inning for the Gents with a walk, and Pratt followed with a bloop single to right. Wallace was at bat with no outs and men on first and second. After striking out twice in a row, Marvin finally made contact with the ball. It was a bouncer between first and second base. Nellie Fox fielded the ball and threw to second base to force Pratt. But Wallace, who was a speedy runner, beat Aparicio's throw to first. Jaco Sworpe was up with runners on first and third.

Sworpe swung at Pierce's first pitch and cracked a line drive to center field. Comiskey Park was the second-largest ballpark in the major leagues—Yankee Stadium was the biggest—and the ball carried to the deepest part. Jim Landis was a fast center fielder, but he couldn't catch up with the ball. It landed over his head and took one bounce before reaching the 445-foot sign in dead center.

Wallace raced around from first and scored the second run on Jaco's hit, but it was a costly one. As Sworpe rounded second base, he slipped and went sprawling into the dirt. He was barely able to get up and limp to third base before Aparicio's relay throw came into the infield.

Jaco hobbled to the dugout. I hoped it wasn't a serious injury. Without him in the lineup, Wallace would be under more pressure to carry the team along. Just what he needed.

Charlie Ross held on, and the Gents won, 2–1. But Wallace had gone another game without hitting a home run.

I called Melissa when I got back to the Palmer House. I

wanted her to check up on Fielding, but mostly I wanted to hear her voice. Absence was making my heart grow fonder.

"Have you seen the *New York Times* today?" I asked her.

"I only read my own stories."

"The story I'm interested in was on the front page. It concerns an IRS investigation."

"Oh, that one. Yes, I know it well. I covered the trial that was referred to in the story. Warner Barnett and Thomas Broder. The story was right. They got shafted."

"Then you must know the star witness, Aaron Russo."

"*Know* him! That's an understatement. The asshole would not leave me alone. I met him at a political fundraiser—for Hugh Addonizio. He's got the wit of a grease monkey and all the sex appeal of an oil change."

"He sounds like your kind of guy. Maybe he'll change your spark plugs for you."

"When I need a tune-up, I'll go to you, Renzler. You're such a handyman."

"How nice of you to notice. The first time I heard of this guy Russo was in this story. Arthur Fielding clipped it out of the paper. But I've got a nagging feeling I've heard the name before."

"Maybe you heard me mention him," she said.

"Maybe. But I think I heard it somewhere else."

"I wonder what Arthur Fielding has to do with him."

"I'm wondering that myself. It could be that he's interested in the investigation. Or he might be interested in Barnett and Broder."

"You want me to find out." It was a statement, not a question.

"I owe you one."

"You owe me fifty, Renzler. And you're going to owe me again. We were right about Tommy Leon and Rudy Appell. They were both caught running numbers at the same time. Served their six months and got out. But I found out something else about them."

"What's that?" I could tell she was waiting for me to ask.

"They were a pair."

"A pair?"

"Of fags."

"How did you find that out?" Melissa was amazing. She had more sources than the Mississippi River has tributaries.

"I talked to a guy who was in jail with them. He said they were lovers."

"It gets lonely in prison, I guess."

"It gets lonely with you in Chicago, Renzler."

"What a sweet thing to say."

"I was only kidding."

19

I was in my usual seat at the bar when I felt the tugging at the sleeve of my jacket. He was a small kid, probably nine years old at most. If I didn't hate little kids, I would have thought he was cute. I offered to buy him a Coke just the same. The bartender took the order with a mixture of annoyance and friendliness as the kid climbed onto the stool beside me. First a chronic hairballer, now a snotty-nosed kid. He didn't like the company I kept, but he remembered my disposition toward tipping.

"They said you're asking about the bats," the kid said. His chin barely cleared the edge of the bar.

"That's right," I said. "What's your name, kid?"

"Jimmy."

"What's your last name?"

"Gibbs."

"Pleased to meet you, Jimmy Gibbs." I shook his hand. It was small, cold, and moist. It felt like a goddamn sardine. "I'm Mark Renzler."

"Uh-huh." He was distracted by his Coke. It was in a tall glass, with a straw and a cherry. He was eye level with the glass, and the straw cleared his head by two or three inches.

"So what's it like to be a big-league batboy?"

"It's okay, I guess." He was looking around the lounge. Perhaps he'd never been in a bar before.

"Do you travel with the team all the time?"

"Nope. This is my first time. My dad's here on business, so they let me come with him."

"I bet it's really exciting for you."

"Yup. I guess so." The kid was a bit aloof for my taste. I would have broken both my arms to be a batboy when I was little. This kid acted like he was underpaid.

"What is it you wanted to tell me about the bats?"

"Someone's stealing them," he said.

"How do you know?"

"I count them every day."

"Smart kid," I said. I was tempted to pat his head, but I was afraid he might be carrying lice. "How many have been stolen?"

He counted on his fingers. I ordered another beer and Coke. "Ten," he said triumphantly after half a minute of counting.

"Are you sure?" I wanted to be certain it was just coincidence that he was missing as many bats as he had fingers.

He looked mildly insulted. "Positive."

"When did you notice them missing?"

That was a question he had to ponder a while. Bats you could count on fingers, but time was a different matter entirely.

"I can't remember." He looked disappointed in himself.

"Do you remember what team the Gents were playing?"

He grinned. I had supplied him with a frame of reference. I was going to be a great father someday, but probably a lousy husband.

"Boston," he said. "Red Sox. Frank Malzone gave me his autograph. It was right after the man came."

"What man?"

"A big guy. Bigger than Mutton!" He stretched out hands vertically to show how big the man was. Of course I didn't need his help to conceptualize.

"What did he want?"

"He wanted to buy some bats. He said he'd pay me twenty-five bucks if I gave him some bats."

"What did you do?"

"I told him I couldn't." There was a note of regret in his voice. A kid could do a lot with twenty-five bucks.

"Good boy," I said. "What did he say?"

"Nothing. He just left. I told him to talk to Ernie."

"Did he?"

He shrugged. "I don't know."

"Have you seen this man around again?"

He shook his head. "What time is it?" he asked.

It was six o'clock.

"I've got to meet my dad in the room. We're going to dinner."

While we were waiting at the elevators, Ernie Mandel and Perry Powers strolled up. Mandel greeted me pleasantly, but I thought he looked a bit surprised to see me with Jimmy Gibbs. Ever since our encounter on the plane, Mandel had acted like my best friend.

I could not say the same for Powers.

"You know, Mr. Renzler," he said, "Mr. Fielding gave you permission to talk with the players. He didn't say anything about talking to the batboy."

"That's right," I answered. "He didn't say anything. And I doubt he would."

"Well, I don't think it's a good idea for you to be bothering a young boy like Jimmy."

"I don't think it's a good idea for you to be deciding what's a good idea."

Powers didn't have a response for that one, and the four of us waited in silence for the elevator. As we got on, Mandel attempted to lighten things up.

"So, have you turned up any leads?" he asked.

"As a matter of fact, Jimmy just told me that a guy offered him twenty-five dollars for a few bats last week."

"Are you kidding?" Mandel sounded genuinely surprised.

I shook my head. The batboy did too.

"Why didn't you tell me, Jimmy?" Mandel's voice was tinged with annoyance.

117

The boy shrugged. "I forgot, Ernie. I'm sorry." He stared at the floor.

The elevator stopped at the sixth floor, and Jimmy got off. "Thanks for the Cokes, sir," he said. "Bye, Ernie. Bye, Mr. Powers."

"Jimmy's a nice kid, but he doesn't have a brain in his head," the Gents equipment manager said as soon as the elevator doors closed. "I can't believe he didn't tell me."

"He probably didn't think it was important," I said. Then I smiled. "After all, he doesn't know what we know, does he?"

I left Mandel and Powers contemplating my question by their door and continued on to my room. Bidwell was waiting for me.

"You should have let yourself in," I joked.

Bidwell didn't laugh. "That's what you would have done," he snapped. "I have more manners."

"Oh, I see." I put the key in the lock. "Why don't you come inside and we'll talk. Is that polite enough for you?"

He followed me in and took a standing position at the edge of my bed. He spoke as if he were reciting a prepared speech. "I thought you were a straight-up guy, Renzler. I'm disappointed to find out you're such a sleaze."

"Life is full of disappointments," I said. I picked up the last two beers off the room-service tray. They were warm. It was time to call for more. "What's bothering you, Bidwell?"

The young pitcher was exasperated. "What's bothering me? You know what's bothering me. First of all, you accuse me of calling Wallace on the phone and get my ass hauled upstairs to lick shit off Fielding's wingtips. Then you go searching through my fucking room."

I offered him a beer. He grabbed it out of my hand and sank back on the bed. If there's a way to sit down violently, he had found it.

"I was only returning the favor," I said.

"What's that supposed to mean?"

It was my turn to act exasperated. "Come off it, Bidwell. I'm getting a little disappointed in you, too. You have a way with words, but mostly it involves lying through your teeth."

He stood up again. "I don't know what the fuck you're

118

talking about. All I want to know is what the hell you were doing in my room."

"Surely you jest."

"I'm dead fucking serious, Renzler."

I was beginning to believe him. I took the cuff link out of my inside jacket pocket. "I was looking for the mate to this," I said. I tossed him the cuff link.

He caught it and stared at it, then looked back at me. "What a gaudy piece of shit. Look at this!" he said. "It's got Babe Ruth's face on it! Are these diamonds?"

"Where did you take your drama lessons? Your act is really smooth."

Bidwell looked at me absently. "You think this is mine? How much money do you think I make? Even if I could afford it, I wouldn't waste my money on a pair of cuff links."

"It didn't cost you a thing," I said. "Your uncle gave it to you."

"My uncle?" Bidwell stared at me, and I nodded. He couldn't match my gaze, so he turned his head away. He picked up the phone. "You need another drink, Renzler. Either that, or you've had too many already."

"William Bosworth Tidwell isn't your uncle?"

"If he is, it's news to me."

I was dumbfounded. I've been wrong on my hunches before, but I'm usually pretty close. This time I wasn't even in the ballpark. I owed Bidwell an explanation.

"Tidwell's nephew plays on the Gents," I said. "Tidwell gave him a pair of those cuff links. He told me his nephew was using another name. I assumed it was you. Whoever it is lost one of them in here. And I didn't invite him in. Can you recall seeing anyone wearing one of those goddamn things?"

Bidwell still looked puzzled, but the smirk was returning to his face. "Nope. But I don't go around checking out people's cuff links."

"You should. Sometimes it's interesting to see what people have up their sleeves."

The beer arrived, and I toasted Bidwell. "I'm sorry," I said. "I owe you one."

"Good. Can I redeem it right away?"

"What is it?"

"Now that Moran's afraid of you, would you ask him to start brushing his teeth?"

20

By the time I got on the plane to New York Sunday afternoon I was ready to go home. Wallace hadn't hit any home runs, and I still hadn't figured out who searched my room. Wallace was striking out a lot lately, but I was striking out more. I hoped talking to Nate and Melissa would pull me out of my slump.

The Gents had won again Sunday behind the five-hit pitching of Braverman. He was throwing better than anyone in baseball. Ned Muhlsinger hit 2 more home runs, bringing his total for the year to 28. That wasn't enough to break any records, but it wasn't too shabby, either.

I sat next to Wallace on the plane, but we didn't talk much. He was trying hard to sleep and not having much success. He hadn't gotten a base hit in his last fifteen times up, and it was beginning to worry him. He was also worried about his wife, his son, and his life.

I told Wallace I was pretty sure someone was just trying to frighten him into pressing. I told him I didn't think he or his wife were in any real danger. Of course, I didn't believe this myself, but I was trying to be reassuring, not realistic.

Actually, there was some truth to what I said. If gambling, as I suspected, was the motive behind the attempts to harass Wallace, nobody would be silly enough to kill him—at least not until he got *real* close to the record. Anyone betting on him not to break the record could not collect if he died. Rita and the kid, of course, were another matter altogether.

Nate was supposed to leave the Wallace house as soon as Marvin got home. I figured anyone who wanted to get at Rita and her son would act while he was away. Besides, Wallace had insisted that he didn't want a bodyguard following him around. Since he was the one we were protecting, it made sense to honor his wishes.

I had arranged through Nate to see Rita Wallace on Monday afternoon. In the morning I was supposed to see Ebel Chapman, the crotchety commissioner of baseball. I had told him I was a writer, and he reluctantly agreed to give me fifteen minutes of his time. It would be a busy day for a guy who just got off the disabled list, and I had to get through Sunday night first.

Melissa and Nate and I went to Jim Downey's, a steak house on Eighth Avenue a few blocks down from Madison Square Garden. Nate and I had gone there a lot during the winter before going to see the Rangers get trounced by the Montreal Canadiens.

I filled Melissa in on the details, starting with Rita Wallace and continuing through Roxanne West. I played my encounter with Mutton Moran strictly for laughs and concluded with William Bosworth Tidwell. When I finished I realized that I'd been subjected to a steady diet of loonies and uglies for the past three days. It felt good to be back among the living.

"You seem to be convinced this thing revolves around the two hoods just because they had gambling records," Melissa said. "Don't you think there might be a simple personal motive?"

"Somebody killed those guys for a reason," I said. "And Rita and Marvin Wallace were both involved. Whose personal motive did you have in mind?"

"Arthur Fielding. After all, he did have an affair with Wallace's wife. Maybe he's jealous."

122

"I'll find that out when I talk to him," I said. "But I'm not sure he'd risk ruining his team's chances to settle a personal feud. He's a pain in the ass and a condescending bastard, but I have a feeling he's a businessman first."

"Aren't you overlooking Rita, too?" she asked.

Nate shook his head. "That's just like a dame," he said. "She *hired* him, for god's sake. And besides, Rita wouldn't hurt anybody."

"Listen to you, Bozo." Melissa elbowed him in the ribs. "You spend two days with her, and your mind is waterlogged with drool. You might recall that she had a fling with Fielding, so why don't you put your pecker away and take out your brain?"

"I'm not saying she's above sharing a snack in the sack. I almost got to first base with her myself. But she wouldn't set up her husband. She's just not that kind of girl." Nate's voice was sulky. He buttered a roll and right-hooked it into his mouth. That meant his feelings were hurt and he wouldn't have anything to say for at least a minute.

"What about this guy Bidwell?" Melissa asked me. "You seem to be looking right past him, too."

I nodded. "The guy's everybody's favorite suspect. He's either the best actor in the world or he's innocent."

"But you think someone on the team is involved." It was more a question than a statement.

"Yes. But it could be anyone who felt like making a few bucks selling some bats. The guy offered the batboy twenty-five dollars. I'll bet he would have gone a few hundred for one of the players."

"What about the equipment manager, Mandel, or Johnnie Haller?" Nate was back in the conversation.

I shrugged. "Haller certainly can't be eliminated. He makes it his business to know everything, but there's a chance he doesn't know his bartender's taking bets. As far as Mandel goes, he sounded pretty surprised when I told him about the guy trying to buy bats. But he and his friend Powers both seem like the type who'd do anything for a buck."

"It's not just the missing bats," Melissa said. "Someone on the team threatened Wallace over the phone. And someone broke into your room."

"The phone call may have been a joke. These guys have a strange sense of humor. Bidwell swears he didn't do it. Moran could have. Wallace made it clear that he doesn't like Moran or Harkness. Just because Harkness said he was eating breakfast with Moran doesn't mean Mutton couldn't have called. And the switchboard girl could have been wrong. As far as the person who broke into my room goes, that had to be Tidwell's nephew."

"Or someone who wanted you to think it was Tidwell's nephew," Nate added.

"That," I said, "sounds a little farfetched."

"As distinguished from everything else that's happened," Nate answered.

"Assuming it was Tidwell's nephew, why would he break into your room?" Melissa asked.

"I've wondered about that. It's possible that he talked to Tidwell and my name came up. I told Tidwell I was a writer, not an investigator. Maybe Tidwell asked him to check up on me. Or maybe he decided to check up on me on his own. Tidwell is just nutty enough to tell the nephew to leave the cuff link in my room to confuse me."

"The question is: Is he crazy enough to try to stop Wallace from breaking Ruth's record?" Nate said.

"The question is," Melissa corrected, "is he sane enough to pull it off?"

Nate grinned. "We haven't even mentioned *my* favorite suspect."

"The acting commissioner of baseball," I said. "Mr. Ebel Chapman."

"Exactly. He's got the perfect motive. He does not want to be made a total fool of in public, as he so richly deserves. He's going to look like a complete moron if Wallace hits sixty-one home runs in a hundred and fifty-four games. Now if we can only connect him with the threats." Nate hated Ebel Chapman the way kids despise leafy vegetables.

"I'll see what I can do," I said. "I've got an appointment with him tomorrow morning. Want to come along?"

"I'd be delighted."

Melissa was nibbling whipped cream off her cocktail straw.

124

She looked dubious, but it may have been the effects of the Irish coffee. It was the specialty of the house.

"What's on your mind?" I asked her.

"Arthur Fielding."

"What about him?"

"I haven't been able to dig up much about him, but I'm planning to look deeper tomorrow. I talked to the guy who wrote the IRS piece Fielding clipped from the paper. His source is mad at him for writing it and won't tell him any names. He doesn't know if Fielding is one of the people under investigation. But I did find out that Fielding's favorite charity is the New Jersey Democratic Party."

"What's that have to do with baseball?" Nate hated politics almost as much as he hated Ebel Chapman.

She shrugged. "Beats me. But I thought it might connect him with Aaron Russo."

"And why would we want to do that?" Nate's question was directed more at me than Melissa.

"Because Russo may be connected to the mob. And the mob is often connected to illegal gambling," I said.

"You're just saying that because he's Italian." Nate was feigning sensitivity about his heritage. He still couldn't get over the fact that his father had changed the family name. From Moresi to Moore, no less.

"I'm saying that because he worked for Hugh Addonizio. That man didn't get to where he is today because of his good looks."

"Perhaps it's time for you to place a bet," Nate suggested.

"I intend to. At a certain bar in New Jersey."

It was one of a lot of things I had to do. And I didn't have much time to do it. In the last few games, Wallace looked like he couldn't have hit a home run in little league. As long as he wasn't hitting, there was less chance someone would be threatening him—and less chance for me to catch someone doing it.

Melissa and I also had a few matters to attend to, and we headed back to my apartment to get started. We got out of the taxi at the corner of 72nd and Amsterdam, and Nate continued on to 79th Street.

Melissa took my arm as we walked along 72nd Street. The

125

temperature had finally dropped into the seventies, and a cool breeze was blowing in from the west off the Hudson River. It was a nice night.

Until the shooting started.

I grabbed Melissa and pushed her down to the sidewalk as soon as I heard the shots. I fell on top of her, and we crawled for cover behind the cars parked along the curb. We were only a few steps from the door to my building. Or, I should say, from where the door to my building used to be. Within seconds it was a massive heap of glass shards.

The shots had come from a car heading east on 72nd Street. There were six in all. I didn't get a look at the car, because I was staring at a dog turd wedged into a crack in the sidewalk. Welcome home.

I could see the heads starting to pop out of apartment windows. I didn't feel like being the center of attention. More than that, I didn't feel like talking to the police.

We hurried into the building. Melissa was shaken up, but she wasn't hurt. To be honest about it, I was pretty shaken up myself. I'd been shot at before, but I've never been hit. There's always a first time. That worried me.

"Never a dull moment when I hang around with you, Renzler." Melissa forced a smile. "I can't think of a better way to cap off the night than being shot at."

"They weren't shooting at us. They were shooting at the door," I said. "And I can think of a better way to cap off the night."

She said she could, too. In all modesty, I'd say we did a pretty good job of it, considering the circumstances.

Pressie was going to shit when he came to work the next day.

21

When I called him in the morning, Nate's enthusiasm for interviewing Ebel Chapman had waned considerably from the night before. At that time he had been giddy with the effects of alcohol. In the morning, he was suffering the aftereffects. It was also 7:30. Not a fit time for man or beast or Nate.

He consented to go, however, when I told him about the late-night greetings Melissa and I had received. Things were beginning to get exciting, and he didn't want to miss the fun.

We dropped Melissa off at the *Times* and continued on to Rockefeller Center. Our appointment with Chapman was at 9:30. We arrived two minutes early. It was a new record in punctuality for me, but I don't think Chapman was impressed.

A secretary greeted us as we entered a glassed-in room. There were three other secretaries behind her, sitting at a row of desks. They were standing guard in front of offices from which I could make out the sounds of business being conducted above the clatter of typewriters.

Our secretary spoke to us in a husky voice. It was the only thing fat about her.

"You must be Mr. Renzler," she said. She extended a slender hand. It had three rings on it. Her nails were painted red, and they were probably two inches long. I was sure she gave great back rubs.

I introduced Nate as my photographer. Luckily we had remembered to bring a camera.

"I'm Pam Masters," she said. She held Nate's hand for at least ten seconds. I couldn't tell which one of them wouldn't let go. "Would you gentlemen like some coffee?"

We said we would, and she went to get some. She didn't have any stockings on, but her legs were golden tan below a silk skirt that barely covered her knees. I would have felt self-conscious for staring, except that Nate was the only person who would have noticed. He didn't, because he was staring at her, too.

She had a long narrow face with firm cheekbones and shoulder-length auburn hair. It was a nice combination. I guessed her age at twenty-three, but you can never tell these days. In a vague sort of way, she reminded me of my old secretary, Sherry Lee Lancaster. If Pam was anything like Sherry Lee, baseball was not Ebel Chapman's favorite sport.

Pam Masters rubbed up against me as she handed me my coffee. She blinked her dark eyes for longer than was necessary and smiled when I thanked her. I didn't object. She was reminding me more of Sherry Lee every minute.

"Why don't you gentlemen make yourselves comfortable," she said, motioning to a leather couch with oak trim. Nate and I had been standing for five minutes and hadn't bothered to sit down. We were distracted, you might say.

"Mr. Chapman is on a phone call right now, but he'll be with you soon. I'm sorry you have to wait."

"We don't mind," Nate said. I could not recall ever seeing him so wide awake in the morning before.

Pam Masters led us into Chapman's office as soon as he got off the phone. The acting commissioner was not as friendly as his secretary, but we didn't expect him to be. He was lagging far behind her in the looks department, too. He was in his

128

sixties, and his face was tanned but wizened, as if he were suffering from too many Florida vacations.

"It takes two of you to do an interview?" Chapman's voice was brittle.

"I'm Mark Renzler," I said. "I brought along a photographer to take your picture. This is Nate Moore."

Nate gave Chapman a hearty handshake. I could see the older man wince under the power of Nate's grip. That would teach him to be irritable with us.

Chapman had the same marshmallow chairs in his office as Fielding had in his. I wondered if they were leftovers from the Hall of Fame.

"This will have to be brief," Chapman said. "I've got a busy day ahead of me."

"Okay, I'll get right to the point then," I said. "Why don't you tell us how and when you came to the decision requiring Marvin Wallace to break the home-run record in a hundred fifty-four games."

"Oh Christ, here we go again. I've answered that question fifty times if I've answered it once."

"Would you mind answering it again?"

"Yes, I would." He paused defiantly. We waited for him to answer. For a moment I thought he really wasn't going to respond. Finally he heaved an exaggerated sigh and spoke. "Fair is only fair. If Babe Ruth had one hundred fifty-four games to set the record, that's all Marvin Wallace should be allowed to break it. It's as simple as that."

"Yes, but you didn't make the rule until the middle of the season," I said. "Why is that?"

"Of course I didn't." The irritation was creeping back into his voice. "There was no worry about someone breaking the record until Marvin Wallace came along."

"Why does it worry you that someone might break the record?"

His blood pressure rose a few points. "It *doesn't* worry me. Stop putting words in my mouth."

"Now that there are more games in a season, I suppose you're planning to amend the rules for anyone with a chance to break a season record," I said. I was baiting him, and he didn't like it.

"Of course not. That would be positively absurd. Which records do you have in mind, anyway?"

"Take the base-stealing record, for instance," I said. "Ty Cobb stole ninety-six bases. If someone—"

Chapman interrupted. "No one is ever going to break Ty Cobb's record. I can assure you of that."

Nate had been silent all along, but he finally spoke up. "Have you ever heard of Maury Wills? He plays for the Dodgers." I was going to add that they had recently moved to Los Angeles, but Nate's sarcasm seemed to have hit deep enough.

The commissioner was insulted by the remark. "Maury Wills is not going to break Ty Cobb's record, young man. And Marvin Wallace is not going to break Babe Ruth's record."

"What makes you so sure?" I asked.

"Class." He said it proudly, as if there were no doubt that he had it, too. "I saw Babe and Ty Cobb play. They had class."

"Modern players don't?"

"It's not a question of modern versus the old days," Chapman said stiffly. "It's a matter of the integrity of the game. I'm charged with the responsibility of protecting the tradition of baseball. The home-run record is the epitome of that tradition. And this is the way I decided to do it."

Chapman looked at his watch. It was gold with diamond inlays, and the dial was shaped like a baseball infield. I wondered if Chapman went to the same jeweler as William Bosworth Tidwell. "I think I've given you enough of my time," he said.

"Just one more question. About gambling."

"What about it?"

"How widespread do you think it is?"

"In baseball?" He sounded incredulous.

"Sure," I said. "I hear there's even a lot of betting on whether Wallace will break Babe Ruth's record."

"I wouldn't know anything about it."

The commissioner was scowling as he got up to lead us out the door to his office. Nate pulled out his camera.

"I want to see you smile real big now, Mr. Chapman," he said. "Come on, be a good subject, say 'Cheese.'" He snapped three quick pictures, and the flash went off in the commissioner's face.

130

Chapman was not amused by Nate's antics. Pam Masters was. She stood up to escort us out, and Chapman turned abruptly and headed back into his office. Her face was red with silent laughter.

"One more thing, Mr. Chapman." I caught him just before he closed his door.

He paused impatiently. Time was money to men like Ebel Chapman.

"Have you ever met a man named William Bosworth Tidwell?"

"No, I haven't. Why?"

"Just curious. He's a wealthy eccentric who's fanatical in his devotion to Babe Ruth. I thought you might have met him at one time or another."

"I meet a lot of people," he said. "It's hard to keep track of all of them."

"You'd remember Mr. Tidwell," I said.

"Then I guess I haven't met him."

Chapman closed the door, and Pam Masters walked us to the elevators. We hadn't made much of an impression on him, but she seemed to be taking a shine to us. It was mutual, I'm sure.

We could hear Chapman yelling for her as she started to speak. She looked toward his office and frowned. "Can I meet you guys for a drink after work?" she asked hurriedly. "There's something I've got to tell you."

Nate nodded like a narcoleptic. He was anything but sleepy.

"Around the corner," she said. "There's a place called Otto's. I'll meet you there at six."

She turned on her heels and strode back to Chapman's office. Nate and I both watched her until she disappeared inside.

"You're looking a little tired lately," Nate said as we stepped onto the elevator. "Maybe I should meet her alone."

I disagreed. "You'll forget to find out what she wants to tell us."

"You're right," he admitted. "But after she tells us, you leave."

"Let's flip for her," I suggested.

"I already have."

22

Rita Wallace looked stunning when she came into my apartment. A few minutes with her, and I'd forget Pam Masters' name. She did not, unfortunately, greet me with Pam Masters' friendliness.

"This is a long trip for me to come in to see you, Mr. Renzler. I hope you have something important to talk to me about." She sounded more tense than annoyed. And she had started calling me Mister again. What a pity.

"If you hadn't walked out on me last time, I'd feel sorry for the inconvenience," I said. "I suppose I could have called you. But that would have been a little embarrassing if your husband had answered the phone."

She blushed. "I don't think that's very funny, Mr. Renzler. We've been through enough lately without you making jokes at my expense. I hired you to *help* me."

"I'm trying," I said. "Only I've been having a bit of trouble getting the truth out of some people. It's made things rather difficult."

132

I got two beers out of the refrigerator and poured us each a glass. I usually drink straight from the can, but being with Rita was a special occasion.

"Mrs. Wallace, your husband is in a lot of trouble. Someone's trying to frighten him, and whoever it is seems to be trying to get at him through you, too. I think I can figure out who's behind it. But I need an assist from you."

She looked quizzical. "What do you want me to do?"

"You can start by telling me how well you know Arthur Fielding."

Her reaction was another classic effort, but this time it was authentic surprise. The beer glass slipped from her hand the instant I mentioned Fielding's name. It bounced off the edge of the desk and shattered against the floor.

"Don't worry about the glass," I offered. "It looks expensive, but I got it on sale at Woolworth's. I've got another one. Would you like some more beer?"

She began to sob, and it reminded me of the first day she'd come to my office. I'd been busting my ass for eight days, and I still didn't know much more than I did to start with. She looked just as pretty now as she had then, but I wasn't as sympathetic. She'd been jerking me around, and I don't like being jerked around. Especially by beautiful women, because I'm a goddamn sucker for it.

She pulled a tissue and a compact out of her purse and began dabbing at her eyes. Being out of paper towels, I wiped the glass shards and beer off the floor with a handful of toilet paper.

I set another glass of beer down on the desk for her. "You look gorgeous," I said. "Don't worry about your eyes."

"How do you know?" she said. It was the first time she'd really looked at me since she arrived.

"Who cares," I said. "I figured it out. That's my job, you'll remember, figuring things out."

She nodded. "I suppose you think I'm a slut, don't you?"

I laughed. Not too loudly and not too long, but I did laugh. "Mrs. Wallace, you seem to be awfully concerned about what I think of you. Don't be. Coming to me is like going to a priest. The only difference is you go to a priest for forgiveness and answers. If you're lucky, you'll get some forgiveness. You

133

come to me for answers. I'll get them for you. But that's all you'll get. I won't give you any sermons, so don't give me any penitence. And, of course," I added hastily, "I'm not celibate."

She shrank back in the chair from my assault. I was beginning to think I was being too hard on her. There you go, Renzler, being a sucker again.

I spoke to her in a soft voice. "Your husband said you were very understanding when he told you he was being blackmailed. You could have been a shit, but you weren't. I admire you for that. Why don't you just tell me about Fielding."

She took a long sip of beer. The story started out shakily, but once she got going, there was no stopping her. She confessed her sin in more detail than I needed to know, or for that matter, than I wanted to know.

"It was last spring. Marvin was with the ballclub in Florida, and Andy—that's my son—was staying down there with Marvin's sister. It got kind of lonely for me, and Marvin wanted me to come down, but spring's a good time for modeling, and I had some assignments. One day I was walking down Sixth Avenue, and I ran into Arthur Fielding. We chatted for a few moments, mostly about baseball and the season beginning, and that was that.

"The next night he called me on the phone. He wanted to meet me in the city for dinner sometime. I didn't think anything of it. I agreed to give him a call the next time I came in. We went out to dinner the following week. I never thought he'd try anything, but I had a few drinks and after a while there we were, back at his penthouse apartment on Park Avenue. Arthur lives in New Jersey, but he keeps an apartment in the city. It's a beautiful place."

She paused for a reaction from me, but I didn't really care much about the condition of Fielding's apartment. "Arthur said some nice things to me that night, and I guess Marvin hadn't been noticing me—or at least I felt like he hadn't been noticing me. It felt good to be treated important for a change, as if *I* mattered, too. Do you know what I mean?"

I said I did, even though I wasn't sure I did. I was still stuck at the part where Wallace had stopped noticing her. I've heard of the law of diminishing returns, but I didn't think it applied to Rita Wallace.

I poured us two more beers while she moved on to the juicy part.

"Arthur treated me so special that night, I just couldn't say no when he asked me to stay. He was so sensitive about the whole thing. I mean, we didn't even—" She groped for a word.

"Fuck?" I said.

She blushed a bit, but not enough to indicate much embarrassment. "Yes," she said, "fuck." There was a trace of a smile on her face, as if saying the word provided a modest thrill. It did for me.

"And then?"

"We saw each other four, maybe five times. I'd call him when I went into the city. If he was free, we'd have dinner, go to his place. It was nice, very nice."

"Are you still seeing him?"

"Oh, no." She was back to being shocked again. "We just went out together in the spring. One night, on his way home, Arthur stopped at my house. Andy was staying overnight at a friend's, and Marvin was due back from spring training the next day. I had told Arthur I didn't want him coming out to the house, and that night I told him again. He said he had to see me before Marvin got back. We had an argument. Not a big fight, but it was our first. By the time he left it was okay. Except Marvin came home half an hour later. He decided to come back early. To surprise me, I think."

"Or to check up on you," I suggested.

"Yes, to check up on me. I told you he's a jealous man."

I nodded. Once again I thought about how I didn't blame him.

"That was when I knew I couldn't see Arthur anymore," she said. "I liked him a lot, and I still do, but I love my husband, and I like having my family."

"What did Fielding say when you told him you had to stop seeing each other?"

"Well, he wasn't very happy about it, I guess. But I think all along we both knew it was only temporary."

"Have you seen him since then—socially, I mean?"

"Yes, two or three times. They have functions for the ball-players and their wives."

"How has he acted toward you?"

"Kind of..." She fumbled for a cigarette and her words. I found a cigarette and a match. She found the words. "Kind of formal, if you know what I mean. He was very polite to me, but I felt like he was talking down to me."

"He has a tendency to do that with everyone," I said.

"I know. That's why Marvin doesn't like him."

"Is there anything else Marvin doesn't like about him?"

"Well I guess they had a dispute over money this year. After Marvin led the league in home runs last season, he was expecting a big raise. Arthur gave him one, but it wasn't as much as he wanted."

"What's his salary now?"

"Thirty-six thousand, I think."

She was right. I remembered reading it in the papers.

"Do you think Fielding still likes you?" I asked.

"Do you mean, do I think he's still interested in me?"

I nodded, and that got her angry again.

"Listen, Renzler, I hope you're not suggesting that Arthur Fielding is trying to get back at me by threatening my husband. That's just not the case. Arthur Fielding is an honest, proud, considerate man. He'd never even think of doing a thing like that."

"I'm sorry," I said. I wasn't, but I didn't want her mad at me. "I just have a question about him that I can't seem to find an answer to."

"What's that?"

"Whoever first made the blackmail threat on you must have known you were seeing Arthur Fielding."

"That's right. I called Arthur as soon as the man called me. He's the one who told me to hire you."

"Why didn't the blackmailer call him?"

She said she didn't know, but that didn't stop her from speculating. "Maybe he thought I'd be an easier target. Maybe he was afraid of Arthur."

I shook my head to tell her that didn't add up. "When a blackmailer picks a victim, he usually picks the one who's most able to pay. In this case, that's Fielding."

136

"So what are you saying?" She spoke in an I-don't-like-your-tone tone of voice.

"There are a few possibilities. One is that Fielding is being blackmailed, and we don't know about it. Another is that there is no blackmailer. Someone is trying to get at your husband through you."

"But I did get those phone calls. I didn't imagine them, you know."

"Yes, that's true," I said. "There is another possibility that comes to mind, but I don't think you're going to like it." I paused for her to ask what it was, but she didn't. She already knew. "Arthur Fielding could be in on it."

"Oh, come on, you've got to be kidding." There was no sign of amusement on her face.

"Rita, someone is out to get your husband."

"I don't care what you say, Mr. Renzler. I know Arthur Fielding, and I know he wouldn't try to hurt me or Marvin. If you don't believe me, why don't you ask him."

"I will." I smiled my charming smile. "In time."

23

Pam Masters was surrounded by admirers when Nate and I got to Otto's. Surrounded may be an exaggeration, but there were three guys lined up like kids at an ice-cream truck. She didn't appear to mind the attention.

Otto's was just like any other midtown bar where people got together after work. There were a few tables, all of which were occupied by men in suits, except for an occasional secretary. The bar also was full, and customers were standing one deep off the stools. Within an hour or so it would empty out, and half the men would catch the bus or train to Connecticut or New Jersey. The others would stay in the city and take a shot at their secretaries, but not before calling home to tell their wives they had to work late.

We got beers at the bar and were almost on top of Pam Masters before she saw us. She appeared to be glad when she did.

"Move over boys," she said, spreading her arms as we approached. "My men are here."

The three business suits stepped aside in deference to her wishes and Nate's size. He had worn his Gents T-shirt in the hopes of captivating her with his bulging muscles. It seemed to be working.

Pam Masters put her drink down on the bar and threw herself at him. "Hey, big fella," she said as she disappeared into his grasp. I could see from the expression on his face that Nate was melting like a goddamn Creamsicle. We hadn't flipped a coin yet, but it looked like Nate had already won the toss and elected to receive. I positioned myself next to imaginary goalposts at the end of the bar while waiting for the kissie-poo to end. After all, I was there on business.

The suits got lost without introducing themselves, and we relocated at a table that had just been vacated by a businessman who'd struck out with his secretary. Nate and Pam sat at one side of the table. I sat across from them, facing the entrance.

Pam Masters said she was twenty-six, so I figured she was twenty-eight, at least. I had been wrong in my initial guess by five years, but who cares. If a woman's a knockout, it doesn't matter what her age is. Unless, of course, she's under eighteen. Then it matters a lot.

"You come here often?" Nate asked her after we ordered another round of beers and a piña colada for Pam.

She said she did, almost every night after work. She lived on 53rd Street, three blocks from the bar and four from her office. She was originally from Brooklyn, and she had made the big move into Manhattan three years before. I could understand why she thought it was fun to hang out at a place like Otto's. Me, I thought it was deadly, but you wouldn't catch me in a goddamn office, either.

Nate continued to ask the questions, and I remained content to listen and watch her answer. Pam Masters was no Rita Wallace, but she wasn't someone you'd throw out of bed just because she rooted for the Boston Red Sox.

"How can you stand working for that guy Chapman?" Nate wanted to know. "He's got to be the grouchiest asshole I've ever met. And for that matter, how old is he? He called me 'young man.' Now, honey, I may look young, but you're staring at a man who's about to turn thirty-six years old."

Nate shot me a reproachful glance as I began to choke on

139

my drink. He was scheduled to turn forty-one on Sunday. And he looked it.

"Oh, come on, he's not that bad." She was giggling at Nate, and I didn't think she felt the sort of loyalty to her boss that good secretaries are supposed to feel. "He's just a little difficult sometimes."

"Difficult! That's the understatement of the year, sweetheart. That man's so constipated, I'll bet his farts sound like sermons."

This was Nate's version of being charming, and Pam Masters was liking it a lot. She tousled his hair with her sharp, shapely fingers, leaned her head against his shoulder and let out a laugh that betrayed her Brooklyn origins. I went to the bar to get more drinks.

As I paid the bartender, I noticed a familiar face leaning over a beer at the front of the bar. It wasn't an especially noteworthy face. It was white, about my age, and it was crowned with a crewcut. It was familiar to me because I had seen it earlier in the day outside my apartment. I had also seen it at the 72nd Street subway station when I was waiting to meet Nate.

I believe in coincidence as much as the next guy, but I also have a sense for when I'm being followed. The face leaned down close to the beer when I looked down the bar. As I began walking in that direction, the face couldn't hide in the beer anymore.

I got within about twelve feet of him before he turned and hurled the mug at me. It came at my head from the left. That's the side I have trouble picking things up from, because that's the eye I'm blind in. Still, my reflexes are pretty good, and I managed to catch the mug before it collided with my face. I tried to sidestep the beer too, but I didn't have much success.

He was a tall, thin, speedy sonofabitch. I say this because he hustled his ass out the door and headed west on 50th Street pretty fast. But I'm no slouch, and I was only fifteen steps behind him when he hit the corner of Seventh Avenue. The problem was, I value my life, whereas he apparently had very little regard for his. The light went red while he was still on the sidewalk, but he bolted into the traffic nonetheless. A lot of brakes screeched and horns honked as a result of his ad-

140

venturous effort. But he did make it across. I was left standing on the east side of the street, swarmed over by a herd of crew-cutted Boy Scouts on their way to Radio City.

I saw the thin man look over his shoulder as he headed north on the other side of Seventh Avenue. I wouldn't forget his face. And I had a few plans for how I was going to change it when I saw him again.

Nate and Pam Masters seemed not to have noticed my absence when I got back to the table. I had probably been gone all of ten minutes.

Pam interrupted me as I described my beer-throwing assailant. "Do you mean the tall guy in the striped shirt? He was sitting at the last stool at the end of the bar?"

I nodded.

"I saw him a few minutes after you guys came in. I think it was Larry Nichols. He works in the commissioner's office. I don't know what he does exactly, but I've seen him around. I always thought he was a pretty nice guy. He asked me out a few times, but I don't really like him *that* much. Why would he want to throw beer on you?"

"Not just beer. He threw the whole goddamn mug," I told her.

"Maybe he's got a crush on you, and he's jealous of us," Nate suggested. I knew he didn't think that's all there was to it, but it was smart to say something for Pam Masters' benefit. She thought we were journalists, not detectives. If she found out we were lying, Nate might lose his shot at sleeping with her.

"I think Larry's a little nutty. I'd watch out for him," I said. "Why don't you tell us what you were going to say this morning when Chapman interrupted you."

"It's nothing that important," she said, pausing while Nate lit her cigarette. "I was just using it as an excuse to get acquainted with Mr. Wonderful." Her reference was to Nate, not me.

"You're so manipulative," I said. "This better be good. I had to get soaked with beer to hear it."

"Okay. If it's not up to your standards, I'll buy the next round. This morning, when you guys were leaving, you asked Mr. Chapman about the guy with the funny name."

"William Bosworth Tidwell," I said.

"Yeah, that's right. He told you he didn't know him. But they had lunch together about two months ago."

"Are you sure?" Nate asked.

"Do you think I'd make something like that up?" She laughed. "I made the reservation for them. Do you want to know where they ate?"

"Sure. And can you tell me what date it was?"

"Are you serious?" She had a dumb look on her face. Dumb but pretty.

"It was at Jack Dempsey's," she said. She pulled an appointment calendar out of her purse and began thumbing through it.

"Is that a record of Chapman's appointments?" I asked. I didn't want to come on too strong, but I was curious to see who else Chapman had been eating beef with in recent days.

"No, this is mine. I just remember which day it was because I had my wisdom tooth pulled the day after." She leaned over the table and opened her mouth. She urged me to look inside. I did, and marveled at her dentist's handiwork. The girl had a set of molars that could turn you into a tooth fetishist. And I've always been partial to bicuspids.

"Here it is," she said. "June twenty-second. That means they had lunch on June twenty-first. Isn't that weird that he didn't tell you?"

I nodded. "You'd be surprised what some people won't tell writers. We're always getting pushed around."

"You poor babies. Maybe it's time for Pam to take you home." She seemed to be talking to Nate, even though she had spoken in the plural. I hadn't expected an invite to her place, and I wouldn't have shared a bed with Nate if we were taking turns with Brigitte Bardot.

I flagged down a cab for myself after they elected to walk the three blocks to Pam Masters' apartment. It was the first time I'd ever known Nate to refuse a ride.

I had spent most of my day with three beautiful women—first Melissa, then Rita Wallace and Pam Masters. But when it came time for bed, it was just me and Fifi Five-Fingers. I didn't care. In the twenty-four hours since I'd been back from

Chicago, I'd been shot at and assaulted with a beer mug. I'd barely eaten a thing all day, and my veins had been transfused with beer. I was so tired I would have given a hooker fifty bucks just to leave me alone.

24

It seemed like a year since I'd seen Mrs. Grayson, and I greeted the old bitch with considerable warmth. That's what a good night's sleep will do for me. For her, apparently, it seemed only like the five days it had been, and she offered her usual unsavory blend of grunt and grimace.

"Do you have an appointment?" she demanded.

I did not have an appointment, because I wanted the advantage of taking Fielding by surprise. People say the most revealing things when you jolt them sometimes, and I wanted to nudge Fielding with a force that would make Babe Ruth turn somersaults in his grave.

"No, I do not," I answered, "and I think Mr. Fielding would agree that I don't need one."

That remark didn't win me any points, and she went back to opening her morning mail. She spoke to her desk. "He's in the lavatory now. You can ask if he wants to see you when he gets back."

I staked myself out on one of the marshmallows while Randy

got me coffee. She was cracking her gum with zeal and appeared to be in a much better mood than the last time I saw her. We chatted for a moment, then I took to reading the *Daily News*. I had barely finished that day's anti-Commie editorial when Fielding returned from the crapper. He was carrying the *Wall Street Journal* under his arm. He seemed surprised, but not dismayed, to see me.

"Well, Renzler, what is it? Have you solved all our problems?" Fielding seemed uncharacteristically cordial. Perhaps he'd spent the night perfecting the squeeze play with Randy.

He surveyed Lipstick's desk for messages. He found one that drained the cordiality right from his face and put it in his pocket.

"I've just got a few questions, Mr. Fielding. It will only take a couple of minutes." I started to walk toward his office, but Grayson's voice stopped me.

"He wants you to call back right away," she said, motioning to the note Fielding had pocketed.

"I have to return a call, then I can see you for a few minutes." His voice had turned brusque.

I nodded. "I can wait."

And wait I did. Fielding's phone call lasted almost half an hour. I went back over the matchups for Tuesday night's game, downing three cups of coffee in the process. The Tigers, thanks to Rocky Colavito, Norm Cash, and Al Kaline, were hanging on to second place, only a game behind the Gents. The series would be a pennant showdown, and the Gents would miss Sworpe in their lineup.

Charlie Ross was scheduled to pitch for New York. The Tigers were putting up Don Mossi, a crafty left-hander whose trading-card picture looked like the dark side of the moon. Casey the Computer was still predicting that Wallace would break the home-run record, though I was beginning to have my doubts. He had to break out of his slump soon, and Mossi was not the one to do it against.

As I switched back to the news section, I could hear Fielding's voice getting louder in the next room. I couldn't make out what he was saying, but it wasn't friendly. Grayson shook her head and began to chuckle, I figured in reaction to her horoscope in the paper. I was wrong.

"You can always tell when Mr. Fielding's talking to Mr. Russo," she said to no one in particular. "He always winds up yelling."

"Aaron Russo?" I asked, quickly losing interest in a story on Mayor Wagner's chances in the upcoming primary.

"I don't know," she said. "I just know him as Mr. Russo. Why don't you ask Mr. Fielding."

"I will," I said as Fielding's voice came over Grayson's intercom.

"Make me a lunch appointment for two at noon tomorrow at D'Angelo's," he said. "And send Renzler in."

Fielding was at his coffeepot when I entered his office. He poured a cup and asked me to get right to the point.

I did.

"Mr. Fielding, I'm wondering why you didn't tell me you had an affair with Marvin Wallace's wife." I was looking at him, but I didn't sense any surprise in his reaction.

He avoided my glance and spent a long time stirring in cream before he answered. When he did, his voice was sarcastic.

"I'm wondering why it took you so long to find out," he said. The man was shrewd. He'd caught my bomb and returned it to me in the form of an insult. I didn't appreciate it a bit.

"I didn't say I just found out. Now just happens to be the time I'm asking about it."

"The answer is obvious, I would think. I didn't want you to know. In fact, I didn't want anyone to know. Who told you, Rita?"

I nodded.

"Damn her. She wasn't supposed to tell you. We agreed on that when I told her to hire you."

"She didn't have any choice," I said. "I'd already heard about it from your players. It's common knowledge, Mr. Fielding. The only person who doesn't seem to know is Marvin Wallace."

I expected the Gents owner to tell me I was being ridiculous, but he didn't. He looked like he had just found a turd floating in his coffee. It was the first time I'd seen him shaken up. I can't say that I felt very sorry for him.

"Mr. Fielding, you've known that the blackmail against Rita

Wallace had something to do with the threats against her husband for a while now, haven't you? You've known about the connection at least since the night I called you from the Wayne police station. We weren't tailing Wallace that night, and you knew it. We were out there to meet the guy who was blackmailing Rita. But you didn't seem the least bit surprised to see Nate and me. Are you sure you didn't have some idea about the connection when you first hired me?"

"Hell no. What are you implying? I don't think I like your point here, Renzler."

"I'm saying you've been holding out on me, and I don't like it. I'm supposed to be doing a job for you, and you're turning out to be my biggest obstacle. And the fact that you knew about what was going on in advance and didn't say anything raises some questions about you."

"Such as?" I thought my voice had been loud, but Fielding's was louder.

"Such as why didn't someone try to blackmail you, too?"

Fielding was silent. He got up from his desk and went to the coffeepot again. The man drank more coffee than I did. He spent a few moments pouring himself a cup before responding. He didn't seem concerned about wasting precious time now.

"Okay," he said resignedly. "When Rita first called me, I assumed whoever knew about us would probably try to blackmail me as well. But then Ed White came to me with that note. I thought there might be a connection, but I didn't know. And I couldn't believe that someone actually had pictures of Rita with me. We had been pretty discreet and still are."

"What do you mean, 'still'?"

"Oh, I suppose she didn't tell you that." Fielding had a smirk on his face that would have put Curt Bidwell to shame. "She probably gave you some line about loving her husband and never being unfaithful again, and I'll bet you believed it."

"Yeah, that's about what she told me, and yeah, I believed her. I generally try to believe what my clients tell me, but she and you have been elevating dishonesty to an art. I don't care much for art. It gets tiresome. So you're saying that you're still seeing her?"

"Not exactly," he said. "But it was only a few months ago,

147

and we only agreed to hold off until it was absolutely safe. I imagine if the opportunity presents itself, she might be persuaded. She's a very pretty lady, I'm sure you've noticed."

"I have."

"Perhaps that's the reason you're so inclined to trust her."

"Perhaps." I got up and walked to the coffepot.

Fielding looked uncomfortable. I was making him feel that way, and it felt good. He was going to be a lot more uncomfortable when Marvin Wallace found out what his wife had done to get in shape during spring training. It was only a matter of time.

"I'm really sorry, Renzler. At first I wanted to tell you everything, but then I thought it might not have to come out. I'm planning to be married in the fall."

I didn't bother to offer my congratulations or ask who the unlucky lady was.

Fielding looked at his watch. He had issued his apology, and now it was time to get back to work. I picked up my newspaper and got up to leave.

"Did Rita Wallace have any other lovers?" I asked him.

He seemed somewhat taken aback. Either the thought hadn't occurred to him before, or the idea of it made him jealous. "I don't know. She's a model, you know. She must meet other men."

"Did she ever mention any names to you?"

"No, I don't think so. I can't recall."

"Try when you get a few minutes. It's important. If you think of any, call me."

Fielding stood up to escort me out. "I am sorry, Renzler," he said. "I feel badly. We're back at square one, and it's all my fault."

He offered his hand, so I shook it. I felt like taking a bite out of it, but I resisted the urge. "Some of it's your fault, Mr. Fielding. But we're a lot further along than square one. I'll be in touch."

As he opened the door for me, I hit him with my ace. "Mr. Fielding, do you know a man named Aaron Russo?"

He paused for a moment before answering, and I thought I sensed a glimmer of recognition.

"No," he said. "Should I?"

"I thought you were speaking to him on the phone before I came in."

He smiled. "Case of mistaken identity. That was *Jack* Russo, my accountant."

25

The visit with Fielding left a bad taste in my mouth, so I stopped for a six-pack before leaving for New Jersey. I was feeling a little deflated. After what Melissa had found out about Fielding's fondness for the New Jersey Democratic Party and Aaron Russo's ties to the IRS, I was pretty sure that Fielding and Russo were connected in some way. After overhearing Fielding's end of the argument on the phone, I was damn certain of it.

Now I didn't know what to think. My only hope was that Melissa would come up with some answers. I sure as hell wasn't going to get any from Fielding.

Nothing looked to have changed in the Garden State since the previous week, except that *The Parent Trap* had been replaced at the Route 3 Drive-In by *The Saga of Windwagon Smith*. Who says there's nothing to do in the suburbs?

Ray Gurella looked positively bored as I strolled to the bar, but his face brightened noticeably when he saw me. The place was dark and deserted, as usual. I wondered how Johnnie Haller

stayed in business and how Gurella stayed awake. I was probably the first interesting customer he'd had since the last time
I'd been in. I felt like I was visiting a friend in a sanitarium,
only I wasn't sure Ray Gurella was a friend.

He mixed me a Bloody Mary and asked if I'd caught up
with Pizza Face the week before. I told him I'd lost him, but
that someone else had found him and lost him again for good.

When I got around to asking Ray Gurella about placing a
bet, he didn't disappoint me. In point of fact, I was pleasantly
surprised.

I shouldn't say surprised, actually, because I suspected all
along that Roxanne West's realty company was a cover for
something. How else did she manage to stay so well fed? But
it seemed almost perfect that her main source of income was
illegal gambling.

Too perfect, to my way of thinking. So before I drove to
her office in Ridgewood, I rang Nate on the phone to let him
know where I was going. To no one's surprise, he was asleep
when I called, having spent the entire night playing slave to
Pam Masters' desires.

I told Nate to expect me back in time for the ballgame. If
I didn't show up by then, he was to come looking for me. He
was practically snoring when I gave him the address, but I
knew I could count on him to remember it. Nate has an impeccable memory—most of the time.

As I left for Roxanne West's place in my Corvair, I had a
feeling I was finally getting close to answering some pressing
questions. The thought made me buoyant, and a little appre-
hensive.

Lilly showed more speed than I would have given her credit
for when she saw me coming in the door. She was hardly what
you'd call fast, but she had at least two hundred pounds to
carry. She managed to get it out of her swivel chair and almost
through the door to the back room by the time I reached the
counter. She was dripping sweat as a result of her effort, and
I let her go into the back room undeterred. I could hear Roxanne
West's voice booming from there, and I figured she was the
person I had to talk to, like it or not.

It only took her about fifteen seconds to get out to the
counter. Lilly trailed behind her, but was partly hidden from

151

view behind Roxanne's vast bulk. They looked like two great suckling pigs jostling for position at the feed table. Roxanne West filled me with disgust, but there was a sense of comic relief about her.

"I told you we can't show those houses," she said.

"No. You told me only Roxanne could show me those houses," I corrected. "And you're Roxanne."

She shrugged. For a normal person it would have been a simple, barely perceptible physical motion. For Roxanne West it was a great heaving movement that shook her enormous breasts like pompons. With it came a spray of perspiration. They really needed that air conditioner.

"I can't do nothing for you," she said. Roxanne talked like she was dumb, but I had a feeling she was smarter than she let on.

"I'm not here to look at the house. I'd like to place a bet." I smiled my charming smile, and it worked its customary negligible effect. She showed no indication of warmth—beyond the involuntary habit of sweating—and if any emotion was at work, it was anger.

"Who sent you?" she demanded.

"Ray Gurella."

"Okay. Follow me in back."

She turned with considerable effort, and I walked behind her slowly into the adjoining room. Lilly stayed out front to watch for customers. I had a feeling there weren't going to be any.

I didn't know much about gambling, but I expected to see a few tables and maybe even a few rooms in back. But there was only one room with a card table, a plastic ashtray filled with lipstick-coated butts, and three folding chairs.

I expected there would be listings for the local tracks and the pitching matchups and odds for the night's baseball games. Instead there was a tattered issue of the *Daily News* that was open to the racing page. I expected to see a cashier who'd record my bet, take my money, and give me a receipt. I was beginning to realize that this wasn't a place to make a bet.

The one thing I didn't expect was to be slugged from behind. You may think it was foolish of me to go into the room unprepared, and in retrospect I have to agree. But at the time I

152

would have felt silly pulling a gun on Roxanne West. Next time I'll take my chances on feeling silly.

I heard him move behind me to my right just as I noticed that there were two different brands of cigarettes in the ashtray. I mention this not because it's important, but just to show that I retain my sense of detail even while my brains are being bashed in. In this case, I was missing the forest for the trees, and the forest happened to be a baseball bat. I think I must have ducked just as he swung, because I felt the bat glance off the top of my head instead of connecting with full impact on the back of my skull. This *is* an important detail, because if it hadn't happened that way, I'd probably be dead.

When I came to, the first voice I heard agreed with my assessment. "You fucking idiot. You could have killed him, slugging him like that. We're not supposed to kill him. We're just supposed to hold him here." It was Roxanne West talking, and she was her usual cheery self.

I heard six voices in all, but there were only three people in the room besides me: Roxanne; Lilly, who was eating a Hostess Twinkie; and Batman, whom she addressed as Chuck. I always hated the name Chuck.

"Who's minding the store?" I asked Roxanne, trying to keep things on a friendly level.

My remark was answered with a slap across the face from Roxanne West's viscous palm. It stung like a sonofabitch, and I could taste blood from my lip. That was the last attempt at conversation I'd be making.

My head felt like it had been used for oil drilling, and my stomach was nauseated to the point where even Pepto-Bismol would have had little effect. My hands were tied together at the wrists with electrical tape. I was sitting on one of the folding chairs. The three of them were standing.

Roxanne West slapped me again, this time with her other hand. It was just as slimy, and it stung even more. My sense of balance was still a little impaired, and I slipped off the chair from the impact of the blow. Batman picked me up by my upper arms and sat me back down. I could tell he hadn't done so out of concern for my well being. I simply made a better target for Roxanne when I was sitting up. If she ever had to lean over, she'd never get up again.

"You're a damn smartass," she said. "I could've let Chuck finish you off, but I didn't. The boss is coming over later tonight to have a talk with you. After he's done you're Chuck's chop." She guffawed at her little joke and came up short of breath.

"Ain't that right, baby?" she asked, nudging the big man in the ribs.

"You bet, Roxy. And this is one punk I'm really gonna enjoy taking some cuts at." Chuck was grinning stupidly and running his hands up and down his baseball bat. He was prime fodder for some wisecracks, but I continued to practice self-restraint. In the interest of self-preservation.

The doorbell rang in the front room, indicating someone had entered. Roxanne West turned to Lilly. "Go out there and see who it is," she ordered.

Lilly stuffed the last two-thirds of the Twinkie into her mouth and padded toward the door. Her words got entangled in her snack as she spoke, but the message was clear: "It's only Ray."

It didn't surprise me to see Ray Gurella stroll into the back room, but it did piss me off. I had taken a liking to him at first, and I was hoping my suspicions of him were incorrect. But he had set me up to be slugged two times now, and I can't say I much cared for him anymore.

He smiled as soon as he saw me. "I see you found the place," he chuckled. "Sorry for the inconvenience."

I didn't reply. Roxanne West did.

She grabbed Gurella by the shoulders from the back and spun him around to face her. "You asshole. You fucking dumb asshole. Why'd you send this damn private eye up here?"

Gurella smiled. "I thought that's what you'd want me to do. I've sent you lots of customers. And I called to let you know he was coming."

"Idiot," she said. Chuck was staring Gurella down, and Roxanne turned to Lilly. Her voice was sweeter than a Sugar Daddy. "Why don't you go home, hon," she said.

Lilly looked dubious. "How will you get home?"

"Chuck will give me a ride. Don't worry. You just go home."

"But what will you do about supper?" Lilly looked positively horrified at the possibility that Roxanne would miss a meal.

154

"I'll manage." Roxanne's expression approximated a smile. She was even uglier when she smiled than when she snarled.

"Remember to put the closed sign up," Roxanne called to Lilly as we watched her saunter into the front room. She turned to face Gurella as soon as the front door closed.

Gurella's smile had begun to fade into a look of uncertainty. Roxanne wiped away what little smile was left with two stinging slaps. She hit him harder than she hit me. He put up his hands to defend himself, which was a mistake, because that's when Batman stepped in.

"You faggot," he snarled. "You're a no-good, cocksucking faggot."

He hammered Gurella with both fists, and the bartender fell backward to the floor. Chuck was about six foot three, and he must have weighed two-forty. Gurella was at least four inches shorter and much thinner. He didn't look like a fighter, and his assailant had taken him by surprise. It was no match.

Batman climbed on top of Gurella and continued to pummel him with both hands. I was powerless to stop him, and I'm not sure I would have, considering how thoughtful Gurella had been to me. Only Roxanne West's shrill commands finally got him to relent.

"Don't kill him, you idiot," she yelled. I had to admit, her voice did have a sense of finality about it. She was one of those people who has natural leadership abilities.

"I want to do him now," Chuck said, picking up his bat.

"No. Not now. Wait till we find out what Mr. Russo wants to do with him."

I broke my vow of silence. "That wouldn't be Aaron Russo, by any chance, would it?"

"Yeah, motherfucker, what's it to you?" Chuck turned to face me and lifted his bat. I was beginning to feel like my question was a bit indiscreet.

"Shut up. Don't tell him anything," Roxanne ordered. "And leave Gurella alone. Mr. Russo might want to talk to him first."

Chuck disagreed. "Russo wants to talk to *him*," he said, pointing at me with the bat. I thought it was considerate of him to identify me with a simple pronoun instead of calling me a faggot, but I kept the observation to myself. "He doesn't give a shit about this queer. And besides, who the fuck is Russo

155

to push me around? I told him after that last time I wasn't going to let him or anybody chew me out again. I mean it, Roxy."

He did indeed. There was a threatening lilt to his voice, and Roxanne seemed to sense it. She didn't want him turning on her. This was clearly a deranged man.

"Okay," she said at last, "but why don't you take him downstairs."

Gurella was cowering against the wall when Chuck picked up his bat. I had thought he was unconscious, but he must have been awake. He made a futile attempt to half run and half crawl to the door. It was no use. Chuck grabbed him by the neck and threw him into the corner. He opened the door to the basement and gave Gurella a push with his foot. I could hear the bartender tumble down the stairs.

Batman closed the door behind himself before going down the stairs. I thought about making a run at Roxanne, but she had picked up a gun off the table. It was my gun. I decided to stay.

I heard a muffled wail from the basement. It followed the chilling sound of wood hitting flesh. The sound made me feel sick to my stomach again. There was the briefest trace of a smile on Roxanne's West's face.

Within five minutes Batman came back up the stairs. The bat he carried was red with blood. He ran his hand along the bat and smiled at me. It wasn't a friendly smile.

"You're next," he said.

26

I figured Roxanne West would get hungry sooner or later. About 6 P.M. she went out for a pizza, leaving me alone with Batman. I didn't much like being dependent on Roxanne West's better judgment for my survival. I liked being the object of Chuck's whimsy even less. Luckily the pizzeria was only a block away, and she called to order in advance.

They didn't consult me about which ingredients to get, and both of them seemed to go for anchovies in a big way. I had a hard time picking them off with my hands tied, but I forced down a piece anyway. It was the first real sustenance I'd had all day, since I'd killed off lunch with another stop at Howard Johnson's. That was a habit that had to stop.

I thought it was damn civil of them to share their dinner with me, and Batman even got so carried away with hospitality that he offered me a can of beer. It was Bud, and on top of anchovies it tasted worse than a urine sample. But the intention was there nonetheless. Aaron Russo had not arrived yet, and from what they said, I gathered he might not get there until late in the evening. I was still alive, and I had to be thankful for my blessings, however small or temporary they might be.

After dinner was finished, Roxanne asked Chuck if he'd like her to give him a lift.

"Aw come on, not now, Roxy," he said. "Not with the assshole here."

But Roxanne West was the sort who couldn't be dissuaded once her mind was made up. "I think it would be fun if we made him watch," she said. Within minutes she had Chuck's pants pulled down to his knees and was working him over on one of the folding chairs.

I don't usually pay much attention to the size of a guy's cock, but I had to admit that Chuck was well-endowed. He looked like he had stolen a roll of bologna from a local deli and soldered it between his thighs. Only a mouth like Roxanne West's could have accommodated it, and she was nibbling away with the ferocity of a bear whose slumber had been recently interrupted. I was glad they hadn't invited me to participate.

I made sure to keep my gaze fastened to the floor, as their sucking and sweating built to a feverish climax. Under different circumstances I would have looked upon their bizarre antics as a spectacle of epic comic proportions, but I didn't dare crack a smile. They finished quickly, and the act was followed by the predictable angry silence that accompanies the end of bad sex.

Chuck helped Roxanne to her feet, and she sat down on her chair and promptly fell asleep. Chuck looked at me as he pulled up his pants, and I was unable to avoid his stare.

"Not a word out of you," he said.

By the time he turned on the radio, the Gents and Tigers were tied at zero in the third inning. But the Gents had two runners on base, and Johnnie Haller was even more frenzied than usual as Marvin Wallace stepped up to the plate against Don Mossi.

I could barely hear Haller say that Wallace had struck out his first time up, above the deafening roar of the cheering fans. A standing-room-only crowd had turned out to welcome the Gents back home. This series against the Tigers was the most important three games of the year, and time was running out for Wallace.

158

Batman got up from his chair and began pacing back and forth across the room. "Come on, you big asshole, strike out," he heckled Wallace. "Come on, you asshole, strike him out," he implored Mossi. I was beginning to think he had less than a hundred words in his entire vocabulary.

Chuck began to jump up and down gleefully as Haller let out an agonizing groan over the radio. Wallace had swung underneath Mossi's first pitch and lifted a towering pop fly to short right field.

"That's it, you cocksucker," Chuck said, drowning out Haller's voice. But he paused uncertainly as Haller's inflection began changing to an excited tone.

"It looks like the wind's taking it. That ball's hit a mile high. Kaline's backing up. He's still backing up. He's backing up full speed now. Kaline's backing up near the wall. He's moving to the foul pole. Kaline's standing at the foul pole now. He's waiting, waiting, it's . . . It hit the foul pole! It hit the foul pole! Home run, Marvin Wallace!"

"Motherfuck." Batman picked up his folding chair and hurled it across the room. It landed in the corner, smashing a row of empty Coke bottles that someone had been saving up for deposits. His face was a ghastly shade of crimson, and I tried hard to avoid his glance. I'd been able to restrain myself during their awkward sexual thrill, but I was having trouble controlling my smile at the thought of Wallace hitting his 51st homer. If Batman saw me, he'd have trouble controlling his anger.

"I don't believe it. I don't believe it. I've never seen anything like it." I could tell Haller was yelling into the microphone, but his voice was barely audible in the jumble of sounds filtering out of the twenty-five-cent speaker. "Marvin Wallace has just hit his fifty-first home run of the year on a ball that looked like it wouldn't make it to the outfield. I said the wind was gusting here tonight, and I was right. Gents lead, three to nothing."

"Cheap. Cheap fucking hit. Cocksucking bastard." Batman was muttering now, but his temper was hardly under control.

He was right, but I didn't care. Although the outfield at Yankee Stadium was the biggest in the major leagues, the right-field foul pole was less than three hundred feet from home plate, shorter than any other ballpark. It was custom-built for

159

Babe Ruth, and now for Marvin Wallace. A few of Wallace's home runs in Yankee Stadium would have been ordinary outs in other ballparks. That may have bothered Batman, but I didn't think it concerned Wallace.

Neither team scored for the next two innings, and Batman's mood gradually changed from violent anger to uneasy sullenness. Roxanne had slept through his outburst, and with her head leaning forward, she had begun to drool onto her blouse. One of her arms hung limply over the edge of the chair, revealing a sweat stain under her armpit the size of a jumbo pancake. The woman was thoroughly repulsive even when she was unconscious.

I think it was the seventh inning when I first caught sight of Nate peering into the room from the window behind Roxanne West. The window was small, and Nate's head loomed large against it like a low-budget Japanese monster on the *Million Dollar Movie*. He was eating a three-pack of Tastycake chocolate cupcakes. Either he had been carrying them around in a hot car for a while, or he had been holding them under his arm. The wrapper was soggy, and the chocolate icing had detached from the cupcakes and stuck to the cellophane like a turd on toilet paper.

Nate held the wrapper close to the window and began poking at it with his pinky. It took him half a minute to complete his labors. He held the cellophane close to the window for me to see. "R U OK?" he spelled out in chocolate.

I checked to make sure Batman wasn't watching, then I nodded. Nate grinned and erased the message with one swift swab of his tongue. He waved to me and disappeared in the direction of the back door.

The next time I saw him, he was inside. He busted through the back door with a heave of his shoulder, and he had already taken four or five steps into the room by the time Chuck knew what was going on. In his right hand Nate was carrying a little-league-sized baseball bat. It looked like a goddamn toothpick as he twirled it in his colossal paw.

Batman got up from his chair and took a home-run swing at Nate with his major-league bat. As they circled each other, bats in hand, the two large men looked like titans competing in a primitive ritual. I saw Nate dance away from Batman's

160

first blow and land two quick jabs with his smaller club. He was big as a bear, but he had the agility of a cat. He would have made a hell of a basketball player if he'd been willing to keep in shape.

I didn't get to watch the rest of their combat, because I was busy trying to wrest my gun from Roxanne West. It took her a moment to wake up when Chuck yelled, and I lunged at her as soon as Nate came into the room. I had the element of surprise, but she had probably a hundred pounds on me and my hands were tied. I crashed into her and upended the chair, sending the gun sprawling onto the linoleum floor. She may have been slow, but she was strong and tough, and it took all my strength to pin her to the floor.

I butted her face with my head, and a stab of pain instantly reminded me of the shot I had taken from Chuck earlier. I couldn't take a free swing at her with my hands tied, but I did manage to pound her with two fists in a hammerlike motion. That was enough to get off her, and when I did I came back down with both knees on her stomach. The fat woman had more wind in her than a hot-air balloon, but the force of my blow knocked it all out. She gasped three or four times before rolling over in a heap like a dead horse. It was a terrible, sickening sound, but a mere trifle compared with the hideous cough that followed. She lost her dinner—and her dessert—in one shuddering retch, and I left her lying in a puddle of anchovies and Bud and I went to grab the gun.

At the back of the room, Nate was standing over Batman, who was pressed face down against the floor. Nate was resting his size-thirteen foot on the middle of Chuck's back and was forcing his bat against the big man's mouth.

"Go ahead, asshole, kiss my label," Nate said. He was grinning like a newlywed.

Nate tied Chuck's hands before untying mine. Together we dragged the big man across the room and dropped him with a splash beside Roxanne West. I tied her hands behind her back and then taped both their legs to one of the folding chairs. They wouldn't be going anywhere for a while.

We were going to go into the front room to wait for Russo, but Nate handed me an envelope that changed my mind.

161

"It's from Melissa," he said. "She said you're going to owe her plenty now."

There was a note inside, which I read first. "Renzler," it said. "Sorry it took me so long, but I couldn't find anything in the *Times* morgue. A friend of mine who works for the *Newark Star-Ledger* came up with this. Love, M."

The photo was from the *Newark Star-Ledger*. It was dated November 9, 1960, and it was headlined BOFFO FETE FOR HUGH. There were five people in the photo, and I recognized three of them.

Congressman Hugh Addonizio was standing in the center, and he looked like he was about to collapse under the weight of an enormous arm that was wrapped around his shoulders. The arm belonged to Roxanne West. She was all prettied up in an evening dress, and she didn't look half bad. There was a man to Addonizio's left whom I didn't recognize, and another one to the right of Roxanne. At the end stood a distinguished-looking gentleman wearing a smile that could have charmed a rattlesnake. It was Arthur Fielding III. The two unknowns were identified as brothers in the cutline that ran underneath. Their names were Aaron and Jack Russo.

I showed the picture to Nate, and he let out a low whistle. "She's right," he said. "You do owe her."

"I owe you, too. What are you doing around noon tomorrow?"

He shrugged. "Sleeping, I guess."

"Would you like to join me for a luncheon engagement?"

"That depends on who's paying?"

"Arthur Fielding."

"I'd be glad to."

I called George Grimaldi of the Wayne police before we left. Ridgewood wasn't his jurisdiction, but he had originally been working on the investigation of Pizza Face's murder. He'd been cooperative about keeping Wallace's name out of the papers, and I figured I could trust him to take care of Batman and Roxanne without getting me involved.

I could hear Grimaldi working over a piece of Juicy Fruit as he came to the phone. He greeted me warmly, as if we were old friends. It felt like a long time since I'd seen him, but it had been less than a week.

"Hello, Renzler, how you doing?" he said. "I got those free baseball passes that Mr. Fielding promised me. He's a real stand-up guy."

"I know," I said. "It's rare that you meet a man like Arthur Fielding."

"That's right," he said. "What can I do for you?"

"This time, Grimaldi, maybe I can do something for you."

"Really. Wouldn't that be nice."

"The man who committed those murders with the baseball bat last week is taking a little nap in Ridgewood. If you get someone over here soon, you might catch him before he wakes up. He killed another guy tonight. He's resting in pieces in the basement. There's a woman with the murderer, a big woman. Her name is Roxanne West. You might need a crane to carry her out. They seem to be involved in some kind of betting operation over here. I don't think they're actually handling any bets out of this place, but it could be some sort of bank. It's in a phony realty office."

"I think I know the place," he said. "A friend of mine pointed it out to me once. Said I could put down some money there. I take it some of the bets are being placed against Marvin Wallace."

"You're quick to catch on, Grimaldi. When are they going to make you the goddamn chief of police over there?"

"Never. There's too much politics in it."

"This may be kind of political, too. I think Roxanne West is an associate of Hugh Addonizio's."

"That wouldn't surprise me a bit. But you're right. It could present some problems."

"I'm sure it's nothing you can't handle," I said.

"Uh-huh." Grimaldi didn't sound as sure as I did.

"One more thing, Grimaldi. Mr. Fielding and I would appreciate it if you'd keep my name out of this."

"I'll see what I can do."

It was 11 P.M. by the time Nate and I got in our cars and headed back to New York. Aaron Russo hadn't arrived in Ridgewood, but that didn't matter. Russo could probably answer a few of my questions, but so could his brother Jack and Arthur Fielding. The answers could wait until the next day. Marvin Wallace had gotten lucky and hit a home run, and

163

before he played again, I'd have a chance to tell him he had nothing left to worry about. I felt certain that with his mind clear, he'd break out of his slump and start slugging home runs again.

We stopped at a bar along Route 46. It seemed like weeks since Ray Gurella had mixed me a Bloody Mary, and the beer I'd had with dinner hadn't done much good. After a shot of Old Grand-Dad and a couple of beers, I was beginning to feel like my old, albeit imperfect, self again. There was nothing left to do except go home, get some sleep, and get set for tomorrow's lunch appointment.

Or so I thought.

As I entered the lobby of my building, I saw three men in blue suits waiting by the elevator. As I got closer, I could see that two of the suits were police uniforms. They weren't waiting for the elevator. They were waiting for me.

The one in the real suit was Inspector Dirk Wirthliss. The other two I didn't know. Wirthliss had been a traffic cop on the police force when I left. He'd come up in the world since then. We didn't know each other very well, but well enough to know we didn't like each other.

Wirthliss was the first to speak. "Are you Mark Renzler?"

"What is this, Wirthliss? You know my name."

His expression was blank. "We're going down to the station," he said. "I want to ask you a few questions."

"Tomorrow." I walked to my mailbox and picked out a few bills and my *Sport* magazine.

"Now," he said. "You're wanted for questioning. If you don't come willingly, I'll get a warrant for your arrest."

"For what?"

"For the murder of Pamela Masters."

164

27

I had two choices, and I didn't like either of them. I could go to the 86th Street station with Wirthliss, or I could make him get a warrant for my arrest.

It was against my principles to' cooperate with the police, especially with a cad like Wirthliss, but I was afraid he might pick up Nate, too. He didn't. There was also a chance I'd be able to get more out of Wirthliss than he did out of me. That one I called correctly.

Pam Masters had been found in her apartment at 11 A.M. Tuesday. She had been strangled, and her neck broken.

"You already know what she looked like, but I'll show you the pictures anyway," Wirthliss said. We were in one of the interrogation rooms, and one of the cops in uniform, Connelly, was with us.

I didn't feel much like looking at the cheap black-and-white photos Wirthliss thrust in front of my face, but I did. Pam Masters looked beautiful even when she was dead. She was nude. There were no marks on her body, except for a wide ugly rope burn stretching across her neck. In one photo her head was turned probably 270 degrees. It was from that photo that you could tell her neck was broken.

I handed the photos back to him. "I hope you made extra copies. You could make a few bucks selling them to your friends."

"Shut up, Renzler. I could arrange for you to have an accident."

"You know better than that. You're going to look foolish enough for bringing me in."

"Oh yeah." Wirthliss pressed his face about six inches from mine. It took every ounce of restraint I had to resist the urge to slug him.

"I see you still have a way with words," I said.

Wirthliss snorted and backed off. He knew I was right. Barney Kenner, the homicide chief at 86th Street, wasn't exactly a friend of mine, but he was a rarity among cops: He was fair and reasonably honest. He didn't go for his cops roughing up suspects at the station—especially when the suspects were innocent and had good contacts with the city newspapers.

"I suppose you have an alibi," Wirthliss said.

"For when? Eleven this morning? I was with a client."

"Hell no. Last night. You were seen leaving a midtown bar with her last night. You and your friend Moore."

"When was she murdered?"

"Why don't you tell me."

"Get off it, Wirthliss. How did you get on to me, anyway? I bet someone tipped you off."

"Maybe." He lit a Tareyton. I could see a slight grin forming behind a cloud of smoke.

"Let's see, who could it be?" I spoke out loud, but the question was directed to myself. "I'd guess it was Ebel Chapman."

Wirthliss choked on his smoke.

"You ought to lay off those goddamn charcoal filters, Wirthliss." I lit myself a Camel and offered him one. He refused it, and so did Connelly.

"So yeah," he said. "It was Chapman. The girl didn't show up for work today, so he got worried about her. He called the police. We went over to her apartment and took a look. That's

166

when we found her. Chapman said you and that big asshole Moore—"

I interrupted. "Moore is big, Wirthliss, but he's not an asshole. You're doing something that psychologists call projecting. It's really you who's the asshole, only you don't know it because you're too busy calling everyone else an asshole."

He stomped out his cigarette furiously. I felt sure this time he was going to hit me. He took two steps toward me and cocked his hand back. When I put up my hands to block the blow, he laughed.

"Look at him," he said to Connelly. "He's scared shitless. Aren't you?"

I didn't answer, and he continued.

"Chapman said you and Moore came to interview him. He said you're calling yourself a fucking writer these days. Since when did you become a writer?"

Wirthliss took my silence as a signal to go on. "Chapman said you were hitting real hard on his secretary. He said she told him she was going out with you last night. We did some checking and found out the three of you left Otto's about ten o'clock. Moore went home, but you went on to her place. You were already drunk, and you probably got drunker. You were a flop in the sack. When you woke up early in the morning, she started giving you shit. Maybe she asked if you were a fag. You were still drunk, or at least hungover. You flew into a rage."

I concluded his story for him. "So I strangled her."

"Yeah, that's right, you strangled her." He was smiling.

"You've got witnesses for all this?" I was getting sleepy, but I was still able to muster a little sarcasm.

It was wasted on Wirthliss. "I got witnesses that seen you leaving the bar and entering her building."

"That's curious. Who saw me entering the building?"

"The doorman."

"Thanks. I'll have to make a point to knock him off before I go to trial. The only problem is I don't know what he looks like, because I don't even know where she lived."

"Bullshit, Renzler."

"I take it you showed him a picture of me."

"No. But he said she was with a tall guy with dark, balding hair."

"That's a pretty complete description."

"It's good enough for now."

"I guess you must have found my prints all over her apartment, huh?"

"We found some prints," he said. "We don't know whose they are. The lab is running a check on them now."

I thought of Nate. His prints *were* all over the apartment. I wanted to keep him out of it for as long as possible.

"That means they can't be mine," I said. "If they were, you would have been able to match them right away. I'm on the station file, you know."

"Yeah, I know." His voice had turned sullen. "But you're smart enough to wipe them away."

"And if I had, you wouldn't have found any prints."

Wirthliss snorted again, but his assistant nodded in agreement. Connelly knew his boss was being a fool, and he could tell I knew he was thinking it. We exchanged knowing looks, but he didn't say anything.

"If you do find any good prints, I'll bet they match up with a guy named Larry Nichols," I said. I didn't want to bring Nichols up, but I was getting tired of hanging around the jail and I didn't want to spend the whole night there.

Wirthliss had turned away from me, but he spun around when I mentioned Nichols' name. "What do you know about Nichols?"

"He worked with Pam Masters. He had a hard-on for her the size of Texas. He was in the bar last night. He threw a mug of beer at me. She said he has a few screws loose. I think she was right. My guess is he went to see her. She let him in, and he killed her."

Wirthliss' expression had gone blank, but it wasn't from lack of interest. "Who are you working for, Renzler?"

"That's privileged information. You know that."

"Come on. The girl was murdered."

"And that has nothing to do with what I'm working on." It wasn't true and I knew it, but there was no way I'd volunteer any more information than necessary to Wirthliss. "Why don't you tell me what Larry Nichols has to do with it. You jumped two feet when you heard his name."

Wirthliss looked deflated. He didn't answer me.

"Nichols is the one who said he saw me leaving the bar, right?"

Wirthliss sighed. "He lives across the street from her. I haven't spoken to him, but he told Chapman this morning after she turned up missing."

"Great. Can I go home now?" I had been sitting on the edge of a table in the center of the room. I started walking toward the door.

"Sure, go home," Wirthliss said disgustedly. "But make sure you go right home. You stay the fuck away from Larry Nichols."

"Of course," I said.

Of course not. I walked to Broadway and got a cab. I got out on West 53rd Street in the block where Pam Masters had told me she lived. I wanted to talk to Nichols before Wirthliss got to him. I had to hurry.

I went into a Chock Full O' Nuts and headed straight for a phone booth in back. There were ten Larry Nicholses in the Manhattan phone book, but only one lived on West 53rd. I was tempted to stop for a cup of coffee. I didn't. It could wait.

Nichols' building was about fifteen stories, and it was narrower than a cocktail straw. I could see from the directory in the lobby that there were only two apartments on each floor. Nichols lived in 3-W. That would mean West.

To get inside I'd have to pick the lock. I could have done it, but it might have taken me a while. A burglary rap I didn't need. I decided to check outside. A narrow alley ran along the west side of the building. It was cluttered with garbage cans and lots of garbage. Not much of the garbage was in the cans. By moving one of them under the fire escape, I was able to hoist myself up to the first landing. The rest was a breeze. The window to Nichols' kitchen was unlocked, and I was able to slip inside silently. I got out my gun just in case he came in to scramble some eggs.

Fat chance.

Nichols was hanging in the corner of the living room beside a floor-to-ceiling bookcase. There weren't many books on it.

But from the few titles I saw, I could tell Nichols was a fan of Norman Vincent Peale. Correction: *Had been* a fan of Norman Vincent Peale.

His feet were about eight inches off the floor. The knot around his neck was perfect. At one time in his life, Nichols had probably been a Boy Scout. The rope was attached to a curtain-rod bracket at the top of the living-room window. The window provided an eye-filling view of the dirty brick walls of the building next door.

There was a dark blue bruise on the left side of his head where he had probably knocked against the bookcase. There was a note on the floor. It was typed on Major League Baseball memo paper. The note was terse: "I loved you, Pam. I'm sorry."

I stayed around long enough to check the type on the note against the typewriter on Nichols' desk. It matched. I would have browsed some more, but I heard a familiar voice at the door.

"Police," Wirthliss said. "Open up."

I went out the way I came.

28

I stopped at the Mayflower Coffee Shop on Broadway and stuffed myself full of bacon and eggs and coffee for a couple of hours. It was still early, but it was too late for me to get any sleep. If I went home to take a nap, there was no way I'd ever get up for lunch.

The murder of Pam Masters made the front page of the *Daily News*. They usually hold page one for at least a double murder, but it must have been a slow news day.

I had two phone calls to make when I got back home. One was hard, the other was easy. I made the hard one first.

I was a bit surprised to find Nate awake at 9:30, but he said he'd gotten out of bed early to be ready for lunch. He hadn't seen the papers, though, and I told him what he'd find when he did. Nate was mad at me for not taking him along to see Larry Nichols, but I told him it was better he hadn't gone. If Nichols had been alive when we got there, he would have been dead by the time we left.

Marvin Wallace sounded sleepy when he fielded the easy

call, and it took me a while to convince him that he wouldn't be receiving any more threats. Despite my assurances, I still thought he sounded a bit uncertain when I hung up. It would probably take him a couple of games to readjust to a normal level of pressure.

After a forty-five-minute shower that failed to wake me up, I called D'Angelo's and changed Fielding's lunch reservation to a party of four. Then I called Sol Feinberg, my lawyer, and told him I'd want him to draw up some papers real quickly in the next couple of days.

If Nate was still mad at me when I met him on Broadway, he wasn't showing it. But he was in a quiet mood, and that meant trouble for anyone who crossed him. We barely said a word to each other during our taxi ride to midtown.

Arthur Fielding was talking with the maitre d' when we entered D'Angelo's. A stocky, balding fellow was standing alongside him. I recognized the man as Jack Russo from the photo Melissa had found.

"There must be some mistake," I overheard Fielding say as Nate and I came up behind them.

"There's no mistake, Mr. Fielding. I changed the reservation."

The two of them turned around as soon as they heard my voice. They were standing face to face with Nate's shoulders.

"Renzler! What are you doing here?" Fielding was alarmed, but he switched on the snake-charming routine immediately.

"We're joining you for lunch," I said, smiling. "You must be Mr. Russo." I offered my hand, but he didn't accept it. "I've heard so much about you."

"What is this?" Russo was not as adaptable as Fielding.

"The four of us are going to discuss Mr. Fielding's taxes," Nate said. He smiled at the maitre d'. "I hope you can find us a nice private table."

The maitre d' looked scared. He was probably five foot six standing on his toes. "We don't want any trouble here," he said.

Nate was still smiling. "There won't be any trouble, my good man. You have my word."

We were led to a booth in the rear of the restaurant. Russo was the first to follow, but it took a mild push from Nate to

172

get him started. Fielding began to sit down beside him, but Nate changed the seating assignments. He sat down beside Russo, and I slid in next to Fielding. If either of them wanted to leave, he'd have to climb over one of us first. Never have I seen two guys looking more in need of a drink.

I flagged down the waiter, and we all ordered doubles. The waiter's hands were shaking as he went to put the drinks on the table, but he wasn't as nervous as the two men who grabbed the drinks out of his hands.

"What should we discuss first?" I asked. "I suppose we could begin with blackmail and gambling, but tax evasion's always good for a few laughs. If Mr. Russo's brother were here, we could talk about something really juicy—like murder."

"You've got the wrong idea, Renzler."

"Why don't you tell me what the right idea is, Mr. Fielding."

"Don't tell him anything, Arthur. He's just trying to trick us," Russo said.

"Well, if it isn't the guardian angel speaking." Nate toasted Russo with his drink. "I wouldn't listen to this guy if I were you, Mr. Fielding. It's his fucking tax advice that got you into the hole to begin with. You'd be a lot better off listening to this detective you hired."

"With a little digging, I could get enough on you to have you thrown in jail for tax fraud," I told the Gents owner. "I wouldn't have to go any further than your friend here or his brother to get it. Isn't that right, Mr. Russo?"

Russo looked at me but didn't answer, and Nate's burly hand fell on his shoulder. "You act like you're not too happy to be here, Jack. That's awfully rude." Nate squeezed the stocky man's shoulder and Russo began to wince. "Now sit up straight and mind your manners. And the next time someone asks you a question, answer it."

I gave Fielding a hard look. "I bet you really thought you were in good when you hired Russo as your accountant, Mr. Fielding. By getting in tight with Russo and his brother, you felt really well connected. But you were too stupid to realize that they could use those connections against you any time they wanted. Now Jack here doesn't exactly seem like a trustworthy

173

fellow. But his brother Aaron's a proven snitch. And he's also responsible for three murders."

Russo looked up at me, surprised, but again he was silent. There was a good chance he hadn't heard about Ray Gurella's untimely passing yet.

Fielding downed his drink in one long swallow. "Now listen, Renzler, I didn't have anything to do with that."

"I know, Mr. Fielding," I said. "You're such a fine, up-standing man. All you did was hop in the sack with your star player's wife and then sit back while a bunch of hoods harassed him."

"I didn't have any choice," Fielding stammered. "They would have exposed—"

"Shut up, Arthur." Russo would have had more to say if Nate hadn't employed the squeeze technique again.

"The style's coming along good, Jack," Nate said. "But I think we'll need to do a little work on the content." He grinned at me. "Proceed, please."

"That's right, Mr. Fielding," I said. "Russo and his brother would have exposed you. But I have no sympathy for you there. It was your idea to cozy up to them in the first place. And then, as if that weren't dumb enough, you stupidly told Jack here about your little spring-training escapade with Rita Wallace. That gave him and his brother two nooses to hang around your neck."

Fielding sucked his ice cubes. He looked desperate without a drink. I ordered another round. "You better take our lunch order now, too," I told him. "These men are going to lose their appetites pretty soon." Nate opted for a double order of ravioli with extra garlic bread and I put in a bid for fettucine Alfredo.

"Okay, Renzler," Fielding said after ordering. "I admit I made a mistake. But I didn't have any part in any killing."

"Mr. Fielding, a mistake is something an outfielder makes when he misses the cutoff man on a throw. You've missed more than the cutoff man. You've missed the whole game. You're an accomplice to murder. You can miss a lot of seasons for that in this state."

Up to that point, Fielding had been able to reach back for some of the charm he was holding in reserve. Now his tank was empty, and his voice was full of panic. "They told me

174

there wouldn't be any killing. They told me nobody would get hurt."

"Who told you? Aaron Russo?"

Fielding looked at Jack Russo before answering, but his companion turned the other way. "Yes, Aaron," he said. "Jack too. But they didn't kill anyone, either. Tell them, Jack. Tell them what happened."

"Would you keep your goddamn mouth shut. These guys don't have anything. It's all suspicion."

Nate's hand assumed the position again. "That's the third time you've been impolite, Jack. Make it the last."

Russo stared at Nate with hatred in his eyes. Pretty soon he was going to lose his temper and do something stupid. Judging by Nate's mood, it would be *very* stupid.

"I can tell you what happened, Mr. Fielding," I said. "It wasn't your idea to kill anyone, and it wasn't Jack's and at first it wasn't even his brother's. These two buddies of yours don't have much to do, except run errands for their political-hack friends and file a few tax returns. They keep busy—and wealthy—by running a little gambling operation. Or maybe it's a big gambling operation.

"Their gambling bank got overextended when someone started taking too many bets against Marvin Wallace. I assume it was a pair of losers named Rudy Appell and Tommy Leon. They both had gambling convictions, and neither of them was very bright. They were so sure Wallace wouldn't break the record they started laying higher odds just to attract more action. When Wallace kept hitting home runs, they began to get worried. Whoever was handling the books—I assume it was a woman named Roxanne West—eventually noticed that the operation was in overheads on Wallace. She's not exactly an energetic sort, so by the time she discovered the problem, it was too late to do anything about it. I'll bet Aaron Russo wasn't too happy when she told him what a beating he stood to take."

I paused for a sip of my drink before continuing. "All Aaron and Jack wanted to do at first was send a few threats to Wallace. They figured he might crack if they applied a little pressure. That's when they came to you. Undoubtedly they told you not to go to the police when Wallace began getting threats. I bet they were real nice at first when they told you their little tale of woe. I'm sure you didn't like the idea very much."

"Of course I didn't," Fielding cut in. "I hated it. I told them I wouldn't have any part of it."

"Of course you did." I couldn't resist parroting Fielding's remarks. "But then they mentioned certain problems you might have with your tax returns if the IRS decided to audit you. And certain indiscretions with regard to Wallace's wife."

I smiled at Fielding and took a forkful of fettucine. Nate was devouring his ravioli, but neither Fielding nor Russo was eating.

"Come on, chow down, fellas," Nate encouraged. "It's not the end of the world. It's just the end of your happiness. Believe me, plenty of people go through life being completely miserable. I hear you can get to like it after a while."

They didn't respond to Nate's attempt to lighten the conversation, so I continued with my story. "It wasn't until Rita Wallace called you and said she was being blackmailed that you realized something was wrong. You called Jack and told him someone was putting the heat on her. You told me you were expecting that someone would blackmail you, too, but I've learned not to believe anything you say. Leon and Appell, working with Russo's halfwit assistant, Chuck, decided to make some cash on their own. Maybe Leon and Appell were going to put the money back into the bank to get off Aaron Russo's shit list. Someone told them about you and Rita Wallace. Was it you, Jack?"

Russo had been maintaining a sullen silence. When he finally spoke, his voice was furious. "What's it to you? I don't have to stay here. I'm getting out of here now."

As Russo tried to stand up, Nate clamped down on the back of his neck. Russo tried to squirm free from Nate's paralyzing grasp with no success. Slowly Nate pushed Russo's face lower and lower until it settled on his plate of linguini. Nate held Russo's head there for about ten seconds and didn't let it up until he had left-handed the last of the ravioli. With white sauce dripping from his tomato-red visage, the chubby man looked like an indelicate blend of northern and southern Italian cuisines.

176

"I warned you," Nate growled. "Now be a good boy and eat your linguini. And clean yourself up first."

Fielding looked mortified as I resumed. "Appell and Leon were lovers. And there's nothing Chuck hates more than fags. I'll bet Aaron Russo didn't like fags, either. Maybe he didn't want any of them working in his organization. Whatever the case, Appell and Chuck went to meet Mrs. Wallace. But Chuck never had any intention of collecting. He just wanted to kill Appell off. He may have been acting on orders from Russo, but that didn't make any difference to him. Leon and Appell weren't getting along too well, and Leon didn't mind having Appell out of the way. At least I assume he wanted him out of the way, because he and Chuck were still working together. Maybe Russo promised him he could have Appell's territory if he stayed on. Leon must have been stupid enough to believe him, because he was stupid enough to go along with Chuck to the house in Totowa where he was killed. Russo was the one who came up with the charming idea of luring Marvin Wallace out there. He couldn't have believed that Wallace would be convicted, but there was always the chance he'd be in jail for a day and miss a game. And, of course, it would shake him up."

I looked at Russo, who had been staring at his plate silently since Nate had showed him where it was. "How am I doing, Jack?" I asked. "Have I missed anything yet?"

"Go on with your story," he said. "I'm getting a real kick out of it."

"That's much better," Nate told him. "Pretty soon you'll be teaching an etiquette class."

"Chuck's a little sick in the head," I said, "and sooner or later Russo would probably like to get rid of him, too. Now that he's killed Ray Gurella—"

"What? Ray Gurella?" It was the first time Russo had shown any interest in the conversation.

"That's right," I said. "Last night, at Roxanne's place. Gurella sent me up there to talk about placing a bet. Roxanne didn't like it, and Chuck liked it even less. He liked it so much less, in fact, that he killed Gurella, above Roxanne's objections. Guess what the murder weapon was."

177

Neither of them made a guess, but Fielding looked sick enough to indicate that he knew.

"Roxanne's place got busted last night," I said. "And I think we may have done Russo's brother a favor. He doesn't have to get rid of Chuck himself, and he's got someone to take the murder rap for him. Aaron was supposed to show up there, but I'm sure he had the good sense to stay away from the place when he saw it crawling with cops. With his political clout I'm sure he'll be able to avoid being charged with murder. But that's where his connections end. And yours too, Jack."

"What makes you so damn sure?" Russo had a trace of life left in him after all.

"I'm going to make sure," I said. "Your political benefactor, Hugh Addonizio, may not be the spitting image of honesty, but after I have a talk with him, he's going to realize that you and your brother have become too much of a liability for him to protect. He's going to drop you two faster than he can say reelection. And just to ensure that he doesn't get any noble motives about helping you out, I'm going to make a few more calls." I paused and smiled—for effect. "To some Republicans."

"You motherfucker." Russo reached into the side pocket of his jacket but came up empty-handed.

Nate grinned. "You wouldn't be looking for this, would you, asshole?" He held Russo's .25 caliber gun in his hand. "You'd do well to find a tailor who can make a suit that doesn't look like a kangaroo costume."

Russo buried his face in his hands and began to sob.

"Your political career is over, Jack," I said. "You and your brother are going to have to start working for a living. *After* you get out of the slammer. And when you do, there's going to be a lot of people out looking for you. Gamblers don't like to be cheated. They like to lose their money fair and square. We're going to get the word out on you in those circles, too. You're going to be like a pair of rabbits wandering around in a cage full of hungry wolves. You and your brother are as good as dead."

"And another thing," Nate added. "Don't start having any thoughts about sending your thugs out after Renzler again. I won't tolerate a repeat performance of Sunday night."

"What are you talking about? What happened Sunday night?" Russo's eyes were wide open.

"Your hoodlum friends shot in the door to my building," I said. "Don't let it happen again."

"I don't know what you're talking about. We didn't do anything to you. Except for that time at Big Johnnie's bar. And that was Tommy Leon's idea."

"I don't care whose idea it was," Nate said. "Guys like you shouldn't get ideas. Just remember this: If you so much as breathe wrong, you're going to long for the good old days when we ate linguini together. You get my gist, Jack?"

He didn't answer, and Nate moved his hand toward Russo's face. "Okay, okay," he said. "Just leave me alone."

Nate smiled. "Good thinking, Jack. Maybe there's a brain cell in your head after all."

I turned to Fielding. He hadn't raised any protest when we were working Russo over, and I thought I knew why. He was beginning to sense the possibility that he would get off easy.

"What about me?" he asked. His business demeanor was returning quickly. Too quickly, to my thinking.

"Well, you won't have to worry about the Russos anymore," I answered. "They don't have anything to gain by bringing you up, except to implicate themselves in a blackmail scheme. I don't think they'll want to do that. Now we're going to have to make an arrangement with the IRS. Because of your impeccable reputation, I'm sure they'll be willing not to pursue criminal charges against you in return for the repayment of your outstanding taxes."

Fielding grimaced at the notion of forking over his cash, but he was smart enough not to object.

"You will also give Marvin Wallace a substantial bonus for his performance this season and increase his salary proportionately next year. We'll work out the figures at a later date. And you'll keep your fucking hands off Rita Wallace. Is that clear?"

Fielding nodded dejectedly. He was a beaten man.

"If I find out you've so much as called her on the goddamn phone, we're going to start talking about big stakes. Like divesting yourself of a baseball team."

That made Fielding gasp, and I didn't blame him. Still, he didn't voice any objections.

I smiled a bit. "And of course I expect you'll be able to give us season passes from now on."

I imagine it took some effort, but Fielding returned my smile. "You know, Renzler, I thought hiring you would give me an alibi if anything went wrong. It turned out to be one of the biggest mistakes I ever made."

"No, Mr. Fielding," I said, "the biggest mistake you ever made was to hire Russo."

29

By the time Nate and I left D'Angelo's at 3 P.M., I was ready to check into a nursing home. I'd been up for more than thirty hours, and they hadn't exactly been uneventful. There were still some questions that I wanted to get answered, such as why Ebel Chapman, the acting commissioner of baseball, had said he didn't know Tidwell, and who had used Melissa and me for target practice Sunday night. But I also wanted to get to the Gents game at eight o'clock. I was pretty certain Wallace was no longer in danger, so I decided to let matters rest while I did the same.

As we walked past the newsstand at Broadway and 50th Street, the front page of the *New York Post* changed my mind.

I had expected the headline to change, but it hadn't changed to what I expected. The death of Pam Masters had been moved to page 2 as part of a story on Larry Nichols' suicide. But the front-page news was about Jimmy Gibbs: BATBOY DIES ON THIRD RAIL.

The story inside was short on detail, but it said he had been killed after the Gents game Tuesday night. His father had come to pick him up but was unable to locate him. He said he had warned his son about playing on the train tracks behind their house, but he often did so anyway. Police believed his death was accidental. I wasn't so sure.

Nate and I got on the subway at Columbus Circle. I wanted to have another talk with Ernie Mandel. I didn't know what hours he worked, but he had to be coming to the stadium sooner or later. If he wasn't there yet, we'd be waiting for him when he arrived.

The security guard let us into the ballpark when I showed my visitor's pass. He didn't know if Mandel was in, so we headed straight to the clubhouse to look for him. It was deserted.

We turned back from the locker-room area and wound our way underneath the grandstand and out toward right field. The public-relations office was located in a small hallway off the main walk. I knew Perry Powers and his staff would be working. I figured he would know where Mandel was.

We could overhear Powers talking on the phone as we waited outside his office. His secretary also was on a call, and from around the corner we could hear the machine-gun sound of two electric typewriters clattering away. I can't say I cared much for Powers personally, but I didn't envy his job. At this point in the season, he had to be drowning in work. I was certain the death of Jimmy Gibbs hadn't made his job any easier.

Nate and I entered Powers' office as soon as we heard him hang up. He was already up from his desk and on his way out. He seemed startled to see me as he looked up, but he was surprisingly cordial.

"Hello, Mr. Renzler. I'm sorry, but I can't talk to you now. I've got an important appointment, and I'm late already. I haven't been able to get off the phone all day. A terrible thing has happened. Little Jimmy Gibbs, our batboy, fell on the train tracks last night and killed himself."

"Jesus, I'm sorry to hear that," I said in the most surprised voice I could muster. I didn't want Powers to know our reasons for seeking out Mandel. "I'd like to speak with Ernie Mandel for a few minutes. Have you seen him?"

182

"Ernie? What do you want with Ernie?" Powers' big brother instinct was taking over again.

"It's just a routine matter. But I'd rather keep it between Ernie and me."

"I'm sorry to say you're out of luck." Powers didn't sound like he was sorry one bit. "Ernie had to go out of town. His father died."

"I'm sorry to hear that." It was my turn to lie. "How long has he been gone?"

"He left on Monday afternoon. I took him to the airport myself." Powers moved closer to the door. He waited, as if he expected us to move with him. We didn't.

"Do you know when he'll be back?" I asked.

The Gents PR man looked at his watch and sighed before answering my question. His cordiality was wearing thin. "You can talk to him tomorrow," he said. "I'm not sure if he'll be coming in tonight. Now I apologize, but I must be going."

Powers moved to the doorway, but Nate and I were still standing in the middle of the room. "Listen, Renzler," he said. "Why don't you go easy on Ernie, okay? He's been having a tough time with his father being sick lately."

"Sure," I said. "Just tell him I'd like to talk to him when you see him."

Powers nodded and left hurriedly, but Nate and I lagged behind. The walls of his office were covered with photographs, pennants, and other baseball memorabilia. It was exactly what you'd expect a PR man's office to look like. We decided to stay for an unguided tour.

On the wall behind Powers' desk were individual photos of all the Gents players and the team pictures from 1957 to 1961. On the opposite wall there were pennants from every major-league team. Several photos of Powers hung on another side of the office. None of them were complimentary. In one he was being held upside down by the ankles by Hawk Harkness and Mutton Moran. They were both grinning stupidly, and with his short, slim build, Perry looked like an undernourished tuna. Scrawled at the bottom of the photo was a message from Moran: "Perry, Don't let anyone ever tell you your not well hung. Mutton."

"Hey, look at this one," Nate said as I was contemplating Moran's sense of humor. "This guy looks just like Babe Ruth."

I studied the picture. It was a black-and-white snapshot that had been enlarged and framed. There were two men in the photograph. One was Perry Powers. He was dressed to mortify in a three-piece suit. The other man wore a baseball uniform. It was a New York Yankees uniform with the numeral 3 on it. He had his arm around Powers, and both of them were smiling. It wasn't Babe Ruth, but there was a definite resemblance.

"That's Robbie Tidwell," I told Nate. "William Bosworth Tidwell's nephew and doorman. Looks like he's also Perry Powers' brother."

"Yes it does," Nate said. "Yes it does."

"The next time I see Perry, I must remember to give him back his cuff link."

"And ask him how he came to leave it in your room."

"Right."

I didn't get to talk to Perry Powers that night, and I didn't see Ernie Mandel, either. I didn't even make it to the Gents game, though I did get to see some of it on TV. I was glad I did.

My eye gave out on me in the sixth inning, but by that time I had already seen Marvin Wallace slug two home runs in his first three times at bat. The victim of his assault was Jim Bunning, one of the best right-handers in baseball. But this was not Bunning's night. The Gents raked him over for five runs in the first four innings and, as I later found out, coasted to a 6–1 win with Braverman pitching. They had pulled out to a three-game lead over the Tigers.

It looked like Marvin Wallace had his swing and his confidence back. He had now reached 53 home runs for the season. To break Babe Ruth's record—and meet Ebel Chapman's requirements—he would have to hit 8 homers in 24 games. With 16 of those games scheduled for Yankee Stadium, Wallace looked like a shoo-in to surpass Ruth.

As I drifted off to sleep on my couch, I dreamed that I was playing second base for the all-time New York all-stars. Babe Ruth was playing right field, and Marvin Wallace was out in left. But Jaco Sworpe had been moved to third base to make room for Joe DiMaggio in center field. I didn't think that was

184

a very smart strategy, because Sworpe is an excellent outfielder. While our team was batting, I decided to discuss the matter with Casey Stengel, the manager of our team. But as I walked along the dugout bench past Bill Dickey and Ed Braverman, I couldn't locate Casey.

He had been fired, Don Larsen told me, and before I could turn away, I saw the new manager waving to me from the end of the bench. Instantly I knew that William Bosworth Tidwell was an inflexible coach. If I questioned his decisions, he would replace me with Johnnie Haller. I hurried back to the far end of the bench and pretended I didn't hear Tidwell yelling for me. But as I went to take my seat, Lou Gehrig got up and blocked my way.

"You should learn to listen to your manager," he said, gesturing at me with his first-baseman's glove. "He's the one that calls the shots."

That's when I woke up.

I was still stretched out on the couch, and the morning sunlight was beginning to seep through the window. Gehrig was standing over me, and it wasn't a first-baseman's glove in his hand. It was a gun.

Babe Ruth and Joe DiMaggio stood on either side of Gehrig. All three of them were dressed in their baseball uniforms. From the expressions on their faces, I could tell they were ready for some serious play.

30

William Bosworth Tidwell was sitting in his leather lounge chair in the computer room when Joe DiMaggio, Lou Gehrig, and Robbie Tidwell, the Babe Ruth look-alike, escorted me in to see him. He was eating a salted nut roll and reading a sports report from his computer. He hadn't started on the beer yet, and he didn't bother to offer me his cream-of-wheat hand. He was wearing his blue Sultan of Swat robe. It was as if he hadn't moved since the previous week.

Tidwell waved at me with a coffee mug when we entered. "I suppose you want some coffee, Renzler."

"I could use about two quarts. Your servants interrupted my beauty sleep."

"Ah, isn't that too bad. They're not servants. They're members of the team. I'm the manager here." He spoke to Gehrig. "Lou, bring Renzler some coffee. And another salted nut roll for me."

Tidwell dismissed Robbie and DiMaggio and motioned to the smaller chair across the table from his. I sat down in it.

"I'm very disappointed in you, Renzler. I had such high hopes for you when I met you last week. You seemed like a straight-arrow fellow. But you deceived me. First you used deception to get in to see me. Then you made trouble for me by putting your nose in my business. Frankly, I don't know what I'm going to do with you."

It occurred to me that he *had* decided what to do with me, but I didn't pursue the point on the off chance that he hadn't. For the time being I was content to drink coffee and listen to his lecture.

"I'm faced with a serious problem, Renzler. My machine put out a new report late last night. It's not encouraging at all." Tidwell's voice was soft and sad. He seemed to have lost most of the vitality he had shown the week before. But it was still early.

"I'm afraid things are not looking very good for the Babe. Thanks in no small part to you, that pissant Marvin Wallace appears to be on a streak again. My machine is now predicting that he will break the home-run record."

"In a hundred fifty-four games?"

Tidwell nodded silently.

"I take it you stand to lose a lot of money," I said. Tidwell's silence had lasted for at least half a minute.

"Money! What do I care about money?" The old man was showing signs of life. "This is a matter of principle, Renzler. I stopped worrying about money years ago, before you were born. I thought you were smarter than that."

I smiled a bit. "I guess it's easier to justify killing a nine-year-old boy on principle than for money."

"How very witty, Renzler. Let me tell you something. I had nothing to do with that boy's death."

"Mandel works for you, doesn't he?"

"I prefer to say that Ernie finds it profitable to perform certain tasks for me on occasion."

"Like killing little boys."

"No." Tidwell's voice was angry. "Ernie did that entirely on his own. You made him very nervous when he found out you had talked to the batboy. I told him to forget about it. He didn't listen to me. That was his major mistake. He was afraid

187

you'd find out he was selling bats to those cheap hoodlums with their gambling operation."

"I thought those cheap hoodlums were your friends."

"How indecent of you to suggest that." Tidwell laughed as he poured himself more coffee. "My, my, Renzler, you really are a disappointment. And here I thought you were so smart. Why, you made Ernie so nervous that he tried to force that batboy into telling him what he told you. It was an accident. Ernie must have gotten panicked and grabbed the boy. When he tried to run away, he fell onto the train tracks. Those were two acts of stupidity on his part. The boy had already told you whatever he knew. Ernie had nothing to gain by trying to find out what it was. And there was nothing to gain, of course, by killing the child. But I suppose Ernie was frightened. Even my nephew shakes at the mention of your name. I could barely understand him yesterday when he called to tell me you had been asking about Mandel."

"That reminds me," I interrupted. "Tell him I have his cuff link the next time you talk to him."

"Oh, yes," Tidwell chuckled. "That was so unnecessary for him to go into your room. I told him not to. And then to lose the cuff link. I'm sorry to admit that pissant is a blood relative of mine. I told my brother I'd watch after him. But he's such a pissant."

"You seem to be getting an awful lot of mileage out of your pissants," I observed. "Without them, you wouldn't be able to conduct any important business, like shooting the glass out of my apartment building."

"Ah, yes, I hope you enjoyed that. The boys told me they had a wonderful time shooting at you. You know, I don't let them go out very often. I was hoping it would frighten you and that lady friend of yours. I thought perhaps it would alarm you to see how vulnerable she is. Ernie can't for the life of him keep a secret, and he told Perry about selling bats to that odious character in New Jersey. I thought you would assume it was those gangsters who were out gunning for you."

"You were right," I said. "That's exactly what I thought."

"Of course I was right. Things work out the way I plan them, Renzler—"

"Except—"

"There are no exceptions. And I hope that's the last time you attempt to interrupt me." Tidwell spoke in a stern, vituperative voice. I was sure he used it with Perry Powers and Ernie Mandel all the time.

I didn't apologize for my indiscretion, but I didn't argue with him, either. It would not be wise to antagonize Tidwell. I was still holding out hope that Nate would notice my disappearance and manage to find his way to Tidwell's estate. It was a long shot, but it was the only bet I could make.

"How are you going to deal with the inevitability of Wallace breaking Ruth's home-run record?" I asked. "That doesn't seem to be working out the way you planned."

"Oh, but it's not inevitable, Renzler. It's not inevitable by any stretch of the imagination—even an imagination as unsophisticated as yours." Tidwell's face was contorted in a mocking smile.

"But your computer predicted it. And your computer does not err."

"That is correct. But there are certain considerations that even my machine cannot determine."

"Such as?" I knew what the reply would be, but I could tell Tidwell wanted me to ask.

"Such as murder, Renzler. I have no recourse but to kill Marvin Wallace."

"When?"

"Tonight."

"Why tonight? Can't you wait? Wallace may go into another slump."

"I think not, Renzler. Something may go wrong. The Gents are going on an eight-game road trip after tonight's game. It's very unlikely, but there is the possibility that Wallace could break the record in eight games. I don't want to kill Wallace on the road. I want him to die at home—in the house that Ruth built."

Tidwell paused and took a long mouthful of coffee. He seemed to be waiting for a reaction from me. I obliged him.

"How are you going to do it?"

"I thought you'd never ask." Tidwell spoke in a cheery tone. He got up and strolled to home plate, then stepped on it twice. It was time for some Rheingold. He motioned for me to follow,

189

and we walked past the computer, busy typing out reports, to a closet in the far corner of the room. Tidwell bent over and opened the lower cabinet door. I could see five baseball bats. He pulled one out.

Tidwell handed it to me. It was a major-league model, and Marvin Wallace's name was inscribed at the end of the label side. "Do you notice anything peculiar about this?" he said.

I swung the bat a few times and ran my hand along it. It felt like the right weight, though it may have been off by a few ounces. It wasn't until I tapped the heavy end against the floor than I noticed the modification.

Tidwell smiled when he saw the look of discovery on my face. "That's right," he said, taking the bat from me. "It's been hollowed out at the end." He pressed his hand against the top of it. After a few turns, the end of the bat unscrewed, and he held a nub in his hand.

Lou Gehrig arrived with two beers, and Tidwell and I returned to our seats. He carried the bat with him.

"I'm sure you've heard about some players putting cork in their bats to make the ball jump," Tidwell said.

I nodded. Hercules Johnson, one of my roommates with the Richmond Sailors, had ruined fifteen bats in an attempt to boost his average. All he got for his efforts was a handful of splinters. One of them went in so deep his hand got infected, and he was unable to play for six weeks. His timing was off badly when he got back into the lineup, and he wound up finishing the year hitting .187. He never made it to the majors.

"This is the same principle," Tidwell said. "Only we're not going to load the bat with cork. We're going to put in something that really pops."

"Dynamite," I said, more to myself than to Tidwell.

"That's right, Renzler. How very astute of you. When Wallace comes to the plate in the first inning tonight, he's going to find that his bat is broken. He's going to go back to the dugout, where Ernie Mandel will give him another bat. That bat will contain fuseless dynamite. It's difficult to find, but I have connections. The first time Wallace makes contact with the ball, POW!" Tidwell stood up from his chair and swung the bat for emphasis, though none was necessary. He was

190

grinning broadly, and his wizened face looked disproportion-
ately horizontal with the framing effect of his furry eyebrows.

"Won't Wallace notice the weight of the bat?"

"A small chance, but I think not. With the explosives in
there, the weight balances out perfectly. I made sure of that.
And it doesn't even sound hollow."

"And what if Wallace strikes out?"

"Ah, Renzler, always the skeptic. Wallace is not going to
strike out without at least hitting the ball. Frank Lary is pitching
for Detroit, and I'm sure you're aware that Wallace hits very
well against him. I think we can count on him to connect with
one pitch. Don't you agree?"

I did, but I didn't say so. The old man was no mere mis-
guided eccentric. He was the craziest asshole I'd ever met.

"And what of the other players?" I asked. "Won't they get
hurt, too?"

"Yes, I did consider that. But the only people who stand to
get injured are the Tigers catcher and the home-plate umpire.
Detroit has a catcher in their farm system named Bill Freehan,
who's supposed to be one of the finest prospects in years. As
far as the umpire goes, who cares? What's one dead umpire?"

"You've got a point there," I said, looking up to see Joe
DiMaggio and Lou Gehrig entering the room. Each of them
was carrying a tray on which there were a tuna fish sandwich
and two bottles of Yoo-Hoo chocolate drink.

"Lunchtime already," Tidwell said. He let out a satisfied
sigh. "I assume you like tuna and Yoo-Hoo."

I didn't want to offend his sense of hospitality, but I felt
compelled to speak up. Yoo-Hoo had to be the most vile blend
of molecules ever assembled by man. "I'd prefer another beer,"
I said.

"Very well then," he answered. "Lou, more beer for Renzler. But leave the Yoo-Hoo. I just might decide to overindulge
today. It's not often that I have such scintillating company for
lunch."

"The feeling's mutual," I told him. "But despite your ap-
parent fondess for me, I suppose it's silly of me to hope you
might spare me the unpleasantness of dying."

Tidwell laughed, discharging brown globs of tuna onto the
table. "*Silly*, Renzler? After all the trouble you've caused me,

you want to know if it's silly?" He paused for a mouthful of Yoo-Hoo. "It's not silly at all, Renzler. It's downright futile."

Tidwell's tone changed from light to serious. "I really am sorry, Renzler, but you've given me no choice. I never would have brought you here if Mandel hadn't killed that boy, but as they say in baseball, those are the breaks. Now I am very fond of you, but I must confess that I don't like you nearly as much as I like myself. I'm sure you understand that."

"What about Mandel?" I asked. "Isn't it likely that he'll get caught. And as you said, he can't keep his mouth shut about anything."

"Yes, that's true. Ernie does run the risk of being apprehended. But I paid him off handsomely, dang it. And there's always the possibility that he might have an accident in the not-too-distant future."

"Perhaps you'd consider paying me off," I suggested.

Tidwell shook his head vigorously. "Not you, Renzler. You can't be bought. Like me, you're a man of principle and integrity."

"I might surprise you."

"No. I don't think so. It will upset me for sure, but I must have you disposed of." He got up from his chair and looked at his watch. "We've still got a few hours," he said. "Why don't we play some baseball."

31

At four o'clock, Tidwell went off to watch *Abbott and Costello*, leaving me alone with Lou Gehrig in the computer room. My feet were handcuffed to my chair, and he was holding a gun in his lap. He didn't say a word.

I entertained myself until dinner by drinking beers and reading a book Tidwell had given me. It was called *Babe: The Greatest Player of All Time*.

We ate dinner in silence, except for an occasional exchange between Tidwell and his nephew. I spoke once or twice, but I didn't have much to say. I didn't have much to eat, either, because the main course was tuna casserole. I was beginning to discern a pattern in Tidwell's eating habits that I didn't especially like. Not that it mattered, since it was probably the last meal I'd be eating. I'd pretty much given up on Nate finding me. It was up to me to escape and get to Marvin Wallace before he came up for his last at-bat. If I didn't, he and I would become just another pair of statistics in the loss column.

For dessert we all had Hostess Twinkies, which I forced

down despite my better judgment. I was going to be needing energy pretty soon.

Tidwell looked at his watch after we finished. "It's time for you to suit up," he told me. "Joe, would you get Renzler's uniform?"

Within a few seconds DiMaggio returned. He was carrying a Richmond Sailors jersey. The numeral 7 was sewn into it. It was my shirt.

"I had it made up special," Tidwell said to me as I pulled the uniform top over my head. "I had Lou order it right after you left last week. Do you like it?"

"Great," I said. "Fits like a glove."

Tidwell ignored my sarcasm. "The game starts in an hour. It's time for me to go to the TV room to relax. I'd invite you to watch the game with me, but I never permit anyone in the TV room while I'm watching. It disturbs my concentration."

"That's okay," I said. "Maybe some other time."

"You're going to take a ride to the Meadowlands with the boys. They're going to drop you off there for a very long swim. When the police find you—if they find you—they'll think you're just another gangster hit."

"Isn't that what I am?"

"I am not a gangster, Renzler."

"Oh, I forgot. You're a man of principle and integrity."

Tidwell grimaced. "I'd prefer if our relationship didn't end on such a sour note, Renzler. I'm very sorry that you've suddenly taken to acting so bitter. It doesn't make me feel good to have you liquidated. I even feel bad about what I said last week. You really could go to your right for those ground balls. I spoke in haste."

Tidwell offered his hand. Reluctantly, I accepted. It was clammy and cold and sticky with the residue of Twinkies.

The Pride of the Yankees pulled out his gun. "Get moving," he said. It was only the second time he had spoken to me, and twice he had said the same thing. What wonderful conversations he and Batman could have had together.

The four of us piled into Tidwell's gold Cadillac. Joe DiMaggio drove, and I had to sit next to him. Gehrig was to my right. He held the gun in his right hand. Babe Ruth sat in back. The three of them still had their baseball uniforms on.

194

As we pulled away, Tidwell waved from the Visitors Dugout. It was the last time I saw the man.

As soon as we reached the main road, DiMaggio pulled into a shopping center. "Okay, Robbie," he said. "Get your ass in there and get us us a six-pack of Schlitz."

"Uncle Billy said he doesn't want you guys drinking beer in the car," Robbie answered.

"Well, he ain't here," Gehrig said. "So get us the beer or we'll leave you in the swamp with Renzler."

Robbie got out of the car without whimpering another protest, and a few minutes later we were breezing south down Route 9W. Gehrig and DiMaggio began giggling like children as soon as they opened the beer. They had carried on the same way on the ride out to Tidwell's. Inside, in Tidwell's presence, you would have thought they were a pair of deaf-mutes. But once they left the house, they acted like two loonies who had escaped from the nuthouse.

DiMaggio drove at a dangerously fast pace along the winding two-lane highway. The speed limit was fifty, but he was taking the curves at sixty and cruising the straightaways at seventy-five. All the while he kept up a steady stream of chatter that had Gehrig convulsed with laughter.

"Yoo-Hoo, oh Yoo-Hoo. More tuna please. And I think I'll have another salted nut roll." DiMaggio made fun of William Bosworth Tidwell's eccentricities, as Gehrig yelled out the window to a pair of young girls walking along the side of the road.

"Come on, you guys, knock it off." Robbie was the odd man out.

"Shut up, you little pissant," Gehrig said in a perfect imitation of Tidwell. DiMaggio was so broken up with laughter, he almost swerved off the road.

"Slow down, Joe, will you? You're making me nervous back here."

I asked if I could turn on the radio, but nobody answered me, so I took an indecent liberty with the dial. Johnnie Haller was already announcing the starting lineups. Bob Shermis was going to be the Gents pitcher, and I was hoping Detroit would rake him over for ten runs. If Shermis pitched a good first inning, Wallace would be at bat within fifteen minutes.

195

"Aw shit," DiMaggio said at the conclusion of the *Star Spangled Banner*. He was staring intently at his rearview mirror. We had entered the town of Englewood, where the speed limit dropped from fifty to thirty-five. We were still going fifty. A local police car was parked by the road no more than twenty-five feet past the speed-change sign.

"See, I told you," Robbie said indignantly. "You should have listened to me."

I turned around to watch the cop, but Gehrig told me to look straight ahead. By observing DiMaggio's expression gradually change from a frown to a smile, I could tell that the police car had not pulled out to follow. If I had been driving in my car, I would have been stopped for sure.

"Fuck you, copper," DiMaggio said. "And that goes double for you, Robbie."

I groaned inwardly as I heard Max Mercer announce that the Tigers shortstop, Dick McAuliffe, had swung at the first pitch and grounded out to Preston at second base. I listened glumly as Mercer reported that center fielder Bill Bruton had taken his first pitch from Shermis for a strike. I should know better than to hope for help from a cop.

As we crossed over Palisades Avenue, though, my hopes rose again. Up ahead I could see two police cars parked along the curb behind a blue Oldsmobile. A cop was standing by the window of the car writing out a ticket. Another one stood by the door to the second police car. He was waving us over with a large flashlight. I didn't like the idea of cops using radar, but I was beginning to think it did have some practical applications.

Bill Bruton hit a fly ball to Wallace in left field as DiMaggio pulled the car over to the curb. If Al Kaline didn't get on base, the inning would be over for the Tigers.

I let out a low cheer as the cop approached the driver's side of the car. Kaline had singled up the middle, and it was up to Rocky Colavito to keep the inning—and Wallace—alive. DiMaggio rolled down his window, and the cop looked at him strangely. I had gotten used to the boys' uniforms, but the cop was meeting them for the first time. I felt like the coach of a baseball team for mentally retarded adults. Then I remembered that I had my uniform on, too.

One thing was certain: I had to get out of that car. While DiMaggio reached across me into the glove compartment for the registration, I slid my hand slowly down the edge of the seat. Gehrig had finished off three cans of beer and stuffed them under the seat. With a little luck I could work one of them loose.

Colavito crashed a home run into the lower left-field seats while DiMaggio was fumbling in his wallet for his driver's license. Norm Cash, the league's leading hitter, was at the plate. Cash took Shermis' first pitch for a ball just as I pulled a can from under the seat. Lou Gehrig didn't notice. The cop did.

"What's that on the floor by your leg, sir?" he asked.

I smiled my charming smile. "It's a beer can." I could feel Gehrig's breath heating up the back of my neck as I turned to face the cop.

"I'm going to have to ask you all to get out of the car."

I turned to Gehrig and grinned. "Better put away the gun for a while, Lou."

I could hear Mercer reporting that Cash had smashed a double into the right-field corner as the cop lined us up at the front of the Cadillac. None of my driving companions said anything, but I could tell from their stares that they were going to enjoy killing me. Even Robbie. I had to get away.

The cop called his partner over, and Robbie, Lou, and Joe all watched as the two began searching the car. I took three small silent steps away from them. Then I pivoted on my heels and took five speedy strides to the driver's side door of the rear squad car.

Robbie was the first to notice my escape, but I had the door closed and the car in reverse by the time the cops heard his yells. I accelerated quickly, and the car lurched backwards, coming within a few feet of crushing my three former captors. Out of my good eye, I caught a glimpse of them sprawled on the pavement as I pulled away and drove screeching down Palisades Avenue toward the George Washington Bridge.

By the time I got the radio tuned in, Al Lewis was doing a pitch for Rheingold Beer. Shermis had retired the Tigers, and the Gents would be coming to bat any minute. As usual, traffic to the toll booths at the bridge was backed up past the

Fort Lee exit. Even if there were no traffic, it would take me ten minutes to drive to Yankee Stadium. As I felt in my pocket for change, I realized my wallet was back at my apartment. I didn't have any money to pay the toll. Behind me, about a quarter-mile back, I could see the other Englewood police car coming after me.

I had no choice. I switched on the siren and cut across traffic to the far-right lane, sending a row of protective cones careening off the bridge and into the Hudson River far below. This was an emergency.

With the siren screeching, traffic began parting for me like the Red Sea had done for Moses. I moved quickly to the left lane and headed straight east on the Cross Bronx Expressway. About a half-mile back, a New York police car joined in pursuit of me with the Englewood cop. Sometime soon I was going to have a lot of explaining to do.

About twenty cars were lined up on the Jerome Avenue ramp when I crossed over three lanes of traffic to exit. I couldn't wait on that line, and there was no room for the cars to move. Braking down to about thirty-five miles an hour, I hurtled the curb and drove up the grassy hill alongside the ramp. Billy Pratt stepped into the batter's box as I ran the red light and took a fast right south on Jerome.

I had almost thirty blocks to drive down the cobblestoned street under the elevated train tracks. I was hoping Pratt would bat true to form and coax Frank Lary into issuing him a walk. Pratt led the league in bases on balls, and now was the best time I could think of for him to increase his lead.

Lary blazed a fast ball in for a strike, but he missed the plate with the next two pitches. I was crossing 173rd Street. The count was two and one. On the next pitch Pratt swung and fouled the ball off into the stands. I narrowly missed a drunken pedestrian as I charged through the red light at 167th. I was seven blocks from Yankee Stadium. The train passed by overhead and drowned out the sound of Lary's next pitch. When it passed, I was crossing 163rd. Barry Preston was coming to bat. Pratt had failed me in the clutch.

The sidewalk outside the home-plate end of Yankee Stadium was mobbed with people when I pulled screeching up to the curb. I muscled through the crowd and desperately tried to

198

make my way through to the authorized-personnel entrance. I didn't know what I was going to do when I got there, because my pass was back home in my wallet.

It didn't take much thought. I could stop to explain why I was there, or I could push my way through. Sometimes the path of most resistance actually offers the least resistance. More is less, or something like that. I went past the two guards with elbows raised, and I didn't miss a step. I hoped they weren't seriously hurt as they crashed to the cement floor.

I could tell by the roar of the crowd that Wallace was coming to bat as I started up the steps to the lower box seats. When I emerged into the bright glow of the ballpark, Wallace was striding back to the dugout. I was eight rows up from the field.

Ernie Mandel was walking toward Wallace with another bat when I reached the edge of the field between home plate and first base. I screamed at Wallace louder than I've ever yelled in my life. It paid off.

The slugger looked up and saw me as I vaulted over the lower-box-seat railing. I didn't have a gun, and again I wasn't sure what my next move would be. Ernie Mandel made my decision for me.

The Gents equipment manager spun around as soon as I got Wallace's attention. He held the loaded bat in his hands, and he began to run the instant I got onto the field. Still holding the bat with two hands, he ran sideways at half speed right over the pitcher's mound and out toward Tiger shortstop Dick McAuliffe. I followed cautiously at about the same speed, and Mandel turned all the way around to face me. He was moving in a backwards trot.

"Get away from me, you asshole," I heard him yell above the thunderous noise of the puzzled crowd.

I slowed to a jogger's pace but still moved methodically toward him. He turned a full revolution, searching the field for an exit. As we got out to shallow left-center field, he made his choice.

Mandel sprinted toward the exit gate behind the monument to Babe Ruth in dead center field. The left fielder, Rocky Colavito, and the center fielder, Bill Bruton, moved in opposite directions away from each other to allow Mandel to pass between them. They weren't about to confront a madman swinging a bat over his head. I couldn't blame them.

Half a dozen security guards finally came running onto the field from the infield box seats to join in the chase. They must have been detained searching for prizes in their Cracker Jacks. Mandel was in deep left-center field now, about fifty feet from the monument. They would never catch him. It was up to me.

And Curt Bidwell.

The rookie right-hander had been warming up in the Gents bullpen along the left-field line when I started chasing Mandel. When I got to left field, Bidwell waved to me in recognition and began to run into the outfield in pursuit of Mandel. The Gents equipment manager was probably twenty-five yards away when Bidwell stopped, took aim, and winged a lightning-fast pitch on a straighter line than anybody will ever draw.

The rap against Bidwell was that he had control problems, but his delivery was perfect this time. The pitch must have been going ninety miles an hour when it struck Mandel in the middle of the back. The sickening sound of the ball hitting flesh cut through the crowd noise like a bull's-eye dart swishing through boar's bristle. It was followed immediately by the ear-splitting explosion of dynamite as Mandel hurtled forward to the ground and the bat shattered into splinters.

By the time Bidwell and I reached him, Mandel had lost enough blood to start his own clinic.

His body shook with tremors as he lay flat on his back in the reddish-brown outfield grass, and from deep inside his stomach came one powerful cough, which twisted his upper body sideways. He choked for a moment, caught his breath, then let out an enormous crimson glob of sputum that would have made Hawk Harkness green with envy. A moment later, a peaceful look fell on Ernie Mandel's face. He was dead in center field.

"What the fuck happened?" Bidwell asked. His face was whiter than the chalk lines around home plate.

"It's a long story," I said.

32

On Friday, the day of the baseball hearing, Melissa and I slept until noon. Between the two of us we had consumed enough alcohol the night before to keep the entire city of New York intoxicated for a year. And that doesn't include Nate's contribution.

The hearing was scheduled for 3:30, and Melissa had gotten the assignment to cover it for the *Times*. We might have slept through, if it hadn't been for Pressie's repeated buzzing.

I staggered out of bed to the intercom. "What is it, Pressie?"

"We got a package, Mr. Renzler. Messenger just dropped it off. You want me to bring it up there?"

I told him I did.

I opened it at the kitchen table, where Melissa and I were guzzling down coffee. It was a small package, and it didn't tick. There was a card with it. I opened the package first.

I don't wear cuff links, but I didn't mind getting a pair. If I could believe Tidwell—and why shouldn't I?—they were worth ten thousand dollars. To a guy who makes fifty bucks a day, that's nothing to sneer at.

I opened the card, half expecting to find a check. I didn't. There was a Norman Rockwell drawing on the front depicting several downtrodden Chicago Cubs standing in front of their dugout and being jeered by a mob of sinister-looking fans. Inside was a brief note scrawled in a hand that I'm sure a criminologist would have attributed to a psychotic. After all, it was the work of a psychotic.

Dear Renzler,

I must congratulate you begrudgingly on a stellar performance. I was quite enraptured by the entire incident while watching it on TV. Of course I did not get to see the conclusion of the game, because I had to make my exit rather quickly. I must tell you that the drive to the airport was absolutely frightening. I have not operated a motor vehicle in almost 20 years, and I had no idea what a proliferation of morons now frequent our highways. I narrowly avoided a serious collision with one of those law enforcement agents you sent to my estate.

I'm off to Cuba by way of Bermuda. Hopefully, I will have arrived there by the time you read this note. They play ball there, you know, and while the level of competition is not even comparable to the questionable standards of Marvin Wallace, it is far preferable to the anomie of an American prison. I expect it will be somewhat lonely without Joe and Lou and Robbie, but as you may have observed, I'm a very flexible person and should have little difficulty adapting to a new situation.

I would ask that you extend my gratitude to young Bidwell for eliminating Mandel. That weasel had it coming to him after selling out to those hoodlums for fifty dollars. And I do hope you'll show some compassion for Lou, Joe, and those two pissant nephews of mine.

Until next time, WBT

It took us almost two hours to get ready, and I stopped by a clothing store on Broadway and dropped ten dollars on a

202

navy blue tie. By the time we picked up Nate and got to the meeting room at the commissioner's office, the hearing was about to begin.

There were probably forty people in attendance, counting all the newspaper and TV reporters, and I had gotten to know quite a few of them over the past couple of weeks. I saw Fielding at a table in front when I came in, sitting with Ed White and Perry Powers. Marvin and Rita Wallace were sitting next to them. At a table near the back of the room, Curt Bidwell was slouched in a folding chair, perfecting the imperfect posture that's essential to maintaining a bad attitude. He had a smirk on his face that you couldn't have wiped off with a snow shovel.

Mutton Moran was sitting beside Bidwell, chewing on a candy bar. To his right Hawk Harkness was staring down at a fistful of napkins on the table. Otto Croaker was across the room doing frog noises for Johnnie Haller, and even Jaco Sworpe had managed to haul himself out of bed to watch the proceedings.

Before Melissa and I reached the front of the room, Marvin and Rita Wallace came over to greet us.

"Renzler," Wallace said, "I'd like you to meet my wife, Rita. This is the man I was telling you about, honey."

Rita Wallace put out her hand. She was wearing the same dress she had on the first day she came into my office, and she looked stunning, as usual. "I've heard so much about you, Mr. Renzler. It's a pleasure to finally meet you."

She teased me by squeezing my hand, and I could hear Melissa's silent laughter beside me. "The pleasure's all mine," I said.

We could have stood there all day exchanging pleasantries, but acting baseball commissioner Ebel Chapman had noticed my presence. He didn't look pleased to see me.

Chapman was sitting at the head of the front table. "What's he doing here?" he asked everyone and no one in particular.

Arthur Fielding took responsibility for answering. "That's Mark Renzler. He's the private investigator I hired when Mandel began threatening Marvin. He did a good job, too." Fielding flashed me a patronizing smile, and I returned it. He still had to be afraid I might blow his ass out of the water, and he was trying to score some brownie points before I testified. That was fine with me. In fact, I rather liked the idea of making Fielding squirm a bit.

"I thought you were a writer," Chapman said to me.

"I wear a lot of hats," I said, tipping the Panama I had dug out of my closet. I tried to make a point of wearing it whenever I thought my picture might turn up in the newspaper. Melissa said it made me look distinguished, and I knew for sure that it concealed the evidence of my receding hairline.

Melissa and I took seats at the table next to Fielding's, and Nate stayed at the back of the room. I wanted him there in case anyone decided to leave early.

Fielding was the first to testify, and, for obvious reasons, he was painlessly brief. The Gents owner wanted to strike a clean public image, and to do that he had to purge the seamy details of Russo's betting operation from his story. He had told me the night before that he was going to ask Wallace not to mention the encounter with Pizza Face in his testimony. I figured Wallace would comply with Fielding's request. The only thing Marvin had to gain by discussing the threats that had led him to the house in Totowa would be the public embarrassment that goes with the admission of blackmail.

I knew the Gents owner was nervous as he began his story, but he handled himself with the same fluid ease and shrewdness that he had used on Grimaldi at the Wayne police station. I had to marvel at his confident manner, but I still felt a twinge of anger that he was getting off so easy.

"Twelve days ago, Marvin Wallace began receiving veiled threats on his life," Fielding said. "There were several phone calls and notes, and one even came from inside the Palmer House Hotel, where our team was staying while in Chicago. It wasn't until that time that I realized someone in our own organization was conducting a systematic campaign to harass and frighten Marvin Wallace."

Fielding paused and poured himself a glass of water from a pitcher on the witness table. "As soon as I learned about the threats, I hired the services of Mark Renzler, a private investigator who used to play minor-league ball in the Gents system. Renzler was a damn good ballplayer, I'd like to add, and he turned out to be an even better detective." Fielding smiled at me, but I met his gaze with poker-faced sobriety.

"At our very first meeting, Renzler raised the possibility that someone in our organization was involved. I told him he was wrong. It turned out he wasn't. *I* was. And I owe him an apology for questioning his judgment. I couldn't believe that anyone associated with the New York Gents would take any premeditated action that would work to the detriment of our ballclub. Even now, even after the events of last night, I'm still having difficulty believing it." Fielding gazed around the room, as if to emphasize his inability to convey his shock in words. He was a first-rate liar.

The Gents owner continued. "I wasn't with Renzler all the time, so I can't retrace all the steps that led him to the discovery that our equipment manager, Ernie Mandel, was plotting first to stop Marvin Wallace from breaking Babe Ruth's home-run record, and later, when it appeared that his harassment techniques were not working, to kill Marvin by rigging his bat with an explosive device."

Fielding paused for a moment—for dramatic effect, I thought—but he was upstaged by an explosion from the back. I joined the spectators in turning around to see Hawk Harkness secreting a soggy napkin into the pocket of his Gents blazer.

"Sorry," Harkness said, grinning. "It's just my post-nasal drip."

"This is a disgrace to the Gents organization," Fielding said. It was not immediately clear whether he was making reference to Hawk or Mandel. "And it's a disgrace to major-league baseball. I, as I'm sure we all do, deeply regret that it ever occurred. And we have Mark Renzler to thank that it didn't end as badly as it could have."

I imagined that my underwear was soaking wet from Fielding's kisses as the Gents owner walked back to the seat beside White. He nodded to me as Wallace took the witness chair.

"I don't really have anything to add to what Mr. Fielding said," Wallace began, "except that I'm sorry all this happened and I'm glad it's all over. And I guess I'd like to thank Renzler and his buddy Nate and my wife for all the help they've been to me."

I turned to the back of the room to see an enormous smile spreading across Nate's face. It took me a few seconds to realize that his smile was directed not toward me but to Rita Wallace.

205

She was returning it, and a moment later our eyes met. We were co-conspirators in a lesser plot. As I looked toward Rita, I felt Melissa's elbow pressing against my ribs.

"Don't be so fucking obvious," she whispered. "Remember, he's supposed to be a jealous man."

"And I guess I owe an apology to one of my teammates," Wallace droned on. Public speaking was not one of the home-run hitter's strong points. "When we began to think that maybe someone on the club was doing the stuff to me, we all suspected Curt Bidwell. I guess it was because he was new and we all thought he was kind of flaky—a lot of us still do, I guess."

That triggered a few laughs from the audience, and when the commotion concluded, Wallace did, too.

"Anyway, Bidwell, I'm sorry," he said.

As Wallace walked back to his seat, Bidwell answered from the back. "Don't be sorry, Marvin. Just give me a cut of that big salary you're going to make after you break the home-run record."

The spectators sputtered with laughter again, and some of them began to applaud. Ebel Chapman put an end to their gaiety by pounding the table with a wooden gavel. The acting commissioner had pulled out all the stops for the big meeting.

"I know we're all getting a bit restless," he said. "But we're almost through. Let's remember that this is an important hearing." Chapman reminded me of my high-school principal. He reminded me of the principal of any high school.

Perry Powers got up next to say a few words on behalf of Ernie Mandel.

"Ernie Mandel was my roommate and best friend," he mumbled into the microphone. I was sure Powers was a fairly competent public speaker, but no one at that moment wanted to loudly declare an association with the Gents equipment manager. "I didn't realize until last night that I didn't know him very well at all. Ernie was a sick man, and I hope you all remember that in the way you think about him. I'm just sorry that I didn't know what was going on sooner, so that I could have helped him and prevented this whole unfortunate series of events from taking place."

Chapman strode to the microphone as soon as Powers was finished. "I think that wraps it up," he said. "And I hope that

206

you reporters cover this as an isolated incident, a regrettable tragedy that we'd all like to put behind us. I don't want to read any reports about the disintegration of baseball or any other such nonsense." He paused, as if he were thinking of some seminal point to add, but he didn't. He simply said, "Thank you all for coming, and let's get back to baseball."

"Wait a minute," Ed White said. "I think Renzler has something to say."

I did indeed.

33

"I'd like to concur with the impression the other witnesses left—that Ernie Mandel acted alone in harassing Marvin Wallace," I said. "Unfortunately, I can't."

I listened to the gasps in the room as I poured myself a glass of water. What I needed was a beer. Sitting at the witness table I felt like a kid giving a book report to an elementary-school class. "Ernie Mandel was part of a conspiracy to stop Marvin Wallace from breaking the home-run record. He was a nobody, a throwaway, and he had help from someone high up in the Gents organization. That person is in this room."

I sucked in a hit of my cigarette and let my gaze fall on Fielding. He was shaking his head almost imperceptibly, sending me a desperate, complex signal. Let the bastard squirm a little, I thought.

"While I was staying at the Palmer House with the team, someone searched my room. For reasons that I won't go into here, I thought it was Curt Bidwell. I was incorrect. The person who searched my room lost something, but he never came back to reclaim it. It was only after I got back to New York that I realized he probably didn't know where he had left it. I'll give it back now."

I pulled the cuff link out of my jacket pocket. "Perry," I said to Powers, "here's your cuff link." I tossed it to him, a perfect throw, but he missed it and it bounced off the table. "Your uncle, William Bosworth Tidwell, gave that to you as a present. You should take better care of it."

Powers stood up after he snatched the cuff link off the floor. "That doesn't prove anything," he said. "So I searched your room. That's because you went to see my uncle and told him you were a writer." Powers was shaking as he talked. His relations with the public were not going so well.

"You're right," I said. "It doesn't prove anything. Not when considered alone. But there's the question of a phone call Marvin received in Chicago. Originally we thought Bidwell made the call, because the switchboard operator said it came from his room. When I searched his room later that day, I found the phone cord stuck under the door leading to the adjoining room. The door was open. It was your room, Perry. You made the call."

"No." Powers was still standing. It was just about time for him to bolt for the door. "Ernie must have called him."

"No, he didn't. As you know, since you were Ernie's roommate and best friend, Mandel went to seven o'clock Mass in Chicago. For what I don't know. Maybe he was praying for forgive—"

I didn't finish the sentence, because Powers had stopped listening. Actually, he may have been listening, but I certainly didn't have his undivided attention. He was busy racing for the door.

Nate stepped up out of his chair and collared him—literally—just as he got to the exit. He picked up Powers with one hand and held him by the back of his neck, as if he were demonstrating the proper way to lift a rabbit. The Gents PR director dangled from Nate's paw as he was carried to the front of the room and set back down in his chair.

"There," Nate said. "Stay put and pay attention. I'll tell you when it's time to leave."

Nate bowed ceremoniously before returning to the back.

"Pardon the interruption, Mr. Renzler. Please continue your story. It's fascinating."

"To understand what Powers and Mandel did, you'd have to have some understanding of Perry's uncle, William Bosworth Tidwell. I spent a few delightful hours with the man yesterday before he tried to have me killed, and I still don't understand him. I suppose it doesn't matter now, because he's off in Cuba. He never really cared for Perry or Mandel, so he decided to let them take the fall."

Powers began to sob furiously as I spoke.

"I first became aware of Tidwell when Arthur Fielding told me a man had offered him six million dollars for the Babe Ruth monument in Yankee Stadium. He made his money, millions and millions of dollars, in mechanical baseball games and computers. The man was consumed passionately, and I suppose you'd have to say maniacally, with Babe Ruth. He was willing to do anything to stop Marvin Wallace from breaking Babe's record, and he did. Fortunately for Marvin, it didn't work."

I was coming into the home stretch, but I wasn't moving fast enough for Ebel Chapman. The acting commissioner interrupted me with a question, but it was more a statement for the purpose of hurrying me along.

"Excuse me, Mr. Renzler," he said. "But could you please tell us what this man Tidwell has to do with the matter at hand? I don't see where this biography is taking us."

"Tidwell has everything to do with it, as you well know, Mr. Chapman." He had tried to make me look foolish, and I was going to enjoy making a fool of him.

"Me? What are you talking about?"

"On June twenty-first you had lunch with Tidwell at Jack Dempsey's. I don't know how much he paid you, but three days later you made the rule change requiring Marvin Wallace to break the home-run record in a hundred and fifty-four games."

I could see people's chins beginning to drop, as if the reaction to my remarks were choreographed. Chapman danced out of his seat.

"That's a slanderous accusation, Renzler. You can't prove that."

"I think I can," I answered calmly. "I don't know how much Tidwell paid you, but I know he gave you that watch you're wearing. It has the same stones and markings as Perry's cuff links. I'll bet there's even an inscription from Tidwell on the back. Why don't you hand it to me, and I'll look."

"No," he said, "get away." Chapman took three steps back, but I hadn't even made a move toward him. "Okay, okay," he said. "I admit it. I did it. But I didn't do it for Tidwell. And I didn't do it for myself. I did it for the good of baseball."

Chapman turned to face the spectators, and the room fell into a dead, queasy silence.

"It's my job, my duty, to preserve the integrity of baseball," Chapman said. I had heard the speech in his office once before. "The legend of Babe Ruth is the legend of the game that we all cherish so dearly. I didn't think it was right for Marvin Wallace to break Babe Ruth's record. It's my obligation to protect the champion's throne from pretenders. I know this may not sound right to some of you, and it's hard for me to say it, but in my judgment Marvin Wallace is not yet worthy of becoming the record-holder. Perhaps in a few years, if he continues to excel. But now, I just don't know."

The commissioner's voice faded out like the end of a song on the radio. His head was bowed by the time he finished speaking. No one else in the room said anything.

Except for me. "That was a fine speech, Mr. Chapman, and I'm sure you won some supporters with your reasoning, no matter how specious it is. But you didn't stop at taking money and making rules."

I spoke now to the audience, not just Chapman. "When Nate Moore and I first interviewed the commissioner, he denied knowing William Bosworth Tidwell. But his secretary, a woman named Pam Masters, overheard him. Mr. Chapman sent a man who works in his office out to follow me to a bar where Nate and I were meeting Pam Masters. Early the next day she was found murdered in her apartment."

Chapman's voice was shrill and angry above the murmurs of the crowd. "I didn't do that. I didn't have anything to do with that. It was that stupid Larry Nichols. He killed her, that crazy bastard. I only asked him to keep an eye on you. I didn't want that girl to die. I loved her."

"I know you did, Mr. Chapman." My voice was lower now, and I was feeling a taste of compassion well up behind my

211

words. But not too much. "That's why you went to Larry Nichols' apartment that same night and killed him. You made it look like suicide, but I saw the body. I saw the bump on his head where you—"

I hadn't expected the commissioner to be carrying a gun. It was the only shot I had called wrong all day. And I was the one he was going to shoot first.

I slid down under the table faster than I've ever moved in my life. It's amazing how quickly your body reacts when you think your number's coming up. But Arthur Fielding reacted, too, and I could see him grab Chapman from behind as I peered out from beneath the table.

The Gents owner was an arm's length away from the commissioner when Chapman wheeled to face me with a .22. I heard Fielding yell, "No, Ebel, don't do it," as he spun Chapman around and landed in a heap on top of him. Then I heard the shot, followed by a solitary sickly moan.

Chapman must have let go of the gun, because Ed White was holding it when I crawled out from under the table to get a better view. Rita Wallace was hunched over Fielding, and the air in the room was dense with the sound of her strangled sobs. Blood from Fielding's chest had spurted all over the front of her dress. For the first time since I had met her, I felt no sexual desire for Rita Wallace, only sympathy. She had suffered alone through her ordeal and it wasn't over yet.

Ebel Chapman was cowering in the corner, closely watched by Hawk Harkness and Mutton Moran. Perry Powers was kicking and clawing in the back of the room, as Nate subdued him with the help of Mule Muhlsinger. Powers had failed in his second attempt to escape. As I put my arm around Melissa, everything in the room seemed to be moving.

Everything except for Arthur Fielding, who lay perfectly still at the front of the room. He had sacrificed himself to get me home safely.

Within minutes a swarm of cops swept into the room, buzzing through the perfunctory duties of a routine murder investigation. Two of them led Ebel Chapman down the center of the room. The acting baseball commissioner's face was ghost white, and his eyes were as empty as an abandoned coal mine. He had been momentarily incontinent, and his gray slacks were

212

stained with urine. At that moment he looked more pathetic than any Bowery bum I had ever seen.

Nate surrendered Powers to one of the cops and joined Melissa and me at the front of the room.

"You've got a story to write," he said to her. "But Renzler and I have the night off. I suggest we take in a sports event."

"No, Nate, no." I shook my head. "I don't think I could stand another baseball game tonight."

"To hell with baseball," he said. "We can go to a ballgame any night. I'm talking about wrestling."

He pulled a pair of tickets out of his shirt pocket and thrust them at me. "Hurry up," he said, "or we'll miss the midgets."

An hour later we were breezing along Route 3 toward the Gladiator's Arena in Totowa, neutralizing last night's hangover by drinking our way into another. Brute Bernard and Skull Murphy beat the Fabulous Kangaroos in two straight falls, and since I had bet on the Aussies, it was my responsibility to spring for dinner.

We found a Howard Johnson's with a liquor license and stayed well into the night, stuffing our faces with the Friday fish offering that's been known to make many a good Catholic boy leave the church at an early age. For one fleeting, boozy moment, I felt almost happy to be in New Jersey.

But just for a moment.

About the Author

Paul Engleman lives in Chicago where he works for a major national magazine. DEAD IN CENTER FIELD is Paul Engleman's first novel, and he's currently at work on·the next Mark Renzler mystery.